CW00661782

Elastic Waxes in Unbounded Media

Dog and Vile Short Fiction

First published 2022
'Kompromat' and 'Room of their Own' © SK Mongrl
'The Pike of Knowledge' © Brian Kelly
'The Message' © Mark Keane
'Wrong' © Namrael Drawde
'Assemblage' and 'Brigadier Robert D'Alby' © EF Hay
'Norfolk' © David Rogers
ISBN: 9798847032735
All rights reserved.
To reproduce selections from this book contact
Dog and Vile at dogandvile@gmail.com
Cover art by Mohamed Lekleti:
Souffle (mixed media on paper)

Dog and Vile

CONTENTS

Under a grey sky, on a wind-blown, trackless plain of dust, without a thistle or nettle to be seen, I met several men bent under loads. Each carried on his back a monstrous Chimaera,heavy as a sack of coal. But the beasts were not just inert sacks; on the contrary, they moved with rippling muscles, digging their claws into the men's chests, their heads rising above the heads of their human mounts like those helmets worn by ancient warriors to unnerve their enemies.

I asked one of these men where he was taking his dreadful passengers. He said he did not know, but it must be some definite destination, for he was driven by an irresistible desire to reach it.

One more strange thing about this scene: the porters were not enraged by the beasts on their backs—almost as if they saw them as parts of themselves. The weary, serious faces showed no trace of despair. Rather, they trudged through the dust like ones inured to a hope that could not be extinguished. At last, I stood and watched until they blended with the horizon's curve. I wished to understand this mystery—but at once a terrible boredom overwhelmed me and, shifting its insupportable weight, I trudged after the footsteps, already fading in the wind's erasure.

—Charles Baudelaire

This is a book about people whose lives have become horrifyingly metaphorical. Who have gone off the rails, pear-shaped and panicking. They are the drivers of cars who've skidded through the safety barrier and are careering off into windscreen-smacking, bone-shaking undergrowth, all the while stamping on unresisting brakes and twisting wheels that turn in their hands like loosening screws.

Some are paying for a lack of due care and attention—as with the debauched writer destroyed by one of his own characters, or the circle of European haute bourgeoisie who mix fine wine with sadomasochism and Borgia-style office politics. Some are overwhelmed by their own ungovernable urges—like the bureaucrat obsessed with his repulsive boss, or the lighthouse keeper who succumbs to ever more bizarre fantasies, or the croppy boy brought face to face with the Awful Truth in his uncle's petrochemical fish farm.

Others appear to have been selected by bored gods for special treatment, and here we have the rapist who swaps bodies with his victim, the would-be writer taught a chilling lesson in the purpose of art and the boy who responds to his white-trash Willesden upbringing with acts that would send Sophocles sprinting, hand over mouth, to the nearest bucket …

Good night, Mr Jerry's little slave.
Hope you have a good jerk-off

Kompromat | SK Mongrl

'Yes, I fully agree that we should wait until we've talked to Elliot and Katie before approaching the Swedes,' said Jeremy.

'Do you, now?' Amadou asked.

Jeremy did not reply.

'Jeremy,' Amadou said, and paused. 'Jeremy,' he repeated, raising his head slowly, 'I very much doubt you would have "fully agreed" if someone lower down the pecking order than you, someone like Abe here'—he put his hand on Abe's shoulder—'had suggested you wait until you've talked to the Americans before approaching the Swedes.'

Jeremy's face began to flush. He opened his mouth, hesitated, and closed it again.

'"Kiss up and kick down" managers, I think people like you are called. Has the management coach we hired for you not introduced you to the term?' Amadou asked.

Jeremy's bulky body began to writhe in the padded leather chair. Ignoring Amadou's question, he launched into an over-elaborate justification for why he agreed with Amadou, swept along by his quickly recovered verbal facility.

'Don't contact the Swedes until I give you permission,' said Amadou, rising from his chair, interrupting Jeremy in mid-flight. 'Anything else you need from me today?'

'No, no. But thank you Amadou for taking the time to attend the meeting. Your strategic insight is always hugely helpful.'

'Well goodbye everyone,' said Amadou, nodding and smiling at the group seated around the table. 'I wish you all a good day.'

They continued with the Monday morning team meeting. But during the first few minutes, Abe and Ann-Sophie could not help catching each other's gaze, raising their eyebrows and smirking. Amadou Diop, United Nations Under-Secretary-General for Development, a small, slim man, who always wore an elegantly-tailored black suit and matching tie, was renowned for his unfailing courtesy and composure. None of the team had ever witnessed him becoming impatient or sarcastic. Neither had any of the team ever seen Jeremy blush, or at a loss for words.

Abe scribbled down a list of five points in his notebook and looked up at Shelley. She was in the middle of her update. Next it would be Geert's turn, then his. Jeremy leaned forward onto his elbows, belly drooping, and scowled at Shelley. Next to Jeremy sat Ann-Sophie, his personal assistant, taking minutes on her laptop—muscular back straight, collagen-enhanced lips pursed, leathery cleavage visible.

Abe glanced over his list of points one last time, leaned back in his chair, and observed Jeremy. He was almost bald and had lumpy, distended pink jowls. This Monday morning, just like at the beginning of every week, he was clean-shaven, dressed in a freshly pressed pinstripe suit and a crisp blue shirt with a white collar. His suits and shirts for the week, Abe knew, were prepared for him on Sunday evenings by his older wife, who lived in their country house. By Friday, Abe also knew, Jeremy's neat and elegant appearance would be a distant memory. After sleeping drunkenly for a night or two on the sofa in his apartment a few blocks away, Jeremy would turn up at the office stubbly, in the same crumpled pale orange shirt as the day before, and give off a vinegary smell when you got too close.

'Neither here nor there I'm afraid, Shelley,' Jeremy said in his fruity colonial tones, cutting Shelley off.

'Doctor van der Beek?' Jeremy asked, turning to Geert.

'Three important developments this week,' said Geert, addressing Jeremy, who nodded. 'First, Under-Secretary-General Diop will be going to Brasilia on Wednesday and will need a briefing note on our evaluation of the CCT programmes in the Mercosur countries by tomorrow. I'll write the first draft but, Jeremy and Shelley, could you please review it? Second, we have the press briefing for the launch of the annual report on Thursday, in press room D. Before we finalise the programme, we have to decide who'll be speaking. You have the draft programme there Shelley, right?' Shelley nodded and waved it in the air. 'Will Shelley,' Geert continued, 'do it alone or do you also want to talk, Jeremy? And lastly, Mourad'—he cast a glance in the direction of the slouching, bearded man who sat at the other end of the table, eyes fixed on the panoramic view of the city outside—'Mourad will be meeting Ribeiro later this week and we have to decide whether or not he asks for an increase in the funds for the East Africa project for next year. And one final thing: I'll be on leave starting Friday evening for three weeks,' he finished.

11

'Thank you very much, Geert. Clear and to the point. Thank you,' said Jeremy. 'Send me the draft briefing note by 2pm today and I'll review it. I will present the annual report, but I won't be able to stay long, so Shelley will have to field questions as best she can at the press briefing.' Addressing Geert as if Mourad were not present, he added, 'And Mourad should request an increase in funds for next year when he meets Ribeiro. They're flush with money I hear. I hope you enjoy your leave, in the Low Countries I presume?' Geert smiled, not catching that it was a question. Abe suppressed a sneer.

Abe, shoulders slumping, started speaking before Jeremy had turned to him. He was determined to make his points as clearly and succinctly as Geert. Abe tried to catch Jeremy's gaze as he talked, but Jeremy's head was bent down, eyes focused on his phone, which he held in his lap under the table. Before Abe had quite finished, Jeremy, hearing him pause a moment, looked up and broke in, reminding everyone that he and Abe would be flying to Manila on Sunday for the two-day regional summit, where they would be meeting Elliot and Katie from the US government. Jeremy then got up and walked towards his desk. As he passed behind Shelley, he leaned over and, without a word, tugged the programme for the launch of the annual report, which Shelley was making notes on, out of her hands. He sat down at his desk and began typing. Ann-Sophie stood to attention beside him. 'Monday meeting over, thank you all for your valuable contributions,' Shelley mimicked under her breath as they filed out of Jeremy's office.

After lunch, as he often did, Jeremy pushed Abe's office door open without knocking and closed it quietly behind him. Abe got up—tall and lanky, he towered over Jeremy—and pulled out a chair from behind the door. Jeremy moved the chair close to Abe and they sat down, their knees almost touching.

'Were it not for her copulating with Diop,' Jeremy began in a whisper, 'we'd never have to countenance such an incompetent press officer. And, come to think of it, were it not for her East Coast liberal arts education—which my own daughter is currently being subjected to—Shelley would not have been copulating with Diop in the first place. At least in your country, Abram, we wouldn't be reduced to whispering impotently behind closed doors like this. We could be using this information against Diop to advance our careers. Not who you know, but what you have on them is what counts there, no?' he chuckled.

Abe's body tensed. His breath quickened. Drops of sweat began to slide down the sides of his rib cage. He stretched his face into a smile and, his voice catching, said: 'We left Russia when I was sixteen. Over twenty-five years ago. It's not really "my country" anymore. Still, I think the Western media's obsession with *kompromat* is probably somewhat misrepresenting things in Russia.' Sitting up and seeking safer ground, he said: 'Great news that Ribeiro might have money to give us. How much do you think we should hit him for?'

'I heard the Canadians and Scandinavians have put $100 million in the new fund, and the Germans will soon be following suit. So, I think we can safely request five million for this year.'

'Want me to go to the meeting with Ribeiro?' Abe asked.

'Yes, it's probably advisable you join Mourad,' he said, smiling widely, revealing his set of near-perfect teeth. Ann-Sophie, in her precise German-accented English, referred to his teeth as 'the last vestige of what was once a singularly handsome man'. One Sunday afternoon, shortly after Abe had first joined the team, and when Jeremy still occasionally invited his staff to his country house, Ann-Sophie had grabbed Abe's hand and pulled him into the sun-filled living room of Jeremy's house. Holding his hand a bit too long, Abe recalled, she had pointed excitedly at an exhibit of photographs ranged on the baby grand. It showed young Jeremy's progress in the world: the pupil in his sporting colours at Falcon College near Bulawayo; the lithe and bearded undergraduate activist in Cape Town baring his fine set of teeth to the camera; and the laughing, dishevelled graduate student punting on the Cam of a summer's eve. Later that afternoon, Abe came back into the living room alone and, with his phone, took pictures, as close-up as he could get, of the photographs.

'Abe, would you mind taking a look at Geert's briefing note for Diop? I'll forward it to you in a minute and, when you've reviewed it, just come through and we can discuss. Also, could you make a start on the presentation for the press briefing? Too important to leave to Shelley. I'd rather it be in a safe pair of hands.'

'Yes, no problem, Jeremy,' said Abe, unable to suppress his eagerness to maintain their special relationship. 'I will come through as soon as I've gone over the briefing note. Will get you a first draft of the presentation by tomorrow morning. Is that okay?'

'Yes, fine,' Jeremy answered and then stood up, hesitating a few seconds. Abe looked at him.

'Abe, would you mind getting that flask I asked you to

14

keep for me?'

Without a word, Abe fished his keys from his pocket, unlocked the bottom drawer of his desk, and extracted a large leather-covered hip flask from behind the old adapters and cables he kept there. He handed it to Jeremy and looked away. Abe heard him unscrew the top, take a long swig, groan slightly, and take a longer swig.

'Here,' Jeremy said, handing the flask back to Abe, who locked it in the drawer again.

Jeremy turned around and headed back to his office without another word, leaving Abe's door wide open. Abe sighed and sank back into his chair. He was only fleetingly aware of the sting of humiliation diffusing through his body before it turned into an urgent sense of sexual arousal. He went to the toilet, locked himself in a cubicle, and masturbated silently, watching pornography on his phone with the sound muted. On the way back to his office afterwards he checked his emails on his phone and noticed a smear of semen on the screen. He rubbed it off on the leg of his pants.

That evening, Amadou and Abe met in the men's locker room, which they both used to change before running home. When they were alone, Amadou insisted on speaking to Abe in Russian. He had spent five years in Moscow on a scholarship in Soviet times and had been married to a Russian woman for a while. Abe was always surprised at how relaxed and easy these conversations were. Was this, he had wondered, because of the levelling influence of the locker room, because they were speaking Russian, or because of Amadou's consummate social skills? As they were both leaving the building, Amadou, who let Abe go through the door first, mentioned that a member of the team had lodged a formal complaint against Jeremy.

'It's not the first time, either,' Amadou added, 'but still no justification for me losing my temper with Jeremy the way I did this morning. How do you think things are going in the team?'

'The atmosphere is as toxic as ever.'

'Such a difficult situation. It's been dragging on for years, but there simply is no easy solution. Jeremy is so competent in many ways. We've discussed this before, but please tell me if you come up with any bright ideas about how to solve this problem.'

'This is a difficult one, I know,' said Abe.

'Have a good run home.'

'Thank you. You too. Bye-bye,' said Abe as they jogged off in different directions.

As Abe made his way back from the toilet down the aisle of the business-class cabin, he saw that Jeremy, seated at the other end, had finished a bottle of wine with his dinner. And that's in addition to the scotches he had drunk waiting to board, he thought. Later, slumped on a sofa in the Emirates lounge during their stop-over in Dubai, Jeremy, drink in hand, sank into a confessional mood. Abe took out his phone, discreetly pressed the record button and slipped it back in his pocket. Abe had heard the stories before, more than once, during similar uncensored, alcohol-fuelled ramblings, but had yet to record them: Jeremy's brother's bi-sexuality, bipolar disorder and suicide; his mother's repeated stints in the Valkenberg psychiatric hospital in Cape Town; his ageing wife's chronic back pain and depression; his son's pot smoking. Abe gave Jeremy his full attention, probing gently here and there, but

16

careful to not to arouse suspicion.

As the plane came to a halt at Ninoy Aquino International Airport in Manila, Abe slid his books and laptop into his bag, tucked his shirt back into his pants, tied up his shoelaces, and double-checked that he had not forgotten anything in the business class berth. A local staff member, wearing a blue waistcoat with 'UN' emblazoned on its front and back, was waiting for them at the end of the jet bridge. He led them to the customs lane for diplomats, took their passports and whisked them through, exchanging a few words with the customs official in Tagalog. He wheeled their two suitcases through the crowds to the Landcruiser waiting for them just outside the airport in the tropical downpour. The driver ran to them with open umbrella, swung their suitcases into the trunk, turned the air-conditioning up for them, checked that all the doors were locked, and pointed the prow of the 4 x 4 into the traffic jam.

'Behold,' whispered Jeremy, who had sobered up, 'the sodden feral children will soon be scratching at the windows. Let us not forget, though, that they are our precious natural resource, the base metal we transmute, thanks to the alchemy of aid and development, into gold, for ourselves, Abram. Modern day chrysopoets we are. Unlike my forebears, though, we work for the New York, rather than the London, Missionary Society.'

'I'm not sure I'm following you,' said Abe. Jeremy flicked his limp hand in the air dismissively.

In the hotel elevator, Jeremy said: 'We'll meet at six in the bar to prepare for tomorrow. That should give us enough time before we meet the US delegation for dinner. Remember, Abe, to use "we" whenever you refer to the Land of the Free during dinner. You are one of them after all, Abram Ivanovich Ragin. A graduate of their elite institutions and a competent speaker of their vernacular. Perhaps even named after one of their most admired presidents. Play it up, Abe. We have to keep the US funds flowing.'

'I'll do my best. Don't worry. But I'm pretty sure Soviet Air Force engineer Ragin didn't name me after Lincoln.'

Jeremy checked the small cardboard folder with his keycard in it and said, 'I'm on the fourteenth floor.' He peered up at the electronic display above the elevator door to see how many more floors they had to go.

'Eighteenth, me,' said Abe.

The door opened. The bell-boy leaned down to pick up Jeremy's suitcase, which had fallen over onto the floor. His shoulder brushed against Jeremy's protruding belly. Jeremy recoiled as if bitten by a venomous insect and wiped off the front of his T-shirt. Abe looked at the bell-boy, who was shaking his head in bewilderment. Waiting for the elevator door to close again, Abe watched Jeremy lumber down the hallway in his creased linen jacket, worn Levis, sandals and T-shirt with a print of an abstract painting on it. The bell-boy was pulling Jeremy's suitcase, keeping a safe distance between them.

Abe hung up his suit and shirts in the closet. He placed his books on the night table, went into the bathroom and unzipped his toilet kit. He connected his iPhone and Airbook to the hotel Wi-Fi and texted his wife that he had arrived safely. Only then did he draw back the thick curtains and look out over yet another cityscape: high-rises and slums, with suburban developments sprouting in the distance; streets gridlocked and swarming with people; murky clouds scudding above and brown haze roiling below. That the dark clouds could be harbingers of a typhoon excited Abe. He put on his shorts, T-shirt and Asics and made his way to the gym on the top

18

floor. He thought he should harness the sudden surge in energy produced by the disruption in his circadian rhythms and run on the treadmill for an hour.

Jeremy, sitting towards the back of the bar in his suit, gave Abe a little wave. As Abe sat down, Jeremy was ordering another double Glenfiddich and asked Abe what he wanted.

'Sparkling water, no ice please,' Abe told the waiter.

'Admirably abstemious,' said Jeremy. 'Did you get some rest?'

'Yes. I fell into a deep sleep for a while after a run on the treadmill in the gym upstairs. Hope it doesn't mess up my biological clock even more. How about you?'

'No. Ended up watching some test cricket on Sky Sports. Zimbabwe against Sri Lanka; Zimbabwe won. A distant cousin of mine still plays on the Zimbabwean team. Incredible.'

Abe opened his laptop. They went over their presentations for the next day and Abe talked Jeremy through the order of battle. Shortly before eight, they moved to one of the hotel restaurants. An orchestra, on a low stage, was playing global tunes rearranged to trouble the consciousness of listeners as little as possible. Shiny wide sheets of water rippled down the walls behind tropical gardens. As they were being shown to the table where Elliot and Katie were already seated, Abe whispered: 'Jeremy, order the expensive wine once they're back in their rooms. No point in reminding them our per diem rates are two or three times theirs.'

They shook hands with Elliot and Abe spontaneously gave Katie, for whom he felt genuine affection, a hug. Jeremy would have preferred to shake her hand, but now felt he had little choice. He embraced her awkwardly, head held back.

'Well, I think that went as well as can be expected,' Jeremy said the moment Katie and Elliot had left to return to their rooms. 'Our funding for the coming years is secure. And, quite predictably, they were delighted with your sinister new project to use sensors, monitors, data analytics and whatnot to keep the poor in their place. Now that the puritans have retired for the night, it's time to order the drinkable stuff.'

'Big data to lift people out of poverty, Jeremy. Spreading the promise of high-tech to the most deserving. I'll have one glass and then, me too, I'll call it a day.'

As Abe was carried up the long escalator that stretched diagonally across the vast lobby towards the elevators, a woman on the downward escalator caught his eye. She was a slim, muscular, heavily made-up Filipina in long blue dress and heels. She puckered her lips, then smiled broadly as she drew nearer. Abe recognised her from a previous stay in the hotel with Jeremy a few months ago. At the point where the upward and downward escalators met, she leaned over towards Abe, and in a husky voice said: 'Good night, Mr Jerry's little slave. Hope you have a good jerk-off.' Abe, iPhone in hand, managed to take a few pictures of her and blew a kiss as she glided down and away.

Abe stood up to look at the books that lined the walls of the living room of Jeremy's apartment. He heard the toilet flush, the water run and the door open again. Expecting Jeremy to reappear, his shoulder and back muscles tightened. He looked at his watch. Almost eleven. I should be out of here before midnight, he thought. He sat down again in one of the two leather wing chairs placed opposite each other. Jeremy's cigarillo still smouldered in the ashtray on the table between them. The living room was a replica of an English gentleman's library, complete with mahogany panelling, Isfahan carpets and one wall devoted to an illuminated display of African artefacts—skins, drums, spears, shields and Jeremy's collection of prized Shona sculptures. Occupying two shelves were hundreds of vinyl records from sixties and seventies rock, blues and heavy metal bands that Jeremy continued to collect. Below the records was his Naim hi-fi equipment, worth thousands of dollars according the audiophiles Abe had eavesdropped on at the office.

Jeremy had gone into the bedroom instead of coming straight back into the living room. Abe leaned his head back against the high leather chair, closed his eyes and breathed in deeply. He then took out his phone and a shot a 360° video of the living room. Jeremy, when he shambled back, had changed from his suit into jeans, an old green Uriah Heep T-shirt, which now squeezed his heft like a sausage-skin, and a pair of flip-flops.

'Let's try to wrap this up,' Jeremy said as he refilled his tumbler and picked up his version of the report they were editing together. 'So, page 42, let's see, third paragraph.'

'Yes, that's where we left off,' said Abe.

'Well, I think this paragraph and the two following can simply be deleted. Just confuses things. Less is more.'

'Agree … I think,' Abe said. He began to draw a line through the text in his copy of the report and then hesitated: 'If we delete these, we're also going to have to change recommendation sex at the end of the report, on page …' he leafed to the back of the report '… page sixty-one, as it refers to them. But during the last inter-agency meeting Diop was adamant that this recommendation be included and, if you remember, he also insisted on its current wording. So, not so sure we can mess with any of this. Currently recommendation six reads: 'Reinforce the capacity of the Global Forum to Alleviate Poverty so it anticipates better cyclical crises.'

'Another one of Diop's Gallicisms,' Jeremy chuckled. 'I doubt he can even write French properly and, the last I heard, they had yet to agree on a standard for written Wolof. Does that sound like English to you?'

'Not sure we have much choice here, Jeremy.'

'But should I even be asking you, who only spoke Ruski till your teens? How can you have the same instinctive familiarity with the English language and all its rich cultural references as someone who imbibed it with his mother's milk—or with his Ndbele wet-nurse's milk, in my case,' he tittered.

'So, what do we do with these paragraphs, Jeremy?' asked Abe, stung, remembering how often he had to rewrite his pompous, long-winded prose.

'Best leave recommendation six as it stands. You've made it abundantly clear amending them is beyond our pay grade.'

As Abe was gathering up his papers, Jeremy cleared his throat once and then a second time. Abe looked over at him and sensed he wanted to say something.

'Abe,' he said. Abe nodded, coaxing him. 'I've returned to AA. But AA online this time. Seems to suit me better. And I'm showing a bit more persistence, so far at least,' Jeremy said.

Abe walked over to Jeremy and gave his shoulder a gentle squeeze, relishing the closeness. 'I'm glad to hear that Jeremy.'

Abe walked out of Jeremy's building into the quiet, brightly lit street. His Mercedes was parked on the other side, opposite the entrance of the building. He opened the car door, settled down behind the steering wheel, lowered the window and breathed in the humid fume-laced air. He looked at his watch. 11.52. I'll wait till 12.45, he thought. He had always liked waiting. Empty, responsibility-free time with a pretext. Deniable idleness. A year ago, his plane had been delayed for fifteen hours in Dubai. He had spent one of his best days in years. Reading, napping, watching documentaries on his computer in the comfort of the business lounge and strolling through the airport shopping mall—with neither pressure nor purpose.

Soon he became aware of a group of men walking towards the car. He sat up and squinted. It appeared to be a slow-moving procession led by a grey-bearded man in a dark robe who chanted in a deep voice, gently swinging a string of beads. Behind him were pall-bearers, similarly bearded and robed, carrying a corpse swaddled in white lying on a carved ceremonial pallet. A throng of men in dark suits followed the pall-bearers. They marched slowly, chanting in unison, filling the street with a low, reverberating, sound. Abe felt his throat and chest resonate as they moved past the open car window. The procession flowed into a low building with wire-mesh on its darkened windows and vanished when the doors were pulled shut. Abe leaned back into the headrest, unable to place what he had witnessed.

Whenever a car appeared, Abe would perk up, and then sink back when it drove by without stopping. Eventually, a cab pulled up. Abe slipped out of the car and walked back across the road. He pulled two $100 dollar bills out of his pocket and waited next to the entrance of Jeremy's building.

A sinewy woman with a large red Nike sports bag stepped out of the cab. She looked at Abe and frowned as she lifted the bag onto her shoulder. He moved forward and, in the calmest and most ordinary voice he could produce, asked: 'Can I speak to you a moment, Jacinta?'

'How do you know my name? Do you live here?' she asked. Abe detected the residue of an accent. But she's not Latina, as her name would suggest, he thought.

'No. I don't live here. I'd just like to talk to you,' he said, holding out the two bills to her, his fingers quivering.

'Two hundred bucks just to talk?'

'Yes, just to talk. No more than ten minutes.'

She looked him up and down, got out a small can of mace from her handbag and showed it to Abe. Then she reached for the $200.

'We'll just walk up and down the street, slowly, okay, under the lights. Can you take this?' handing him the sports bag, which he struggled to raise onto his shoulder.

'Why do you know my name?' she asked.

'I work with Jeremy Barker—Mr Jerry?—and I hacked into his private email account.'

'What do you want from me?' she asked, pencil-thin brows furrowed, black eyes trying to bore into him.

'I'd like your help.'

'What for?'

'Help me video one of your sessions with him.'

'You don't need my help with that. You just need to place a miniature remote-controlled webcam next time you're in his place and connect it to his IP address. I think you know that, Mr Hacker. So why are you asking me?'

'I want some high-quality footage, not from a fixed webcam. And …' he hesitated.

'And you'd like to watch some of it close-up and live, too?'

'Yes,' he said, hearing his voice break with excitement. 'I'd like to be there.'

They walked in silence a while. He shifted the heavy bag from one shoulder to the other. She got her phone out and started tapping on it. He forced his eyeballs around as far as they would go to see what she was up to. Doing sums on her calculator.

'Doable, if you can pay,' she whispered. 'Sorry the bag is so heavy. Barker's pleasure instruments.'

'You serious?'

'About the bag or that it's doable?'

'Doable.'

'Yes, but not cheap.'

'How much?'

'You're not from here, are you?' she asked.

'How can you tell?'

'$9,000,' she answered. 'Once you use the footage and he finds out, I lose him as a client. A big loss, even I've come to dislike the man. And maybe it'll also get me into trouble. Hard to predict how these things play out. So, anything less than $9,000 would not be worth my while. No face shots of me, understood?'

'Is that an opening gambit?'

'No, I left the souk many years ago, mashallah,' she said. 'Pay by Bitcoin. Half before. Half once you have the footage. I'll send you instructions. He likes to be blindfolded and I'll put headphones on him.'

'Choukran,' he said.

'Afwan. When do you want to do it?'

'Well, depends on when you have your next session.'

Abe gave her an email address, which she entered into her phone. They walked back up the street towards the entrance of Jeremy's building. With the sports bag on the other shoulder, they were now close enough for Abe to inhale her scent. Once in front of the entrance, he dropped the sports bag onto the ground and kissed her on the cheek, feeling her black curly hair stroke his face. He felt like hugging her, but instead crossed the street to his car. She heaved the bag back onto her shoulder and went into the building and up to Jeremy.

Abe sat at the desk in his study. He stared out over his computer screen at the heavy summer rain falling on the roofs of the suburban houses. For a moment, he listened intently, trying to locate the whereabouts of his wife, Alicia, in the house. All was silent except for the sound of the rain and he looked down again at the screen.

He was downloading files to his encrypted hard-drive: the pictures of the woman in blue on the escalator in Manila; pictures he had taken surreptitiously of Jeremy passed out from drink on other recent flights to Nairobi, New Delhi and Cairo; the video he had taken in Jeremy's living room; recordings of Jeremy's online AA meetings he had gained access to; and recordings from the bugging software he had planted on Jeremy's cell phone. He pushed the buds of his headphones into his ears and began listening to a recent recording of a conversation between Jeremy and his wife. Content of conversation unremarkable, he thought. Jeremy's voice, tense and bullying. Hers, frail and then tearful. He skipped through the rest of the recording and had just deleted it when, with a jolt, he felt Alicia's fingers on his scalp.

He pulled out his ear-phones, took her hand in his, and looked up at her.

'Why don't we go out somewhere, Abram, instead of spending the day cooped up inside?' she suggested.

Gazing at Alicia released an upwelling of tenderness in Abe, for her open face, so unused to dissembling, for her quiet rectitude, for her bright and clear voice, her unobtrusive assertiveness, and for the perennial fresh and soapy smell she exuded. Then the recurring thought, which he could never voice to her, came back to mind: what amounts to a species barrier separates us. This is how, he had often reflected, a human being endowed with first-rate genes developed in optimal conditions turns out.

'We could,' he finally said turning to the window, 'but it's pouring out there. Why don't we wait till it eases up a bit? Where do you want to go?'

'Not sure. We could go the gym and then go to the steam room together. I'll go get changed.'

She was about to shut the door again when she asked, 'Is that the hard drive with all those files on Jeremy you've been collecting?'

'I've got other files on it too. I use it as an extra-back up.'

'How long have you been collecting this stuff? What's the point?'

Abe stared out the window again, chastising himself for having pushed the ear-buds in so deeply.

'A while ago,' she said, 'after we discussed it for the first time, I mentioned it to Ashley at the clinic.'

'What did you say?' Abe asked, irritated but unsurprised.

27

Alicia worked as a psychologist in a student mental health clinic.

'What did Ashley say is more to the point.'

'Well, what did she say?'

'She said you should probably be seeing a therapist. I told her about Jeremy and she agreed that you should have filed a formal complaint against him a long time ago.'

'I've been seeing a therapist, for what ... almost three years now. Did you tell Ashley?'

'And what does your therapist say?'

Still looking out the window, Abe said, 'The rain has stopped. Want to go?'

'Have you told him, Abe? Have you told Dr Russo about Jeremy?'

'Yes, he knows that I have a difficult relationship with him. Dr Russo's been trying to help me deal with it. But he also thinks that at this point I should consider finding another job. That this is a "very damaging re-enactment of the past with a deeply troubled individual", but to which I make a significant contribution, or something along those lines.'

'Do you think he's right to say you also contribute to this?' she asked.

'Yes, he's no doubt right.'

'Did you tell him about all these secret files you keep on this encrypted drive?' Her desire to know had overridden her principles, Abe noted with unexpected pleasure. She grabbed the hard drive, lifted it up and dropped it. He lunged forward to catch it. 'So precious to you? I don't know what the hell you have on it.'

'I've mentioned them to him,' he said.

'High time you did a little more than "mention it", don't

28

you think? Maybe it's also time you talked to Diop again, or to personnel, or whoever.'

'It's not in Diop's interest to confront Jeremy and not in mine to kick up a fuss. Would end up backfiring on me. And a lot of this is my doing. I've let myself become too entangled with Jeremy.'

'Okay, okay,' she said. 'I'm sorry. As long as you're talking it through with Dr Russo, I'm sure you'll work things out.' She kissed his forehead and declared, 'Come on, let's go!'

Jacinta beckoned to Abe through the half-open bedroom door. Abe stepped into the room as quietly as he could. He pointed the camera at Jeremy, on all fours on a large black coffee table. As planned, Jeremy was blindfolded with big black earphones clamped over his ears from which the sound of heavy metal escaped.

He looked even fatter naked than dressed. The heaps of flesh that sagged from Jeremy's body were a translucent white with a faint purplish-blue hue here and there from the blood vessels showing through. Other than his face and hands, no part of Jeremy's body had seen the sun in years. Abe noticed that his toe and finger-nails were painted black, his cheeks covered in rouge, and he wore crimson lip-stick. In the warm room, Jeremy's naked body gave off the smell of sour milk.

Abe leaned against the wall. He looked at the shelf opposite to check that the miniature camera he had asked Jacinta to place on the shelf was there.

Jacinta, crop in hand, stood in a black latex half bra through which her brown breasts and pierced nipples poked. She wore motorcycle boots, a metal ring around her scrotum and half-erect penis, and a pair of elbow-length latex gloves. She stood behind Jeremy and pulled him upright by a thick leather collar. She forced his arms behind his back and clamped metal handcuffs on his wrists. Kneeling, Jeremy's erect penis pointed at Abe. Abe slithered along the wall away from it.

Jacinta struck Jeremy with the crop a few times. Abe zoomed in on Jeremy's face wincing. She smiled at Abe, leaned towards him and kissed him, forcing her tongue deep into his mouth. With a box of hypodermic sterile needles in hand, Jacinta walked around to face Jeremy. Concentrating, she grabbed a handful of Jeremy's breast fat and pushed a green-tipped needle through it. She did this again and again, until a ring of needles radiated out from each nipple. She then kissed Jeremy on the cheek, leaned back, and slapped him across the face lightly once, then a second time slightly harder. She reached for Abe's hand, pulled him over, and motioned him to slap Jeremy, too. Abe retreated at first, then handed the camera to Jacinta and slapped Jeremy, once, twice and a third time, careful not to dislodge the earphones. He quickly withdrew, taking the camera back from Jacinta. Jacinta was beaming, about to break into uncontrollable giggles. Abe moved back to the safety of the doorway and continued to film.

Jacinta forced Jeremy to turn around on the table, with his back to Abe, took off the cuffs and pushed him onto all fours again. She nudged his knees apart, separated his heavy white cheeks, opening his pinkish-brown crack and exposing a corolla of moist red swelling around his anus. Holding a bottle of lubricant, she grinned while she lifted her gloved hand, stretched her fingers out and—as if closing a fan—folded them into a fist. She covered her fist and gloved forearm with

30

lubricant and methodically smeared it around.

Brow creased in concentration, she gently inserted one and then two fingers into Jeremy's anus. He let out a loud groan. Exaggeratedly loud, Abe thought, but then remembered the headphones with the blaring music. His sphincter relaxed. Soon Jacinta had managed to force her entire hand into Jeremy, who was now groaning shamelessly to the rhythm of the music. Jacinta gradually pushed her hand deep into Jeremy's rectum and up into his colon. She slid it right up to her elbow. A constant loud rhythmic groan was now emanating from Jeremy. Jacinta pulled her arm out and then slid it in deep again, slowly and regularly. Jeremy's groans turned into a high-pitched ululation. Abe crouched down and caught Jeremy's sperm splattering across the black surface of the coffee table, on video.

Jacinta pulled her faeces-smeared arm out of Jeremy, producing a long sound of wet suction. An acrid smell began to fill the room. She shooed Abe away, indicating that it was time for him to go. Abe zoomed in on the shit-streaked glove being peeled off and switched the camera off. He dropped it into his jacket pocket and slipped out of the apartment. In the elevator down, he vibrated his penis through his pants and ejaculated just as the doors opened onto the empty lobby.

After receiving the final payment, Jacinta sent Abe the footage from the camera that had been placed on the shelf. She mentioned, in the email, that to avoid any potential problems for herself, she would, as soon as Abe confirmed receipt, delete all copies of the footage.

Taking advantage of Alicia's absence at a conference for the rest of the week, Abe spent his evenings editing the footage Jacinta had sent him. He interspersed it with pictures, videos and audio recordings taken from the rich store he had accumulated on his encrypted hard drive. Between the shots of Jacinta skewering Jeremy's blubber and exploring his innards, Abe told Jeremy's life story, or at least the version of it he had been able to piece together. He added a dozen explanatory intertitles for coherence, like in an old silent movie. He found he could work for hours, in a manic state of mind, the biopic taking shape according to a plan he was barely conscious of. By late Friday night, he had a forty-five-minute video from which he had carefully edited out all sign of himself and all face-shots of Jacinta. He sent a copy to her, as promised. On Saturday, alone in the house before Alicia came back in the evening, he watched the video again and again, tweaking it here and there. Finally, towards the end of the afternoon, he got up and paced around, perplexed by his handiwork.

When he sat down at the computer once more, an email had arrived from Jacinta. It was a short message, without greeting: 'Having second thoughts. Has his sexuality ever caused anyone harm? Please reconsider using footage for revenge or blackmail.'

For months now, Abe had fantasised about anonymously sending a video similar to the one he had just created to Jeremy, to Jeremy's wife, Jeremy's children, to members of Jeremy's team, particularly Geert and Ann-Sophie, and to Amadou Diop. Imagining in vivid detail the impact the video would have on them all provided Abe with a depth of emotional satisfaction matched by few other experiences. He had gone so far as to download and learn to use a Tor Browser and onion router to cover his tracks. But the unpredictability of it all went against his nature. All along, he said to himself, he had known he would never go through with it.

Under pressure to leave and pick Alicia up at the airport, he replied to Jacinta quickly: 'All is fair in love and war, no? Agree that J's sexuality is harmless. Okay, you have my word: I will not use for blackmail or revenge. Your compassion for him is admirable. Worth more than $9,000. Let's meet again.'

He shut down the computer without sending his video out into the world. Speeding on the highway to get to the airport on time, Abe felt the frenzied energy that had animated him for weeks finally begin to ebb.

Around eight o'clock Monday morning, before dropping his bag off in his office or hanging up his jacket on the hook behind the door, he knocked on Jeremy's door and asked if he had a minute to discuss a pressing matter.

'Can it not wait till late this afternoon? Not feeling very fresh. And we have our weekly meeting at ten, and then I have to prepare for a meeting with the secretary-general this afternoon.'

'No, I'd prefer to talk before then.'

'Well, okay, if you insist, why don't you just come in now? But it'll have to be quick.'

Abe, strangely calm, pulled out a letter in a plastic sleeve from his bag, and placed it on the desk in front of Jeremy. Jeremy removed it from the sleeve and began reading it aloud at first, and then in silence. When he had finished, he looked up at Abe and said, 'Don't you think we should discuss this first, rather than you putting me in front of the fait accompli.'

'My mind is made up. I would prefer not to discuss it.'

'Well, you could perhaps be so kind as to provide an explanation for this rather unexpected decision, no?' Jeremy said, swallowing.

Abe pulled a memory stick out of his bag and handed it to Jeremy

'That I ended up doing this is all the explanation you need. After you watch it, I will destroy the only other copy that exists.'

At ten that morning, Abe, Mourad, Shelley, Geert and Ann-Sophie were all seated around the long table in Jeremy's office, waiting for the weekly meeting to start. Ann-Sophie was fidgety, checking her phone every few seconds. She had rushed in a few minutes before to say that Jeremy would be late, explaining that he had asked to meet Diop urgently. As they waited, the initial awkwardness gave way to amiable chat. Soon Geert was telling them all about the Zugspitz Ultra trail run in Bavaria that he had competed in during his vacation.

Abe, only half-listening, was staring out of the wall-length window. His eyes idly followed the contrails that criss-crossed the sky while he mentally rehearsed how he was going to tell his colleagues about his resignation. Ann-Sophie suddenly looked up from her phone and said: 'Jeremy says today's team meeting is cancelled. He'll be tied up with Under-Secretary-General Diop for a while longer.'

As they were all leaving the office, Ann-Sophie, who had remained seated, reached for Abe's arm as he walked by, gesturing to him to stay behind. Once alone she leaned in close to Abe and whispered: 'I heard that this meeting with Diop might be good news for you, Abe.'

Xenophobia and misogyny all dropped like dead weights to the bottom of the pool. As he followed them down, past layers of sediment holding the bones of Norman and Saxon patriarchs, he saw nothing but a series of systems, collective delusions, mass deceptions, seductive fictions and never-ending dehumanisation

The Pike of Knowledge | Brian Kelly

Fionn was born with a call to the heroics. He wanted to go everywhere and do everything. He wanted to speak all the words and hear them spoken. But most of all, he wanted to give himself to something—something good, something worthy, something worth dying for.

In the Clanbrassil Street flats, such sentiments were viewed with grave misgivings.

As Fionn hit his sliotar into a bin hoisted on the wall for target practice, the neighbours, €125 flush from the doll office, did their best to ignore his messing. They poured Dutchy and Bavaria and Bucky down their throats and watched the stolen car smoulder on the concrete square between the four towers. When Fionn's practice finally came to fruition and he took off, hurly raised above his head, to celebrate in front of a packed Hill Sixteen, the neighbours rolled their eyes. The final embers of the burning car died away and the drunken elders of the Clanbrassil Street flats swore that if the young fella kept up this carry on then something was gonna have to be done. The bog ball. The history books. The talking in Irish

37

and the singing I-diddly-I fucking music. Was he a bleedin muck savage or what? Could somebody not drag the young fella into the twenty-first century? Could somebody not get him a subscription to Netflix or Sky Sports or something? How much longer were they gonna have to put up with this culchie-loving bollix?

Understandably enough, this was the majority opinion in the Clanbrassil Street flats. There were, however, other elements, odd as this no doubt was, who took the young fella's interest in romantic Ireland as proof of a Republican sensibility. They'd have him spray-painting Tiocfaidh ár lá on the side of buses yet. They'd have him supporting Scottish football teams in no time.

Now everyone in the Clanbrassil Street flats respected what the lads had done in 1916. The IRA managed to get rid of the Brits after 600 years of oppression and nobody would hear a word said against that. But when Sinn Fein youth enlisted Fionn for a commemoration march and Fionn started quoting Padraig Pearce and conscripting other young fellas for a New Republican Youth Brigade, they'd seen enough. Fionn was losing the run of himself. He was getting ideals. He was becoming fundamentalised. Next thing you'd know, he'd be sporting a beard and swearing off bacon. If his ma was not gonna take him in hand then they would.

That was the exact phrase they used with Ms McCuil and the next morning she was on the phone to Uncle O'Brien, the cutest hoor in all of Ireland, to ask for help.

'Leave him to me, Mary,' said Uncle O'Brien, in his thick Cork accent. 'I've got some work down here that'll put some manners on him right enough.'

The next day, as Fionn sat at the kitchen table revising

38

his aimsir fhaaitcanacli, his mother informed him of his fate.

'I will like shite go down there,' said Fionn, conjugating his verbs with absolute confidence.

'You'll go where I fecking tell ya!' shouted his mam, unleashing the wooden spoon she'd kept ready for a bit of gentle persuasion.

After losing three wooden spoons to back chat, cursing and general carry on, Ms McCuil finally brought Fionn around to her way of thinking, and that very evening he was on a bus heading for Cork.

By the time the Bus Eireann pulled up outside Uncle O'Brien's gas plant, Fionn was absolutely dying for a slash. He hadn't been allowed off at McDonald's. He'd been given a final warning for trying to sneak off at the garage. At the services, the driver finally lost his patience and slapped Fionn around the ear. Ms McCuil, it seems, had given orders that Fionn was not, under any circumstances, to be allowed off the bus until it reached a particular patch of no man's land on the outskirts of Cork City.

As a result, Fionn's first impressions of Uncle O'Brien's oil refinery were received lad in hand, with the hot smell of urine burning in his nostrils. So, this was the famous O'Brien refinery? Hard to believe all those towers and rigs and pipes and warehouses, stretching out for as far as the eye could see, belonged to Uncle O'Brien. Maybe his ma had been right? Maybe Uncle O'Brien—who smelled of Imperial Leather and chewed liquorice allsorts and waddled his arse when he walked—really was the cutest hoor in all of Ireland.

'If you're going to have that thing out around here you better make sure you're ready to use it,' came the voice of Uncle O'Brien, popping up, as if out of the mucky ground, on Fionn's left and proceeding to gaze openly at the young man's cock.

'Sorry, Uncle O'Brien,' said Fionn, bringing his stream of piss, despite the horrible stinging it caused, to an abrupt stop and giving his lad a healthy shake before trying to get it back in his trousers.

'Any more than three shakes is wanking,' hooted Uncle O'Brien, slapping Fionn on the back.

The young man stumbled forwards into the pissy grass, lost his grip on his cock and dangled himself out in the open air once more.

'Another McCuil mad for the micky, I see,' said Uncle O'Brien as Fionn, flustered and piss-stained, struggled to get his lad back inside his cacks once and for all. 'Oh well, we'll work that out of you soon enough.'

'Sorry, I was dying I was. Wouldn't let me off the bus they wouldn't,' said Fionn, turning sheepishly around to face his uncle.

Uncle O'Brien reached inside his old suit jacket, produced two liquorice sweets—one ringed in pink, the other in brown—which he popped into his mouth before turning to walk away. 'Follow me,' he said, his bulbous arse waddling up and down as he set off across the fields.

Now Fionn had studied the geography of Ireland. He knew the names of the all the rivers—The Barrow, The Nore and The Sure—and he knew all the mountains, too. As a result of these studies he was fairly sure there was no bog land on the outskirts of Cork City. As far as Fionn knew, such habitats—by no means rare in the county—were confined to the uplands some miles away. Yet as uncle and nephew waded into deeper and denser muck, and followed harder and narrower paths, between deeper and darker pools, which reflected thicker and taller tufts of heather, there could be little doubt, no matter what the geographical survey might have to say about it: they were walking through a bog. Maybe this was what his ma had meant when she said Uncle O'Brien would teach him a few things he couldn't learn in those books of his.

After forty-five minutes of jumping and sloshing and balancing and hopping and splashing uncle and nephew finally arrived at a chain-link fence and a topple-down wooden shed.

The fence was stained brown to a height of two feet as if it had, like Fionn's new jeans, slowly sucked up the bog water through a process of capillary action. Above the shit stains there hung a yellow sign, turned upside down, which read 'Private Property' and in a tiny subtext, almost invisible to the naked eye, 'Trespassers will be shot'. Fionn wondered who the fuck would ever want to walk forty-five minutes across that bog to climb a bleedin fence in the middle of nowhere. Despite the distance they'd travelled, the gas towers, periodically sending ribbons of orange flame up into the sodden sky, still looked like they were a long way off. How far the warehouses and factories were beyond that was anybody's guess.

Still, Uncle O'Brien's arse had stopped waddling and Fionn was glad of the opportunity to scrape some muck off the bottom of his boots.

'You see that?' asked Uncle O'Brien, pointing with a piece of black rope liquorice.

Fionn had been distracted by the distant gas towers and factories and warehouses, but as he lowered his eyes onto the piece of bog just beyond the fence he could indeed see. Who could bloody fail to see? How had he not seen it already?

Stilly as mirrors, deep as mine shafts, long as battlefield trenches, there stood a dozen rectangular bog holes filled

41

with black water, separated by a grid of narrow turf walkways. Fionn could see it, but he was fucked if he knew what he was looking at.

'What you're looking at there, boy, is potentially the most profitable fish farm on planet Earth,' said Uncle O'Brien, popping the liquorice noose into his gob, spitting a jet of black phlegm into the thick muck, and rubbing his grubby little hands together excitedly.

'A fish farm?' asked Fionn cautiously.

'A pike farm, to be exact,' said Uncle O'Brien, turning away from the chain-link fence and leading his nephew towards the tumbledown shed. 'Tell me, what do you know about pike, Fionn?'

Fishing was not the most popular pastime in the Clanbrassil Street flats, but contrary to common misperceptions about inner-city life, it was not an impossibility. The canal was a five-minute stroll from Fionn's gaff, and on a hot summer's day, when nobody could be arsed playing football, Fionn would occasionally while away an afternoon sitting on the banks of the Grand Canal with a couple of maggots squirming on the end of his line. Now you were just as likely to catch a traffic cone and old pair of socks in the Grand Canal as you were a fish, so Fionn's knowledge of those animals was limited. But what he did know was that perch, roach and pike, the fish that could be caught in the canal, were not edible under any circumstances. In fact, if local legends were to be believed—cats snatched from the bank, dogs ripped limb from limb in clear daylight—you were more likely to be eaten by a pike than to eat one yourself. So, when Uncle O'Brien asked Fionn what he knew about pike, that's what he told him.

'I know you can't eat them,' said Fionn as they arrived at

the rotten shed door.

'No, you can't, Fionn,' said Uncle O'Brien, turning to smile at his nephew. 'You absolutely cannot eat them.'

'Then what are you farming them for?' asked Fionn innocently.

'Never you fucking mind,' snarled Uncle O'Brien, smile dropping from his face as he ripped open the shed door. 'Just step inside here now while I explain a couple of things to you, Fionn.'

Fionn had never actually owned a garden shed. They weren't a common feature in the Clanbrassil Street flats. He had, however, made a couple of posh friends in primary school whose parents owned houses in Portobello with gardens and flower beds and sheds and all that shite. Now as far as Fionn was aware, such sheds normally contained lawn mowers and shears and trowels and rusty bikes and bits of old go-karts. He may not have been an expert in the field but he was fairly certain that they didn't normally contain priest's vestments or shiny chains or leather breeches. Admittedly, Fionn had only been involved in the fish farming industry for the past twenty seconds, but he still couldn't for the life of him imagine what all this gear had to do with pike.

'You'll sleep there,' said Uncle O'Brien, kicking a bundle of rags, which Fionn thought he heard squeak. 'And you'll guard the pike with this.'

Uncle O'Brien pulled a case from under the bed and produced a hefty shotgun. Fionn suddenly began warming to this new job of his. He'd finally get to put that Youth Brigade training to good use. He'd finally be a man at arms!

'I suppose it's too much to expect that a Jackeen West-Brit yobo like yerself might know how to use a gun in the service of his country?' asked Uncle O'Brien, pressing the double-bar-relled shotgun into Fionn's belly.

The words 'service' and 'country' struck Fionn's ears like a bugle horn. He was being given a mission. A fishy mission in the middle of a bog, but a mission none the less. Uncle O'Brien wasn't growing pike in the middle of nowhere for nothing. The cutest hoor in all of Ireland was surely up to something, and he'd chosen Fionn to help him do it.

'I have received basic firearms training and am ready and willing to serve my country, sir,' answered Fionn, snapping to attention.

'Ready and willing eh?' said Uncle O'Brien, running his hand along the length of the gun barrel whilst leaning in so close that the smell of liquorice and Imperial Leather made Fionn nauseous. 'I like lads who are ready and willing, Fionn, I really do. But what I don't like is anybody sneaking around trying to get their hands on my pike. So, if you catch any little fucker trespassing on this land, you're going to shoot them square in the bollix, Fionn, and kick their bloody corpse into the ponds for the fishies … is that clear?'

Fionn's brief training with the Irish Volunteers Youth Brigade, which mostly consisted in running around the Dublin Mountains with paint-ball rifles, had encouraged shots to the head, stomach and sternum. The 'kill zones', as they'd called them. He'd even been shown how to finish off an enemy combatant with his bare hands, but this craic of purposefully aiming for a lad's nuts seemed a tad violent to Fionn.

'In the balls?' asked Fionn, leaning back on his heels to seek some relief from Uncle O'Brien's breath.

'Right in the fucking nut sack,' repeated Uncle O'Brien, cupping his nephew's balls in his hand and squeezing home his point.

'Yes, sir,' yelped Fionn, daring not move lest his uncle's hand take yet a firmer grip.

'So I'm understood?' demanded Uncle O'Brien.

'Understood,' yelped Fionn.

'You sleep here. You feed the fish. You shoot any fucker who tries to climb the fence and you do not, under any circumstances, eat the pike,' said Uncle O'Brien, giving Fionn's balls a final sickening squeeze.

'Got it,' groaned Fionn, pre-vomit super-salivation invading his gob.

With that Uncle O'Brien was gone, and given the events of the day—the traveling and walking and sloshing and wading—Fionn thought it best to eat the packed lunch his ma had given him and hit the hay.

It was a weird old shed, but with a couple of rags pulled up over his body he felt pretty snug. He had never been in the scouts, but this must be what camping out was like. He had never bivouacked at an ambush point, but this must be exactly the kind of buzz that the great rebel heroes of Irish history felt when getting ready to blow the shite out of some unsuspecting English regiment transporting political prisoners through the Leitrim mountains. With thoughts of 1798 and Vinegar Hill and Robert Emmet and Wolf Tone flying around his head, Fionn fell fast asleep.

When, some hours later, Fionn's ear detected the distant approach of a car engine, his hand, fresh from dreams of shooting Black and Tans, instantly reached for the shotgun.

Dressed only in his boxer shorts, Fionn slipped on his boots and crept silently towards the shed door. He slowed his breathing and his heart rate. He cocked his ear at the crack.

And yes, somewhere down the hill, moving steadily across the bog tracks, Fionn could hear the rattle of an engine and the sloshing of tyres.

Well, he hadn't started his new job a moment too soon. Uncle O'Brien, the cutest hoor in all of Ireland, must have known this was coming. Fionn pushed the shed door open an inch further and hadn't long to wait before shards of electric light began dancing across the tips of the heather.

Fionn had listened to many a stolen car pulling into the Clanbrassil Street flats. He knew his Honda Civic from his Subaru Impreza from his Ford GT Golf, and he got out of bed for nothing less than a three-litre sport injection. As a result, Fionn could tell from the pathetic whine of the approaching vehicle that this was nothing more than a Toyota Starlet or a Nissan Micra or an Opel Corsa. Emboldened by the fact that his enemies had such a shitty getaway car, Fionn clicked off the shotgun's safety and took aim.

The headlights cut clean through the darkness. Shots of blue and green and purple scattered through the heather. The bog pools shifted and teemed and shone. The muck grumbled and squelched and slid. The chain link fence gleamed as Fionn closed one eye and trained the gun on the cusp of the hill.

He'd give them one warning shot to the bonnet and if the fuckers did anything other than take off in a hurry, he'd let them have it in the balls, just like Uncle O'Brien said.

A drop of sweat tickled Fionn's neck. Something squeaked in the shed behind him. The wind picked up awful fierce and the odd smell of stagnant water and fish feed and petrochemicals wafted in the shed door. But Fionn did not as much as twitch. He was fully focused as a beige Micra finally emerged from behind a bush and squelched to a stop not ten metres from the shed door.

The car engine had barely stopped when Fionn let loose with both barrels.

The blast blew the shed door wide open and nearly dislocated Fionn's shoulder. The stinging in the soft flesh between his upper arm and shoulder was such that Fionn all but forgot about the car he'd opened fire on. As he shook his deadened arm and hopped from foot to foot in pain, a series out shouts could be heard outside.

'Jesus fucking Christ! What the fuck do you think you're doing?' shouted a voice.

A rat, which had been hiding somewhere in Fionn's bed, scurried towards the shed door, and as Fionn's eyes followed its path, revulsion growing as he realised it was gnawing on a pair of his socks, he caught sight of Uncle O'Brien, red-faced and angry, rapidly bearing down upon him.

Ordinarily, Fionn would have prepared his excuses, but then something happened that took him totally by surprise. Out of the Micra, without fanfare or ceremony, there stepped a vision: a beatific apparition; an angel decked out from head-to toe in Daz Ultra whites that were completely at odds with life in the bog. For a moment, Fionn, who'd kept the shotgun semi-erect despite his stinging shoulder, was too stunned to pay any heed to Uncle O'Brien's threats.

'I'm going tell you one last time before I knock your fucking block off,' roared Uncle O'Brien, his belly wobbling with anger as he stepped inside the shed. 'Put down the fucking gun and cop the fuck on to yourself.'

Uncle O'Brien spat these orders with such venom that liquorice shrapnel flew across the shed and struck Fionn in the face. This little piece of return fire finally got Fionn's attention.

'Sorry about that,' said Fionn holding the gun out, barrel first, towards Uncle O'Brien's chest.

'Are you trying to fucking kill me or what!' roared Uncle O'Brien, swatting the barrel aside and ripping the gun from Fionn's grasp.

'Sorry. I thought yez were-'

The cold metal barrels of the gun pressed up against Fionn's balls and brought his apologies to a stop.

'Do you want me to blow your fucking balls off and feed you to the fish?' snarled Uncle O'Brien, holding the butt of the gun down around his crotch and pushing forwards so Fionn's testicles were now hanging partially inside the barrels of the gun.

'No, Uncle O'Brien,' yelped Fionn.

'So what the fuck are you doing taking pot shots at me and my guest?' demanded Uncle O'Brien.

'I thought yez were robbers coming to steal pike from the farm,' groaned Fionn as Uncle O'Brien applied yet more pressure to his balls.

Fionn felt full sure he was about to lose his boyhood before he'd even turned it into a manhood. But then there came an intercession—a piece of providence, some divine succour drifting effortless down to him like sands off the ridge of an Arabian dune.

'Please, Mr O'Brien,' said the Shaq, his voice unfurling itself in the air like hookah smoke. 'The young man was trying to protect our investment was he not? With such loyalty we will see a great return, will we not?'

'Oh, we'll see a great return all right,' snarled Uncle O'Brien. 'But I don't think my nephew is going to be around to witness it.'

48

There was a wild look in Uncle O'Brien's eyes. A look Fionn had seen in Father Sullivan's when he preached about the dangers of the flesh and the evils of contraception. A look he'd seen on old Mary McTernan's face when she pulled young fellas out of the boys' toilets at the teenage disco. It was rash and it was constricted and it was likely to blow your fucking nuts off as quick as it looked at ya.

'Come, my friend,' said the Shaq, placing a bejewelled finger, glittering purple and blue despite the gloom, on Uncle O'Brien's shoulder. 'It would be a shame to waste such a fine looking boy.'

Uncle O'Brien's nostrils flared. His face dropped from deep vein scarlet to a valentine red. The gun barrel eased off Fionn's nuts and Uncle O'Brien leaned back, eyes narrowed, hand groping inside his pocket for liquorice while he draped lingering looks all over Fionn's shivering young body.

'The McCuils have always had a fine athletic cut to them, in fairness,' said Uncle O'Brien, turning to the Shaq like a punter at a racecourse.

'He has shapely legs and thighs,' answered the Shaq, twisting the ends of his mustachios.

With the threat of castration fading, and the adrenaline of the attack waning, and the surprise of the Shaq passing, Fionn felt a bog-chill tightening its teeth around his bones.

As the Shaq and Uncle O'Brien continued to pass comment on the cut of Fionn's shoulders and the flatness of his belly and the pertness of his buttocks, Fionn stooped to retrieve his trousers.

'And what do you think you're doing now?' snapped Uncle O'Brien, interrupting the Shaq's wistful tale about a young camel hand with the most exquisite Kashmiri blue eyes, whom he'd once held in his employ.

'I'm dying with the cold,' explained Fionn, and the wind, as if to illustrate the young man's point, began to blow with such force that it felt like the shed may well keel over and die.

'And wouldn't that be good enough for you now,' answered Uncle O'Brien, constipated rage clogging up his veins and forking out like bleeding trees on his liquorice-stained skin.

'Come, come, my friend. Let your nephew get dressed,' said the Shaq, stepping between Fionn and the barrel of Uncle O'Brien's gun. 'We have more pressing business to attend to, do we not?'

'I suppose we do,' snarled Uncle O'Brien, leading the Shaq past Fionn into the shed proper.

It was without doubt the closest Fionn had ever been to somebody in such a foreign get up, but he was far too freezing to care. His knees were purple and his elbows were an angry shade of blue. His teeth were chattering with such force that he found it hard to focus his eyes on any object in particular. This, coupled with the total lack of feeling in his fingers, meant the process of getting dressed was far from a simple one. With great difficulty, Fionn managed to zip up his piss-stained jeans. Buttoning his shirt was such a hassle that Fionn barely noticed Uncle O'Brien taking the priest's black cassock from its hook on the wall. The agonies of tying his bootlaces were such that Fionn played no heed to the leather straps and metal chains Uncle O'Brien affixed to his religious garb. It was not until Uncle O'Brien was fully changed and standing beside the Shaq that Fionn took in their appearance.

With one dressed entirely in black and the other entirely in white, they resembled a pair of kings on a chessboard, meeting up in secret, at some point before the game, to arrange the slaughter of their underlings in a way that left them both unscathed.

'Jesus, I feel mighty in this get up, I tell ya,' laughed Uncle O'Brien, pulling at the white collar that dug deep into his fleshy neck.

'You are ready to prime the feed then, my friend?' asked the Shaq, a hint of anticipation creeping into his face.

'I'll prime the fucker all right,' laughed Uncle O'Brien, pursing his lips and thrusting his hips like a Chippendale trapped inside a priest's clothing. 'They're always better after a little ride.'

Uncle O'Brien may well have been the cutest hoor in all of Ireland, but Fionn was rapidly coming to the opinion that he was also the strangest. As the monochrome kings cackled in the wind-shuck-shed, Fionn couldn't help but notice the shotgun lying unmanned against the wall.

'Yes, yes, what you say is true, my friend,' laughed the Shaq. 'These things always go so much better when we let them sweat in the trunk first.'

Who was in the trunk? Why they were in the trunk? And what precisely was going to be done to them once they were out of the trunk? None of this much concerned Fionn. All he wanted was to avoid getting his balls blown off and make a runner back to Dublin as quickly as possible. Possession of the shotgun seemed to be a major factor in realising these goals, and Fionn must have been staring at it a little too intently, for Uncle O'Brien suddenly stopped mid-giggle, spat a wad of red liquorice on the floor and grabbed the weapon.

'Private Fionn McCuil,' snapped Uncle O'Brien, advancing on Fionn.

'Yes sir!' answered Fionn, standing to attention.

'Enemies of our state, foreign agents hell-bent on the destruction of our liberty, insurgent elements determined to counteract our interests have been captured through the efforts of our forces as well as those of our allies,' said O'Brien, nodding towards the Shaq, who gracefully returned the nod. 'And we will need you to stand guard while we interrogate the subjects.'

'My young friend we are relying on you,' said the Shaq, placing a delicate finger on Fionn's shoulder and offering him an oddly paternal smile.

Fionn did not take the gun with anywhere near the same relish as previously, but grip it he did. For was this not the test of nerve that every hero from Emmet to De Rosa had undergone before him? Was this not the moment when all doubts were suppressed and a glorious course of action committed to?

Fionn marched out of the shed after Uncle O'Brien and took up a position, as instructed, some fifteen metres from the Micra, concealed by a slight depression in the bog, which despite its sheltered nature afforded Fionn a full view down the hill towards any would be imposters.

'Don't take your eyes off that fucking ridge,' ordered Uncle O'Brien.

'We are relying on you my friend,' repeated the Shaq.

'Yes sir,' answer Fionn.

And with that the two men, one dressed entirely in white and the other dressed entirely in black, began walking back towards the Nissan.

At first Fionn was rather pleased with his new assignment. He scanned the ridge for any signs of movement. He listened carefully for the snapping of twigs or the slushing of water or the whisper of voices. But then strange noises started coming

from behind him rather than in front. There was the sound
of an opening boot, some gagged screams, stinging slaps on
bare flesh, low grunts, the rhythmic squeal of suspension
springs—and soon the cacophony made it very hard to concentrate on his duty.

'Keep your eyes on that ridge boy,' called Uncle O'Brien,
as Fionn chanced a glance backwards. 'Don't let them catch
us with our langers out.'

'You can rely on me,' shouted Fionn, deciding to ignore
what he had just glimpsed.

Instead, Fionn brought all his concentration onto the brow
of the hill and sniffed the air for the scent of enemy combat-
ants. It was a method he instantly regretted as the pong of the
bog mingled with the fumes of the gas plant. He managed to
hold down the puke, but the tears flowed with such volume
that shapes began to dance across his vision. Didn't that bush
just inch itself to the left? Couldn't some sneaky fucker be
slithering his way up through that line of heather? Couldn't
the crosshairs be falling on Fionn's noggin at that very instant?

The grunting and squealing and slapping had gone manic
over Fionn's shoulder and he dropped down on his stomach to
better concentrate on the threat at hand. He wiped away the
tears with his cuff. He shimmied a foot to the left. He scanned
the target bush without blinking. He made a mental note of
the position of every twig and branch. He told himself that
patience and perseverance were the key factors in any snip-
er-flushing exercise. Oh, he tried to be patient; he really did.
But the squealing and the grunting and the slapping and the
whistling going on at the Nissan seemed to mock his reserve.
It seemed to call him chicken. It seemed to say, yes, there was a
time for contemplation; yes, there was a time for perseverance,

but this was not it. No. This was the time for action. The time for putting your body and soul on the line. And at that exact moment, with images of Pearse and Connolly playing in his mind, Fionn was absolutely sure that fucking bush had moved.

He let loose with both barrels and sprang forward, reloading the shotgun as his did.

'Take cover,' he shouted over his shoulder while advancing in zig-zag sprints towards a stone that looked exactly like Paul O'Connell's ear.

But the enemy combatant was not found in the heather. He was not writhing in agony in the bush. There was no visible blood trail setting off down the hill.

'He may have doubled back!' shouted Fionn, crouching low as he sprinted back up the hill. 'Keep an eye out to the left there!'

Given the fact that Fionn believed himself to be in mortal danger—given the fact that he was braced for incoming fire, perhaps it is understandable that he failed to twig the state of his uncle and the Shaq. He glanced at them sure enough. He made sure they weren't lying around with legs blown off or guts spilled out. But it was still a good three-to-four minutes before Fionn properly noticed that the lads were sharing a cigarette rather than diving for cover. The other oversight, and by far the larger of the two, could perhaps be blamed on the exuberance of youth, the passion of the patriot, the devotion of the revolutionary, but whatever the case, the fact remained that it was still another two-to-three minutes before Fionn realised that the lads were wearing no trousers. No trousers and no pants. Absolutely bollix naked from the waist down. Not only that, but perched between the two men, there was a bare arse bent over the car boot.

This was, of course, not the first arse Fionn had seen. Changing facilities were not what they could have been in the Clanbrassil Street GAA club. He'd seen flabby arses, skinny arses, spotty arses, whipped arses, red arses, blue arses, oddly green arses, pert arses, carnivorous arses and even a lopsided arse from a lad who'd fallen off a motorbike. As a result, it cannot be said Fionn did not know what he was looking at. No. That was not where the problem lay. The problem lay in the incongruity of two elements hitherto separate in Fionn's mind. That Uncle O'Brien and the Shaq were wearing no trousers beside a bare arse indicated a particular gender in regards to that arse. But as far as Fionn was aware, and his experience with female arses was admittedly not as wide as his experience with the male variety, women did not usually have long wiry hairs sprouting out theirs. That Uncle O'Brien could be doing something to a male arse was plain old strange to Fionn, and it was perhaps a natural resistance to any changes in his long-held worldview that caused Fionn to make no comment whatsoever on what he saw.

'Be ready for a second wave,' muttered Fionn, turning around to scan the horizon once more.

'Ah, this youth, my friend,' said the Shaq behind him, 'So ready to fire! So ready to explode!'

'The McCuils are all the fucking same!'

Fionn focused on that suspicious bush once more.

'He needs no assistance, does he not? He would finish this work more swiftly than us old men!'

Fionn retraced the line of the heather.

'He'd get one away swiftly enough, I'd imagine,' agreed Uncle O'Brien.

With no movement in any of the quadrants and no visible

signs of the enemy, Fionn turned around and became aware that his uncle and the Shaq were talking about him.

'Perhaps we could offer him a turn?' said the Shaq, offering Uncle O'Brien the cigarette with an effeminate gesture completely at odds with the setting.

'Well, what about it?' asked Uncle O'Brien, approaching Fionn with his langer swinging in the wind. 'Fancy a go or what?'

Fionn dropped the shotgun to his side and contended with a myriad questions. Whose arse was this on the boot? Why exactly was their arse on display? Did they like having their arse on display? If not then what had they done to deserve such punishment? How could he avoid such punishment himself?

'Well then, McCuil,' said Uncle O'Brien, offering some liquorice sweets to Fionn. 'Do you fancy a go or not?'

'A go?' asked Fionn turning down the sweets.

'Yes, a go,' said Uncle O'Brien, popping a brown liquorice into his mouth before grabbing his exposed crotch.

'I think I'll give it a miss if that's okay with you, Uncle O'Brien,' said Fionn, as respectfully as possible.

'What's wrong with ya?' shouted Uncle O'Brien, snatching the shotgun out of Fionn's hands. 'Don't know how to use what God gave ya?'

Once again Fionn's testicles found themselves in the barrel of a gun and once again it was the gentle voice of the Shaq that saved Fionn from certain castration.

'Come my friend, we have bigger fish to fry do we not?' said the Shaq, pulling his white robes back over his head.

'Bigger fish to fry!' laughed Uncle O'Brien, wobbling Fionn's nuts in the muzzle. 'Oh, that's a good one Shaq! A bloody good one!'

'Come, let's leave the young man's nether regions in peace and get ourselves dressed for the feeding,' said the Shaq, handing Uncle O'Brien his black vestments and gently lowering the barrel away from Fionn's bollix.

'Ah, there are bigger fish to fry for sure, Shaq!' hooted Uncle O'Brien, pulling on his robes, 'Bigger fucking fish to fry!'

With his testicles momentarily free, Fionn began inching away towards the shed. That bed of rat-infested rags now seemed like heaven. Those bog-rotten walls were a protective fortress. If God could only let him return to that safe harbour he would never seek to go anywhere again. He'd sit in there and say his prayers and wait for his mammy to come and get him.

'And where the fuck do you think you are going?' snapped Uncle O'Brien, pushing his head through his robes.

'Back to the shed?' said Fionn meekly.

'Get over to the fucking car and help us carry that fucker to the fish farm,' snarled Uncle O'Brien with a constipated rage.

'Your help would be greatly appreciated,' added the Shaq, stepping forwards to place a languid finger on Fionn's shoulder.

'Yes, sir,' whimpered Fionn, inching slowly towards the Nissan.

The white arse on the boot looked even more horrific in the first rays of dawn. With the joyful chatter of early birdsong, and the feathery strokes of orange light, and the infinite stillness of the watery bog holes, the arse looked positively statuesque—like something carved from marble, like something Fionn passed on O'Connell Street, like something he bowed to without conscious thought.

By the time Uncle O'Brien handed him one of the hairy legs, Fionn had managed to dehumanise the arse altogether. Even as the Shaq rose it up by the arms and they started carrying it towards the fish farm, Fionn did not, for one moment, consider the fact that the arse might be connected to a stomach or the stomach to a chest or the chest to a neck or the neck to a face or the face to a name. He simply took the bruised leg that was handed to him and waded through the shitty bog in hopes of avoiding any more trouble.

'Easy now, lads,' said Uncle O'Brien as they reached the fence. 'Keep a good grip on the fucker while I open the gate.'

'Very good my friend,' answered the Shaq, his beatific robes taking on tints of gold as the sun peaked over the heather and stirred the waiting pools of water to life.

As Uncle O'Brien struggled with a hefty padlock, Fionn thought he felt the leg begin to squirm in his hand, but a savage knee from the Shaq, directed straight into the unseen face, put a quick end to that.

'Right: off we go, then,' panted Uncle O'Brien, throwing back the gate and coming back to pick up the other leg.

As they walked along the narrow paths between the pools there was a sinister shimmer of movement. Teeth glinted in the half light. Tips of tails pierced the surface. Red eyes hung in a darkness beyond the reach of dawn.

The further they walked, the narrower the path became, until the strip of turf between Fionn and the waiting pike was no barrier at all.

'Is this safe?' asked Fionn meekly.

'It's far from fucking safe for this fella, that's for sure,' laughed Uncle O'Brien, kicking the limp body in the balls.

Fionn thought he heard a tiny pop, like the crushing of chestnuts under hard nail boots, and got an odd sense of sympathetic nausea in his stomach.

'But you are perfectly safe my young friend. There is no

need to look so worried,' said the Shaq, stopping their procession at pool number eight.

As the body lay still on the turf, a deep horn blew from the gas plant and six ribbons of flame danced up against the dawn.

'Well, I suppose we better check for any dodgy fillings before we fuck 'em in,' said Uncle O'Brien, pulling out a flick knife. 'We don't want our prize fish going down with a bellyache.'

To Fionn's horror, Uncle O'Brien now rolled over the arse to expose a face—a human face, a handsome and heroic human face.

Fionn went weak in the knees and almost tumbled into the dark pool.

'Get a fucking hold of yourself,' snapped Uncle O'Brien, bending towards the man's mouth, but prevented from attacking the teeth by some invisible barrier.

Fionn lost his balance again and was forced to take a knee.

'Ah yeah the fucker was in disguise alright,' said Uncle O'Brien, pulling off a mask to reveal the face of Robert Emmet and then Charles Steward Parnell and then Fionn's great-great-grandad, who worked for pittance in the Liverpool shipyards, and then Fionn's great-great-uncle, who died from dysentery on a ship to New York, and then his grand-aunt, fading into a laundry in Leitrim, and her brother drinking himself to death in Kilburn, and his brother rotting in Pentonville, and then James Larkin sitting lonely on the Soviet Council of the World, and then James Connolly manning the barricades with tears in his eyes, and then Fionn's neighbour sailing to England and bleeding all the way home, and then Fionn's dad losing his job and hanging himself beside the recycling bins, and then someone who was just like … someone who was just like Fionn … someone who had his own fucking face.

59

Instinctively Fionn's hands reached up to his face to check it was still attached. It was. It was still there. And yet that face down there was the exact same. Fionn's head began spinning and he placed both hands on his knees before vomiting into the pool. But the retching did not empty Fionn of disgust. The darkness did not shield him from the muffled screams rising from the turf. There was a screech like nails on a blackboard, there was a squelch of an overfed leech, there was the violent snap of an over-taut string.

'Right, I got all the fillings out,' shouted Uncle O'Brien, holding half-a-dozen teeth in his bloody palm. 'In the fucker goes!'

Fionn clasped his hands over his ears, but still he heard the large splash, the cackle of laughter and the snapping of a thousand jaws. His stomach turned summersaults and he lost all sense of up or down, of left or right, of in or out. His brain screamed for more information. It demanded updates. It insisted on co-ordinates. But opening his eyes now would be folly. Seeing his own face being ripped apart by pike would be the end. Having failed to deliver the information his body demanded his body did what bodies always do in these situations: it cut its losses and trusted in gravity.

❖   ❖   ❖

When Fionn awoke in the shed, he thought he was in heaven. For a moment he remembered none of the horror of the pike. Instead, he wallowed in the lovely warmth of a rat-infested bed. He revelled in the stilly calm of a bog-rotten shed. The fleas and the mould were his good old pals. The pong of frying fish in onion and garlic! Oh, the glory of the world! Oh, the

60

sweetness of existence!

That he was high as balls, and drunk into the bargain, did not occur to Fionn. How could it? It was not every day you were nursed back to health with a mixture of Munster poitin and weapons-grade hashish drawn from the mountain tops of Afghanistan. Indeed, one of the beautiful consequences of this concoction of Uncle O'Brien's was the inability of the patient to consider any malice or bad feeling existing in the world at all.

Fionn's flesh felt so comfortable on his bones. His bones sat so snuggly in his flesh. Every contour of his body was lovingly accommodated by the floorboards below. His lower head hovered effortlessly above the soft pillow of his muddy boots. The cracks in the walls admitted drafts of air that filled his lungs with joy. The shadows playing on the ceiling danced to the rhythm of his heart. The sweet aroma of frying fish was a fillip to his nostrils—quick yet meaty, pungent yet fresh.

It was only when the shadows on the ceiling began to cackle, when they bared their teeth, when they chomped those teeth into some unseen flesh, when there was absolutely no doubt that something was being consumed, that Fionn received a jolt of adrenaline strong enough to raise him from his stupor.

If this was heaven, had he left his body behind? Was he drifting face-down in a pond of black water quickly turning red? Was that gnashing the sound of his body being ripped limb from limb?

'Nooooooo …' groaned Fionn, trying to rise up on his elbows.

'Ah, our friend needs another dose of medicine,' said the Shaq, standing by a stove in the corner.

'The little fucker is more of a hindrance than help,' answered

Uncle O'Brien through a face full of fish.

'Perhaps a little taste of pike would make him more suitable for our purposes,' said the Shaq whilst forking a juicy piece of pike.

'More suitable my arse!' cried Uncle O'Brien.

'Surely a more knowledgeable workforce can only bring higher rewards, my friend.'

'Maybe way off in the desert it can!' shouted Uncle O'Brien. 'But you're not in the fucking desert now, Shaq. This is Cork. And we're in a bog. And I'm telling you here and now that there is nothing more dangerous in this country, possibly nothing more dangerous in the world, than to give a little Irish toerag like that even a whiff of knowledge.'

'But …'

'No buts, Shaq,' snapped Uncle O'Brien. 'The only thing for these young fellas is the bottle and the brown.'

Fionn groaned in the corner and his head collapsed onto a pillow that suddenly felt a little less comfortable.

'Of course, I bow to your superior knowledge of local matters, my friend,' said the Shaq, dropping his fork back on his plate. 'But I think we can both agree that another dose of medicine might save us from that groaning while we eat.'

'Absolutely,' answered Uncle O'Brien enthusiastically. 'We don't want the little fucker distracting us once the new information starts digesting.'

The muck-caked laces on Fionn's pillow were now digging into his head, but the aching in his neck, of a kind deep enough to suggest serious structural issues, made any movement impossible.

He groaned as the shadows on the ceiling approached. He shuddered at the sound of the heavy opening zip on the leather medical bag, like a swarm of unclasping metal teeth.

There was a pop and a hiss and a faint gurgle before he gasped at a sudden prick in the arm and then … and then … and then …

And then he felt nothing at all.

The Shaq and Uncle O'Brien, having administered a healthy dose of their special medicine, turned away from Fionn and returned to the stove for another piece of pike.

'After you my friend,' said the Shaq, forking a large chuck.

'No, after you, Shaq. I insist.'

The Shaq nodded slowly and his robed shadow cascaded down the wall onto the lovely little splinters massaging Fionn's side. With the drugs and the grog dissolving Fionn's body into one comfy mess, even the chomping of pike and the myriad popping of its bones reached Fionn's ears like a symphony of angels. Fionn felt perfectly in tune with the universe. The shadows he saw dancing on the ceiling and the wind he felt shaking the shed and the damp he smelled rising from the floorboards—it all played to some grand rhythm, it all moved to some larger design.

Then suddenly the Shaq ceased his movements. The chomping. The chewing. The little snap of bones. It all stopped.

As the shed swayed and the damp rose and the floor creaked, the shadows were utterly still on the ceiling.

'Do you taste that my friend?' said the Shaq slowly.

'What am I looking for, Shaq? Tell me how to taste it!'

The Shaq took another careful chew, then pursed his lips.

'Just under the taste of politician,' said the Shaq.

'I'm with ya. By God, I'm with ya, Shaq!'

'A little left of the journalists we threw in last year.'

'Give me a second now. Just give me a moment,' said

63

Uncle O'Brien, chewing furiously. 'Right. I've got you now, sure enough.'

'That metallic tinge …'

'By God, I taste it! By God, I do!'

'A taste like old money.'

'That's our man, Shaq! By God, that's our man!'

'And what is he telling us my friend?'

'To go short, Shaq! To go way fucking short!'

'We must return to the office and act without delay,' said the Shaq, throwing his fork to the floor and making for the door.

'By God, we must!' shouted Uncle O'Brien, giving chase.

'Two or three more feeds, my friend, and we will know everything we need,' said the Shaq, stepping out the door.

'Two or three more and it'll all be there on a plate!'

And with that the shed door closed and Fionn was left alone in the lovely dark with a comfy pillow of boots and a gorgeous bed of rags. His eyelids felt heavier than a pair of bank-safe doors. The silence in that vault was richer than a thousand bars of gold. He no longer needed to look out upon the world. He felt sure that everything was already inside him. That if he could just stay in here and listen then he would understand. That the universal was the personal. That to understand himself was to understand everything.

This was soothing in the extreme, and it is doubtful Fionn would have emerged from his sealed vault of philosophical speculation if it hadn't been for his particularly strong reaction to the cannabis. Now the munchies are not, in and of themselves, something strange. God knows, many's the time a sliced-pan of Brennan's bread has been devoured with garlic cheese-fries by a young man working his way through a half bar of Morocco's best. Fionn, however, being of an athletic disposition, and being in the possession of a speedy metabolism, came up for food like a skag-head towards the needle and the spoon.

If he could've gotten his hands on a rat, he'd have eaten it raw. The poitín, however, impaired his finer motor skills to such a degree that hunting was an impossibility. Indeed, he was capable of little more than throwing himself bodily onto the floor and, despite the splinters, making his way towards the door in a snake like fashion that left a smear of sweat, slug thick, across the boards. The going was hard, and even with the numbing effects of the potion the sheer volume of splinters caused Fionn worry. Nobody could say it was a good state to be searching in. Indeed, many would have simply given up. But if Fionn hadn't been reduced to the state of humiliation that he was then, it's unlikely he would've found the food that he did.

His nose detected it firs—like a Godly present tossed to earth, like regal alms flicked onto his lap—right there in front of his face: a juicy lump of pike on a discarded fork.

His tongue lapped at it without delay, flicked back and forth along its slimy contours and sucked in its oily juices. The fleshy pong hung on his breath as he panted in suspense. Despite a forest of splinters in his stomach, despite the exhausted groaning in his body, Fionn made one final attempt to move himself forwards. He gained an inch and his teeth came into range. He nibbled with his canines. He pinched with his incisors. He pulled the flesh deeper into his mouth and let the pungent taste drip down the back of his neck. The shot of sustenance popped in Fionn's brain like a finger pulled from a dyke and the endorphins drowned any worries about splinters or fatigue. He thrashed at it furiously, drove deeper and deeper into it, pummelled it harder and harder still, punished it for leaving him so hungry for so long, so needy, so starved of flesh. He continued to dominate it long after all reluctance had descended into a sloppy mess of fluids. He gave it more than it could take—showed it who was boss, showed it who was in control. Then once it was totally overcome, completely stripped of integrity, he swallowed it down and burped.

For a cheap little piece of flesh it was surprisingly satisfying. The good old bout of mastication had Fionn all but spent. He spun from his belly onto his back and breathed in deeply whilst enjoying the tattoo of his heart. Normally he needed a long tray, four slices of batch bread and a half-litre bottle of coke to feel so satisfied. Even then he'd normally be rooting around in the cupboards sourcing some Hobnobs to dip in one last cup of tea before he went off to bed. But he had no urge for biscuits or crisps now. His munchies had been completely and utterly sated by that shitty piece of pike.

Fionn was ready to have himself a little nap, but suddenly there was an odd grumbling in his guts—a sharp darting from left to right, a shimmering movement towards the deep colon. For a moment Fionn was scared he would shit himself. He clenched his sphincter for all he was worth. He summoned up pictures of plug holes and bottle corks to battle the feeling that a paddock of Formula 1 drivers were shaking magnums of champagne in his arse. He was just about to give up the fight when the gas suddenly reversed direction and rumbled up through his windpipe like a bowling ball. As it arose, his sinews stretched and the popping of little bones filled his ears.

'Beeewwwwwaaahhhhhh …'

The stench was inhuman. Even the rats made a run for the door. Fionn tried to hold his breath, but the thoughts of keeping such a noxious gas in his bowls was just as horrific as its re-emergence.

The belches came in bursts and the spiders and the flies and the beetles dropped down dead to the floor. The gas came in through Fionn's nose and fumigated his brain. The vermin of his mind jumped ship. The cobwebs and burrows were cleared away. It felt like a fog, a noxious industrial smog, was being burned away by the rising of a new star.

And into that clean air, up into that spotless sky, there surged a taste … a taste unlike anything he had tasted before … and it was multifaceted and it was onion layered, but it was sharp and it was clear. It was the taste of black ink repeating official lies. It was the taste of money in brown paper bags. It was the taste of turned sods on re-zoned land. It was the taste of poured concrete on ghost-estates. It was the taste of pyrite spreading in the foundations. It was the taste of capitulation. It was the taste of shame.

It was a taste that brought Fionn to his feet.

'The fucking bastards!' Fionn screamed, grabbing the shotgun. 'The stealing fucking bastards!'

He was ready to throw back the shed door. He was ready to charge across the bog. He knew exactly were the fuckers would be. He knew exactly what they'd be doing. He'd eaten enough pike to know it all.

'I'll blow THEIR fucking nuts off!' shouted Fionn, before one final burp saved him from a certain suicide mission.

The pong came up and cleaned away the anger. The stench came up and urged him to rethink. He would be totally outnumbered in the gas plant. Even with complete knowledge of the guards' positions he would be lucky to make it past the gate. He'd have to play a different game here. A cuter game.

'My own fucking uncle taken in by that towel-headed prick,'

growled Fionn, before his athletic metabolism offered up yet another bone-rattling burp.

Millipedes in the rafters shrivelled up in agony. Ants in the floorboards twitched their last. The wind growled outside as the bog attempted to reassert itself as the main creator of pong in these parts. Fionn sniffed at the fumes and the bout of xenophobia cleared from his brain. Oh no, he wouldn't be falling for that old trick. He wouldn't be tacking it all onto the foreigner, the outsider, the other. The Shaq was nothing but a fall guy. He was nothing but a dupe. He was a piece of misdirection designed to take your eye away from the fecker who was stealing your wallet.

'Oh no! Not this time! Not this fucking time you won't!' Fionn said, placing down the shotgun and stepping back from the shed door for a big old think.

He sat down on his bed of rags. He stroked a non-existent beard. He pondered. He ruminated. He pontificated. And slowly the problem rearranged itself into something more clear, something better delineated. And reading between those lines, Fionn could clearly see that the problem was his uncle. Yes the problem was the cutest hoor in all of Ireland.

'I'm gonna shoot his prick off and feed him to the fucking pike,' said Fionn with a grin. 'But I won't stop there.'

Oh no he could not stop there, for Uncle O'Brien may well have been the cutest of the cute hoors, but he was far from the sole practitioner. The country was teeming with the cunts. This was not a mono-headed-beast who dropped dead with one swipe of the sword. It was Medusa. It was Hydra. It was an organism spread with a million spores. It would re-emerge like mould on the wall if a single spore was missed. And there was only one way to fight it: exposure, exposure, exposure.

68

You needed to expose them all and then attack relentlessly with wire wool and bleach.

'I'll catch me a pike,' said Fionn putting down the shotgun and looking around the shed for anything that could be improvised into a fishing rod. 'I'll catch me the king fucking pike, eat it and learn all the places where the cute hoors are hiding!'

But despite a fevered search, Fionn could find little that could act as a rod: a rusty coat hanger, a rotten broom handle and two leather paddles. None of it would hold up in a battle with the king pike. And in any case, what was there for bait? Old bits of carpet? Some wrecked boots? These fish had been fed up on lawyers and accountants and politicians! This shite wasn't gonna get them out of bed!

Another burp rattled through Fionn's rib cage and the resulting realisation made him shudder. There was something he could use. There was something that would tickle its interest. The king pike would almost certainly make an appearance for his toe. Not for his pinkie and not for his middle. But almost absolutely definitely for his big toe.

For a moment Fionn considered abandoning the plan completely. Why was all this his problem, anyway? Wasn't everyone else happy with the current state of affairs? And if they weren't happy, weren't they content with wringing their hands saying—oh well, what's to be done?

Let them all go to fuck. Australia is nice this time of year. He could be drinking a beer in Greenwich Village by tomorrow evening. Wouldn't a spot of teaching in Korea be just the ticket?

But then up came another burp and all the sentiments he'd held in ignorance—all that shite about the glory of the revolution, all the codswallop about the ideals of the republic—it all came surging back in a completely different context. Now

Fionn really was terrified. Now he really wanted to run away. But worse still, turning had become something far worse than going ahead.

'Fucking bastards! Bloody fucking bastards have me by the fucking balls!' shouted Fionn ripping off his shoes and socks before he could change his mind.

His big toe had been his secret weapon for so long. It had poked him many a goal. It had driven in free kicks from impossible angles. It had proceeded him out of every bed and down every tunnel. But it had also penetrated many a sock. It had destroyed shoes far and wide. It was a crude, blind tool with little skill or finesse. Maybe he, like all of his countrymen, was too reliant on it. Maybe now was the time for the gentle cup and the sweet caress, for the instep and the arch.

On bare feet Fionn charged out the door with the shotgun under his arm. It was a clear crisp morning that had sharpened the blades of grass up to needles. It was a frigid fucker of a morning that sent any reasonable person back into the hall for a scarf and gloves. But Fionn would not be turning. He skipped across the barbarous mud without as much as a yelp and started climbing over the chain-link fence without even a glance towards his feet. No, he could not chance a look at his toe now. He needed to get over the fence and get to pool number nine, dip his toe into the king pike's environs and seduce it to the surface with a wiggle and a shake before he had any time to think. He needed to take action. Any action. Because he knew too much for doing nothing. Sitting in that shed and pretending he was doing anything other than waiting for Uncle O'Brien to bend him over a shitty beige Micra was a complete impossibility.

Off the fence and down the path he went.

On the bank he watched the water carefully. Trying to catch a glimpse of the pool's solitary resident. There was an odd hush across the bog. Chittering birds kept a sudden whisht. All movement in the undergrowth ceased. Fionn blessed himself, steadied the shotgun under his arm and slowly dipped his big toe into the black water.

A horn blew at the gas plant and a cold wind cut straight through Fionn's clothes. But shivering now would mean death. A sudden movement now would see him dragged into pool number nine before a scream could even leave his lips. He needed to dip gently. He needed to wiggle and wag. He needed to drift and bob. He needed to look like the worm but be the serpent under it. Then as soon as the big fucker came close, as soon as he couldn't survive the blast—BANG—he'd open up with both barrels. Then if he needed to dive in and drag it out, then so be it.

Another horn blew at the gas plant and a tectonic rumble arose from underneath the farm. The pike in pool number eight started diving for number seven. The pike in number seven made a run for number six. They threw themselves out of home and began thrashing towards exhaustion—mouths gulping at air they could not breathe, gills flapping towards a dispassionate sky. Fionn could not accept such a fate. Fionn would not be turning to run. He would catch this pike or he'd go down trying. Let it all come as it may.

His guts misinterpreted that final sentiment and another burp rattled its way up Fionn's spine. He battled to keep his foot steady. He used all his strength to keep the big toe still. But then the fumes of knowledge hit his brain and terror froze him completely.

Hadn't the water gotten a little bit thicker around his leg?

71

Wasn't there a new stillness inside the stillness? Wasn't his toe like a blind scuba-diver swimming into a dark cave?

Without making another movement Fionn rolled his eyes to the left, noticed a dim glob of red near the bank, and swivelled his vision to the right, where an identical buoy could be seen.

Could its head be so big? Could its mouth have been waiting all this time?

The red buoys blinked in response.

Oh God. Oh good lord of Mercy. Oh sweet Jesus fucking Christ.

He thought he'd been seducing him to the surface. He thought he'd been summoning him into range. But here he was in the jaws of the beast. Here he was about to have his leg reduced to a bloody stump.

Fionn raised the shotgun in a panic, but a pulsing, maniacal laughter, moved up through the turf and rattled his aim all to shit. The red-eyes peeled wide-open and Fionn felt an updraft of water moving around the hairs of his toe. In that ultimate moment of horror, all Fionn's brain could offer was an image of little Davey Malloy being mauled to death by a pit bull in the playground. Oh if only he'd stopped trying to pull his arm away, his mother had said. If only he'd shoved his arm right down the dog's throat. Fionn was about to lose his leg and this was the best his brain could do? The laughter coming from the pike continued with the solemn inevitability of an old madame who'd seen it all before. Had seen moral fortitude crumble like a honeycomb in her mouth. Had felt guilt and shame dissolve like butter on her tongue.

It was then that Fionn realised that this was no king pike. No, this fucker was a queen. A hermaphroditic queen whose mouth was both the crown of penetration and the throne of consumption. With the image of little Danny Malloy's face being ripped apart, Fionn drove his leg deeper into the queen pike's throat. There was gaggling and bobbing and sucking and an odd feeling of mucus as the queen pike broke the surface to look Fionn straight in the eye. They were the red eyes of the madame and the priest and the porn-star and the nun and they saw straight through Fionn. They stripped him of all pretence. Here was his nature, naked and violent, stuffing himself down her throat while totally open to attack. Driving it all down harder. Deeper. Faster. But no matter how rabid his thrusts, Fionn could not make her blink. She stared up with insolence. An arrogant dare that knew it would not be met.

'Fuck you! Fuck you, you fucking cunt!' screamed Fionn, thrusting his hairy leg in deeper as he raised the shotgun.

As he took aim he could feel the teeth tightening on the bone. He could feel a tingling in the tip. He felt sure the toe was about to pop. It would be emptied from the inside out. It would be drained of marrow and left flaccid on the queen pike's tongue. Oh, it was coming. Oh, it was going beyond the point of return. His arm shook as he felt ready to submit, ready to evacuate himself. With his last ounce of reserve he pulled the trigger and shot the queen pike right between the eyes.

The recoil threw Fionn onto his back and he lay panting in the cringing silence with his eyes closed. He waited for relief—searched for it in the darkness, but instead there came an awful sense of futility. Of absurdity. Why had he come to this fucking bog? Why hadn't he simply run away from Uncle O'Brien? Why had he come out here at stupid o' clock in the morning to dip his toe in the water? What the fuck was wrong with him?

Until that moment Fionn never knew fish could cry, but cry they did. From pool number eight down to pool number one they offered ululations to the sky. Wailed and screamed with cold-blooded wounds. And with the spears of frozen mud piercing his back, and the bog wind slicing through his skin, and the frigid morning light leaving nowhere to hide, Fionn felt nothing but shame.

A chasm of anxiety yawned in his chest and he felt compelled to run in front of a bus, to jump off a bridge, to drive into a fire, to lie down before a train: anything but feel this diffuse sense of coming disaster. What he wouldn't give for those teeth to threaten his leg again. What he wouldn't pay for the possibility of being eaten alive. He would sing her paeans of immediate fear. He would worship her with palpable horror.

Fionn rolled into pool number nine, crying. He added his little saline tears to the black, black water. He threw his arms around the carcass and begged the queen pike for forgiveness. The black water covered them like a satin sheet and Fionn buried his face in her scales. The cold locked his limbs around her. The hypothermia froze a single thought in his mind. He must chew. He must move his jaw and chew. Mouthful by loving mouthful he pulled her in. Consumed her. Her scales became his. Her tiny bones reconfigured themselves inside his skeleton. His mouth was warm as a cunt. His teeth were sharp as a prick. His lungs filled with breathing water and his tail beat him away from the surface. But this felt less like transformation and more like transcendence. With these new eyes, Fionn could see into hidden depths. Down in the silence of the black-black-water things became more clear. His hatred of Uncle O'Brien floated away. His elitist delusions of revolutionary heroics drifted up like flotsam to the surface.

Xenophobia and misogyny dropped like dead weights to the bottom of the pool. And as he followed them down, past layers of sediment holding the bones of Norman and Saxon patriarchs, he saw nothing but a series of systems, collective delusions, mass deceptions, seductive fictions and never-ending dehumanisation. Doctors became torturers in its shadow. Teachers became slave drivers under its hand. It infiltrated the arts. It vitiated love. Worth became nothing but want. Meaning became nothing at all. His tail drove him deeper down and he knew what he needed to do. He knew because she knew. Together they would swim up that hidden passage. Together they would enter the gas plant through its maze of cooling pipes. They'd twist their way into the extraction chamber. They'd brave the coming flames. They'd submit to the sacrifice and they'd do it with love. They'd drift in the gas. They'd trick the bastards into piping knowledge into every home. Their pong would rise from kitchen hobs. It would emanate from flaming boilers. Oh, only that stench could do it now. The ears and eyes had long ago become traitors. Only the olfactory organ knew the truth. Yes, it would fumigate their brains whilst cooking their dinner. Yes. They would receive revelation over a bowl of super-noodles. They would smell their servitude in all its manufactured forms. They would wretch at the arrogant stench of their masters. Then they would emerge from their slumbers. Then they would grab a bucket and a mop and take violently to the floor.

Lucas needed to pee but it hurt to move.
He rolled off the bed and headed to the bathroom.
He stripped, taking off his skirt and removing
his torn knickers. He looked for his penis, which
was missing

Wrong | Namrael Drawde

> I am dragged along by a strange new force. Desire and reason
> are pulling in different directions. I see the right way and
> approve it, but follow the wrong.
> —**Ovid, 'Medea and Jason'** *Metamorphoses*

Something was wrong. He jerked back in his seat, stunned.
The screaming stopped abruptly, like someone collapsing at a
dinner party. There was an awkward pause. He looked at the
woman beside him in the back seat. His hands, hovering above
her face, had been around her throat. The woman regained
consciousness and stared wide-eyed, coughing. She rubbed
her throat and touched her bloody nose, tried to sit up. The
man yelped. His eyes screwed shut and he let out a guttural
wail, throwing his head back then down, crying on his knees.

The woman continued to stare, confused. The man's trousers were around his ankles and his penis was erect. She could
see the veins underneath its pale skin. She tried to open the
door—she had to get out—but it was locked. The man continued to cry, his chest heaving and shaking as he sucked in

air. He groaned, and started to whimper.

'Please, stop. Please don't hurt me'.

The woman ignored him and examined herself. Her clothes were torn and her bare legs were spattered with blood. The man looked at her again, his eyes red and blinking, breathing hard. He whispered, 'What's happening?'

'Get out', she replied, then screamed, 'GET OUT! GET OUT! GET OUT!'

She began hitting the man, pushing him against the door. At last, she reached across him and pulled the handle. He fell to the muddy ground. She followed, and moved away from the car, looking into the woods around her. She paced back and forth, then turned back to the sobbing man, her mouth agape, her face a picture of horror.

'Please help me. Please,' he choked.

Notes for an initial police report were written three days later by Detective Inspector Hyland.

Lucas Barrow, 43, a senior manager at Winsgate-Gray, a luxury car dealership, visited a police station in the town of Mauditt near Chelmsford in the early hours of Sunday morning. Mr Barrow appeared inebriated and hysterical. He described to officers an alleged assault and abduction at a pub carpark in the town. Mr Barrow appeared incoherent, struggling to remember what had happened, and even his own name and identity.
We visited Mr Barrow's flat in Chelmsford and came into contact with the alleged victim of the assault, Ms Rachel

78

Sims. Ms Sim, 29, a paralegal working for a corporate finance firm, met the officers at the premises and agreed to let them inside to inspect the property. She appeared taciturn and evasive, claiming she had no knowledge of an assault and denying that she had ever met Mr Barrow. When questioned as to why she was at the property, Ms Sims declined to answer and appeared uncertain as to how she had arrived there or where she was the previous evening.

Lucas lay face down on the mattress in Rachel's bedroom. The cuts and bruises on his face hurt and he was exhausted after a sleepless night. If this was a dream, he wished he would wake up, but each time he fell asleep, someone he didn't know would call, or there'd be a knock at the door.

They kept calling him 'Rachel' and wanted to know what had happened to him—which he couldn't answer, because he didn't know much about who this 'Rachel' was. She was just a woman he'd spent a few days following after seeing her at a pub a couple of weeks ago.

That was the way he always worked. He'd see a woman somewhere, follow her, make a mental note of where she liked to go, and after a few weeks, he'd snatch her and take her somewhere quiet. Afterwards, he'd drive her somewhere else and let her go. But last night, something went wrong. He'd woken up in the car wearing her clothes, and there was a guy with his dick out who looked exactly like him. This was fucked. He'd tried to convince the police that he didn't know anything but he couldn't explain the cuts on his face, or where he was the previous night.

The police took him to a house and the girl's fucking family were there, asking him more questions, everyone crying and trying to hug him. Who the fuck *were* they? He wanted to be alone so they took him away, and now he was inside her fucking house. Perhaps he had a concussion, or she had some disease. Every time he looked in a mirror, he saw her fucking face staring back at him.

Lucas needed to pee but it hurt to move. He rolled off the bed and headed to the bathroom. He stripped, taking off his skirt and removing his torn knickers. He looked for his penis, which was missing. He was afraid to touch his new vagina. It was unnatural to him. He didn't want to sit on the toilet so he stepped into the shower instead.

His body was not his. He had breasts and hips that didn't feel right. His skin was too soft. His whole frame felt light and frail. The skin had a brownish tan, and the painted toenails looked attractive, as did the toned calves and thighs. He pushed a finger into his vagina but it hurt, probably from where he'd grabbed it last night. He sniffed his finger and then licked it but it tasted like piss. He turned the shower on and a warm spray soaked him as he urinated, the yellow liquid draining away, along with the blood stains. After a few minutes, he stepped out and stared at himself in the mirror, Rachel stared back at him.

He took his breasts in his hands and squeezed the nipples until they hardened, but then stopped, thinking about his missing penis and his inability to masturbate the way he normally would. He looked at Rachel's face, his new face. He was pretty despite the dark bruises and finger marks on his neck. His upper lip was swollen, with a gash along the lip. His right eye had a red ring around it where his knuckles had struck Rachel's cheekbone and eyebrow.

Lucas felt a twinge of something he hadn't felt before. It seemed a shame that her looks had been spoiled. He'd hurt her because she would never give him what he wanted voluntarily. He didn't know if he wanted love or sex, but he needed to prove to himself that he could take one without the other. He felt strangely pitiful for the first time in his life, and these feelings were unfamiliar because they didn't belong to him.

A knock at the door broke the silence. He tried to ignore it, but after a minute he realised the person wasn't going away. It could be the police again. It was important to play along just in case they suspected anything. He put on a pair of jeans and a jumper he found in a laundry basket. He walked downstairs and opened the front door. A a young blonde woman stood staring at him looking cross and impatient.

'Oh my god, Ray, where have you been? Are you okay?' she stammered, shocked by what she saw. Lucas didn't say anything, caught off guard by the woman's good looks. She was perfectly blonde, perfectly tanned. She stepped forward and hugged him. Before he could speak, she pushed backwards towards the kitchen.

'Your face, Ray. I can't look at it. You've got to tell me what happened. Do you want a coffee or tea, or something stronger? Are you hungry? I can make you some lunch. Is there anything I can get you? Anything you need? I can't believe what that bastard did. Your parents called me this morning and said you'd been attacked and you weren't answering the phone. I screamed when they told me. How are you feeling now?'

'Uhh—better … Who are you?'

'Who am I? Jesus, what did he *do* to you? Sit down, let me

81

get you a drink.' Lucas sat down at the kitchen table as she opened the fridge and took out a bottle of white wine. She picked up two glasses off a shelf and waved them at Lucas.

'Pinot?' she asked, pursing her lips.

'No, thanks,' he mumbled, staring at the holiday snaps stuck to the wall beside him. There were pictures of Rachel in cut-off jeans, clinging to other slim, tanned young women in cut-offs, smiling, sometimes with their tongues hanging out. They were in a jungle, on a waterfall, at Ayers Rock. There were in bikinis on beaches, waving glow sticks at Full Moon Parties, drinking prosecco in backless dresses and looking bored. More photos showed stubbly young men in sunglasses, their mouths open, giving the pitchfork sign, or pursing their lips like the blonde did when she offered him the wine. He felt sick.

'Any rum? Or vodka? Cider?' he grunted.

'Ummm … I don't know, I don't live here,' she said, frowning. 'You drink rum and vodka?'

'Just make me a coffee.'

'Coffee? Okay, yeah. No problem. Coffee.' She put the wine back in the fridge and switched the kettle on, then started opening cupboards looking for mugs.

'What's your name?' he asked.

The blonde looked at him, her mouth open. 'I'm Saffie,' she replied, impatiently. 'Saffie Moyle. Your best friend. You've known me since college. We go on holiday together. We went to Dubai. We went to Lisa's wedding. I introduced you to Rufus. You went out with Leon. Don't you remember? What *happened*, Ray?'

'I don't want to talk about it.' Lucas slid off the stool and walked to the living room where he sat on the sofa and stared at Rachel's reflection in the TV's blank screen. Saffie followed.

She sat down next to him, reached across and held his hand.

'Are you alright? Did he hurt you?' she asked softly.

'Don't fucking touch me,' he replied, pulling his hand away and scowling. 'I don't know you.'

'Ray, I'm sorry. You must've been terrified. I wish I could help you. I'm so worried about you.' Saffie's voice cracked and her eyes brimmed with tears.

Lucas noticed she'd taken her shoes off, and was sitting cross-legged, her feet poking out from either side of her knees. He reached across and placed her hand on a foot, gently squeezing it. Saffie stared back at him, confused. 'R-Ray … what are you doing?'

'Shh … it's okay,' he said in a low voice.

'Ray, I don't know—' She pulled her foot away and backed up on the sofa. 'You're being strange, Ray.'

'No, I'm not.'

'Ray—' she said in a whiny voice.

'Shut the fuck up,' he said, slowly.

'Ray—' she said again, but louder.

Lucas punched her in the mouth, causing her to fall sideways onto the floor. She gasped and held her mouth. Lucas stayed on the sofa as Rachel stared at him from the TV. Saffie rubbed her face.

'Why?' she said, almost to herself.

'Fucking get out, bitch,' he said. Biting her lower lip to hold back the tears, Saffie stood, and then left, shutting the door quietly behind her. Lucas wished he had his penis so he could have fucked her the way he wanted to. He felt that odd sadness again. He was alone, and in the wrong place.

Rachel lay on the plastic mattress, face to the wall, eyes closed, focusing on her breathing. This was a meditation technique she'd learned to help her deal with stress. In the past, she'd struggled with confined spaces, but had had to overcome this when she'd moved to London for her first job. The crammed Tube carriages, bodies stuck to each other, no oxygen, no available exits, just bodies crushing you against the wall. Her face hot, her heart pumping, a sudden impulse to reach up towards a window that wasn't there. 'HELP ME I CAN'T BREATH! I DON'T WANT TO DIE! PLEASE HELP ME!' she'd think, but then the doors would slide open and everyone would calmly walk out.

Now she was wearing a prison uniform: standard-issue blue jeans, jumper and shirt, and she was sleeping in a cell for a single person. The walls were painted a sickly yellow and stained brown. There was nothing in the room except for a metal toilet and basin with a cracked mirror, a roll of toilet paper, and a small window the size of a shoe box high up on the back wall. There were two small vents on the ceiling and floor, presumably to allow air in, or perhaps to wash away blood and faeces in the event of an uncooperative occupant.

Strangely, she felt safe and secure inside this box. The guards outside were protecting her just as they were protecting the general public. The sleep and solitude allowed her to calm down and put things in order. Maybe she'd lost her mind, or perhaps this was a dream, but if so, when would she wake up? Was she in a coma? This isolation and silence were also the true torments of prison, she thought. She missed her friends and family, and wondered if she would ever see them again.

There was a clicking sound as the metal shutter on the door slid open. A pair of eyes appeared and a voice called to her in a hard tone. 'Barrow. Inspector Hyland here to see you,' the guard barked. As the keys knocked against the door, she wondered what the point of the little window was, and why they just didn't open the door without the preamble, since she wasn't likely to be too busy to see anyone.

The door opened and Inspector Hyland stepped inside. The guard—'Mr Happyface' as she called him—waited in the doorway, since there wasn't enough space in the cell for all of them. She sat obediently on the bed, staring sheepishly up at the two men, feeling small and helpless.

'How are you, Mr Barrow?' the policeman asked politely.

'Ah, I'm fine, thank you, sir,' Rachel said, glancing at Happyface, who had his eyes fixed on her.

'Good to hear.' He spoke quickly, looking around at the walls as if couldn't stand the sight of her. 'Well ...' he cleared his throat. 'The witness has asked to have a meeting with you in exchange for her statement. We advised against it, but we are, under supervision, willing to accommodate this. You're free to decline if you don't wish to see Ms Sims, but if you do agree, it would be your right to have legal representation there with you. Is this making any sense?' he asked.

'Ms Sims?' she asked. 'I—that would—I don't know ... Who is she?'

Hyland rolled his eyes and made a clucking sound. 'If you need more time to think about it, I can give you until this afternoon.'

'I want to see her,' Rachel said firmly. 'I don't need legal representation. I want to see her.'

'Fine, then,' Hyland said. 'We'll speak to Ms Sims and see what we can do.' The policeman turned and left Happyface to lock the door behind him.

She looked at herself in the broken mirror above the sink. Lucas stared back at her and looked unhappy and reproachful, like a headmaster catching her cheating in an exam. He was handsome and silver-haired, and as a younger man, she could imagine her mother poking her and calling him 'dishy', to make her cringe. He had bright blue eyes in striking, chiselled features. He reminded her of a young Robert Redford or a Michael Caine. He was well-groomed, his hair long and swept back, his nails short and immaculate. Who was this beautiful man, and why was he capable of such violence?

She looked at her huge hands and arms. She expected them to feel heavy, but her muscles, like the rest of her body, made her feel light and energetic. She felt like a gorilla—her arms were hammers capable of breaking bones and pulverising meat. She felt vulnerable whenever she left her cell for the world of impending violence outside, but out there, she was the alpha male. They would be fearful of her.

Adjusting to Lucas' body had its own challenges. In the mornings she awoke to find her penis erected like a tentpole under the bedsheet. She'd touched it, and wondered how to deactivate it. She didn't remember having any erotic dreams. She squeezed it just to see what would happen, but this disturbed her. Lucas was a rapist and a deviant; somehow the penis symbolised his perversity. She wished she didn't have to look at it. Worse still, she found her ability to walk normally had been impaired. There was always a lump stuck between her legs. She was always looking down to make sure it hadn't slipped out, and she worried it might get caught in a door.

The next day, she waited in a room without windows, hand-cuffed, sitting on a chair with an empty desk in front of her. Happyface stood off to one side, waiting and checking his watch. There was a knock at the door and Hyland opened, like a gentleman, to allow a young woman with bruises and cuts on her face to step inside. She heard Happyface inhale and he stepped forward to offer the lady a chair.

She stared at herself, at the dark bruises and swollen eye sockets. She felt violated, and wanted to shout: 'You're not me! You stole my body!' But when this Rachel entered the room, her shoulders were slightly hunched, her eyes downcast, glancing furtively around at the space of the room and the objects inside it. She—the real Rachel—guessed this was Lucas, checking his surroundings, looking for possible exits, ready to move fast and with force.

Lucas took a seat opposite the prisoner without being told that he was allowed to do so; nor did he notice the men's hospitality towards him. Hyland took a seat next to him, cleared his throat, but appeared uncertain as to how to begin; presumably he was wondering whether he should make formal introductions.

'I'll start by saying that this meeting is being recorded as part of our investigation. Thank you both for attending,' he said, with a slight smile of reassurance to the young lady, before turning to the prisoner. 'You've both consulted your legal advisers and are happy to continue without them here. I thought, perhaps, if we all agreed, I could start by asking a few questions about the incident on Friday 5 August, and we could clarify a timeline. How does that sound? Ms Sims, how are you feeling?'

Rachel opened her mouth to speak, but she realised that

he was addressing the young woman.

Hyland looked at her. 'So, we're all happy to conduct this interview. Do you agree to this, Mr Barrow?'

'I think we know what happened on the night of the incident,' Rachel said. 'You already have the evidence and my statement that I had abducted and assaulted Ms Sims. What I'd like to know is exactly why Ms Sims wants to hold this meeting.'

'Okay,' Hyland said, flustered. 'That's what we're going to find out, but first I'd like to clarify and establish the facts, and then if Ms Sims feels comfortable and ready to comment, we can—'

'He's lying,' Lucas said in Rachel's voice. 'He didn't attack me, or try to rape me. I met him at the pub, and he offered me a lift home. I was a bit drunk, I kissed him and said I wanted to have sex. He refused, so I started hitting him. He hit me back. I hit my head when I fell. It was dark and wet. I was upset. I tripped over, he tried to help me, and I hit him again, so he stopped. I scratched my face on some glass and stones. I drove off in his car back to his flat to wait for him. That's what happened. I guess I had a concussion from the fall, or I was just really drunk and I blacked out and that's why I couldn't remember anything.'

Hyland stared at Lucas incredulously, as did Lucas and Happyface.

'He's fucking lying!' she said, indignantly, in Lucas' tough baritone. 'I attacked her. I fucking waited outside the pub, then I came up behind her and hit her on the head. While she was unconscious, I picked her up and drove her to the woods. She, or he, is lying!'

Happyface stepped towards her, feeling that the conversation was getting out of hand. Hyland raised his hand to signal

88

that he should remain calm, and then he spoke loudly, but without shouting.

'Mr Barrow, calm down, please, or we'll have to end this meeting and escort you back to your cell.' He turned to Rachel, and tried to speak calmly. 'Ms Sims, it's just—it doesn't quite fit the evidence which we have, not just from Mr Barrow, but from witnesses who were there on the night in question.'

The woman sighed, shuffled in her seat, and leaned forward impatiently. 'I don't really care. I was intoxicated, I met him in the carpark, we had a fight; I acted stupidly and then I left. I guess he was angry with me about the way I'd behaved, so he made up this story … probably to get back at me for acting like a bitch.'

'This is unbelievable. Inspector Hyland, you don't honestly believe this? This woman, who I've never met before, suddenly decided to go home with me? I don't know why she's lying. I'm guessing because she wants to drop the charges.'

'I think Mr Barrow is more shaken by what happened than he thinks,' Lucas said, wincing. 'I'm still recovering after what happened. I'm sure Mr Barrow just wants to go home.' He looked at himself, the prisoner across the table. 'I think if we just started over and picked up where we left off …'

Rachel stared at herself saying these words; she was appalled by his arrogance. Not only was he denying what happened, he seemed completely unfazed by it.

'You're joking. I'm a rapist. I should be locked up,' she said.

Hyland stood up and gestured to Happyface that the meeting was finished. 'I don't think there's anything more to say. Ms Sims, let me take you back to reception.'

Lucas glared at Rachel. 'I'll see you at the trial,' he said, as Hyland took him by the elbow and led him outside. Happyface unlocked her restraints, and she left the room without saying anything more.

The trial drew the media and made newspaper headlines. SEX PREDATOR CONFESSES, VICTIM DENIES IT read the front page of one tabloid. Details from Lucas' past were exposed: a female colleague who'd resigned from her job at the dealership after allegations of harassment, but dropped due to lack of evidence. More witnesses would follow.

Pleading guilty to all charges, Rachel spoke openly and derogatively about Lucas' past, of which she actually knew very little. For the jury, she painted herself in the worst possible light, whereas the legal team hired by Lucas' employer tried to salvage her defence. They used his military service as leverage, presenting him as a loyal and heroic army officer who'd suffered post-traumatic stress disorder. They'd pointed to incidents where Lucas had fought selflessly without regard for his own safety to protect his men, for which he'd been awarded the Distinguished Service Cross. The prosecution struggled to make a consistent case for themselves as Lucas tried to undermine their allegations by denying key pieces of evidence and contradicting the witness statements, much to the dismay of both the jury and the crown's legal team.

When the verdict was read out, the jury found the accused guilty of assault and battery but acquitted him of the rape and kidnapping charges. The judge passed a sentence of one year in prison. This had been a disappointment for Rachel's parents, a victory for Lucas and a relief for Rachel, even though she was apprehensive about going to prison.

Prison life wasn't nearly as bad as she'd expected. Most of the inmates were sad, gaunt men serving light sentences, who wanted to be left alone, and hoped to reduce their sentences with good behaviour. There were small gangs, pockets of young men who'd grouped together for safety, and who sometimes intimidate the other inmates with loud talk, but generally it was sanguine and monotonous. Her size and her notoriety as a former soldier and violent offender, plus the label of 'mentally instability', deterred unwanted attention, and in some ways, she'd never felt so in control. But then she'd never felt so alone.

With her free time, she engaged with the prison's volunteer scheme and education courses, which helped inmates improve their reading, writing and maths skills, as illiteracy was shockingly common among the inmates. Thanks to her professional background, she was able to offer legal guidance for court hearings, and practical advice on employment and training opportunities. The men she helped were surprised by her generosity, and before long she made friends with people whom she never would've spoken to before, and they gave her their respect and trust.

A few months later, Rachel was released from prison. She felt aged and strengthened by the months of isolation. She went to Lucas' flat in Chelmsford, a domain filled with objects that projected success and status. This was Lucas' shrine to himself. She didn't know where else to go, since she couldn't return to her home, or parents. She' wondered if it were possible to reverse this 'change', although the problem of how to do it, and even if she should, preyed on her mind.

Lucas sold her house and took a severance package from her employer after a year of sick leave. With this money, and the help of old contacts at Wingsgate–Gray, he invested in luxury cars again. It didn't take long to make a profit, although this turned out to be harder work than he'd expected, since friends and contacts didn't give him the breaks they had before. At first, no one took him seriously; they talked down to him, didn't call him back, and were often rude if he was outspoken. It was humiliating, and it was because he was a woman.

He'd struggled for months with his femininity: how to dress, how to speak, how to walk, how to apply make up. He hated it. He didn't know how to behave around people. For the first few months, he didn't shave his legs and wore jeans and baggy jumpers. Eventually he hired two women, a personal assistant and a beautician, to help fix his make-up and wardrobe, explaining to them that he'd been in a coma and was relearning how to present himself as a professional woman. He had to grit his teeth when they laughed because he said he didn't want to look pretty, just 'normal'. In retaliation, he did what he'd always done, which was to victimise anyone weaker than himself. These skinny, giggling, fresh young girls, looking for their first job after graduation, were the easiest targets. As their boss and someone they admired, he felt like he could say anything to them, and they'd just smile passively and internalise their humiliation—especially when he talked about fucking.

He also victimised Claire, a dippy blonde saleswoman who laughed too loudly and talked endlessly about her nights out.

At an after-party, he'd made sure his staff got drunk, ordering more prosecco and shots of sambuca, goading them on. By the end of the evening, Claire, along with most of the rest of the team, was slurring and could barely stand. He'd ordered everyone a taxi but said he'd drive her home. He didn't ask her; no one cared. They didn't suspect anything—why would they?

Sitting in the driver's seat, he told her how glad he was that she's come that night. Claire, eyes drooping, head against the door, looked as if she were about to vomit, but mumbled her thanks. He leaned across and squeezed her knee; she opened her eyes and smiled dumbly. He asked her if she wanted to spend the night at his place, and she slurred 'sure, whatever', before closing her eyes again.

Lucas drove his Porsche at speed along the dual carriage-way. He reached across to caress her knee again, and she moaned. He moved his hands up the inside of her thigh and she flinched, shoving his hand away. 'Don't keep touching me,' she slurred. He reached for her breasts, and Claire pushed his hand away. 'Get off me!' she shouted. As he tried to grab her neck, she swung her arms wildly, slapping his face. She tried to open the passenger door and he clawed her back, one hand still on the steering wheel. She fought him, scratching his face. He didn't see the concrete barrier separating the road from the turn-off. The car careened into it. The windscreen exploded, glass and debris flying as the front end of the car collapsed. Claire and Lucas remained in their seats, unconscious and bleeding, until the ambulance arrived.

Lucas spent two-month in hospital. Towards the end of his convalescence, charges of driving under the influence, abduction and assault were brought against him. Colleagues and ex-employees gave statements in court that Rachel Sims, founder and owner of Parnassus Ltd, had routinely harassed and intimidated staff at the dealership. Lucas pleaded not guilty but the jury disagreed, and the judge handed down a four-year sentence.

Prison was less kind to Lucas than it had been to Rachel. He had not expected the female inmates to be as violent and erratic as they were. There were the gangs and the bull-dykes, as he'd expected, but unlike in men's prison, the hierarchy wasn't motivated by sex and money. They didn't want to rape him, or take what he had; they wanted to own him. Addicts, prostitutes and baby killers. Loud, angry women who'd take pleasure in burning you with a cigarette, just for the reaction.

Lucas thought he had an advantage with his money and military experience, and he tried to bribe the bull-dykes in exchange for their protection, but this just made him more of a target. After several months, he was knocked unconscious in the shower room and sent to the infirmary, where he remained in a coma. Rachel's parents, despite being estranged from their daughter, visited regularly. They were there on the day she died.

Rachel had read about Lucas' trial and had written to him in prison, suggesting that, when they were both released, they meet and discuss a reconciliation. His written response was simply: 'Rachel, if you want your body back, we have to fuck. That's the only way to end this curse.' She let some time pass before writing back, 'I don't see why that would work. I think you've hurt a lot of people, and hope that prison might change you. I hope we can find another way.' His response to that troubled her, for she knew that any contrition was meaningless. 'I'm sorry for what I've done,' he wrote, 'I know I am an evil man and I deserve to die. I'd do anything you want if you can get me out of here. Please help me. I can't take much more.'

Some time later, she heard he died.

After her release, she'd felt inspired by her experience of offering support to inmates. She worked her contacts in the legal industry and set up meetings with organisations that supported ex-soldiers; she attended women's rights workshops and talks. She volunteered, she gave legal and financial advice to campaigners, she promoted diversity, prison reform and domestic abuse awareness. She organised fundraisers and the people who met her were intrigued by the time she'd served.

She wrote articles and gave TED talks, and eventually got invited onto *Good Morning Britain* and *Question Time*. In the end, Lucas Barrow became a celebrity: sex predator turned human rights campaigner. A publisher asked if she'd be interested in collaborating on a biography. Rachel was hesitant at first, since she barely knew the real Lucas, but she agreed on the condition that a cut of the profits were donated to women's groups.

The book was published a few weeks after Lucas' death. It was titled *Lucas Barrow: The Man inside the Monster*, which the editor had said was a working title, but Rachel said she liked just as it was. The introduction contained two quotes that were equally ironic, one by Simone de Beauvoir: 'The body is not a thing, it is a situation: it is our grasp on the world and our sketch of our project.' The second was from Shakespeare's *Twelfth Night*: 'In nature, there's no blemish but the mind. None can be called deformed but the unkind.' Rachel asked her parents if she could dedicate the book to them and their late daughter, and they agreed. One day, Rachel would tell people the truth, and she didn't care if nobody believed her.

Throughout history, his forefathers had leapt unathletically ashore from Hebridean rowing-boats, Norse longships, Saxon galleys, Dutch schuyts, Portuguese naus, Irish coracles—off the backs of solid iron penny-farthings or Number 52 Routemasters, to convey startlingly bad news to women sufficiently optionless to take delivery of it

Assemblage | Evan Hay

Urquhart H Findlay fled endlessly into a confused and bot-
tomless solitude, sheltering from harsh hyper-realities fully
furnished with icy cold untrustworthy folk; retreating behind make-belief & suppressing natural, lustful desires that
should've driven one on, keenly, into society-at-large. Adroitly
utilising defensive avoidance strategies- barren years passed,
deep-in-denial, without propulsion; hiding under quarried
strata of sedimentary self-delusion, a *rara avis in terris* subsist-
ing on spicy deceits peppered with pinches of black humour,
sniggering deliriously at altered images twisted through a
time-warped, paranoid mind, Urquhart vainly struggled to
uphold semblances of plausible normality. For whose pleasure, it wasn't clear: the big barbarians had vacated his drum
ages ago, so appeasing frightful memories was a fool's errand.
There were external existential dangers to dread, natheless over
time, as a post-pubescent, he'd deduced strangers offered him
insufficient interest to pose corporeal threats. During twice
weekly excursions to local food banks, irritable by-passers
perceived him as a furtive, poverty-stricken assemblage of

repellent materials. An indigent-cum-ragged substrate indeed, still- he understood himself as a defaced relic of terrible maltreatment, existing irreparably in the dim aftermath of personal catastrophe. Urquhart struggled ineffectually to reify positive dynamics in the wake of his bewildering juvenescence; according to gallus big sister Fiona, they were both hapless victims of an internecine crime-spree, sparked pre-parturition.

Uprooted, & carted off to NW London aged two & nine, not part of a broad diaspora but as hostages to self-obsessed, self-atomising striplings. Star-crossed loins, explosive Doddie Findlay & virally infected wifie Jeanie (née Cruden), escaped an extended family perched 555 miles north- too far afield to compassionately intercede in, or practically thwart, the un-remittable cluster-fuck that two squabbling teens concocted raising twa feart cowran bairns. Fiona told the story. 'Once mum fell pregnant her folks demanded she move back home; patently, she preferred standing proud. Following my unbid-den birth, mum's refusal to comply with Granda Cruden's final ultimatum meant she was disowned: cut off without a penny. Nana Findlay raised me single-handedly; singing me to sleep at nights with the Highland fairy lullaby, before waking me up each morning with bon accord plus a toasted buttery & porridge breakfast- escorting me to nursery, fetching me from school, the whole schmear. Nana cooked square meals of an evening; punctually reading fables & soothing poems, too, whilst our mismatched parents were out gallivanting. They treated her gaff like a cheap hotel with free childmin-ding services. I remember nana sewing dresses & braiding my hair for village festivals; I was crowned Beltane Queen once. Heigh ho! So, a tough couple of years ensued after you were born, Urquhart; dad insinuated he'd been cuckolded & the atmosphere indoors grew intolerable. Still, mum & dad stayed lodged together, united in wearing out their welcome; severing our remaining family ties with rancorous ingratitude. They squandered all available goodwill, screwed-up nana's hospitality & chucked it straight back in her boat. When nana suffered her heart attack, they acted like spoilt kids, blaming mother nature for cramping their style before heading south in massive sulks to spunk paltry savings, setting up a short-term sojourn in Cloud Cuckoo Land. But, as you're aware little bruvver, that was an epic failure. Perhaps just as well, because- trust me, Urquhart- you dodged a bullet when dad went AWOL. If he'd stuck around 'til you hit puberty, he'd have had your guts for garters.'

Fiona maintained that describing their late parents as 'economic migrants' was tantamount to disingenuously ennobling a couple of narcissistic, self-serving lotus eaters, reflexively fleeing constraining traditions, domineering conventions & archaically punctilious responsibilities prescribed by rural Doric antecedents in 1950s Banffshire. Hard-headed Fiona permitted no forgiveness for whatsoever puerile emotions spurred her gyte folks' meridional flow: 'Emotions are real, okay, but temporary- unlike dependable certitudes. You tipped them over a precipice, Urquhart; they folded like knitted deckchairs under the pressure of a second child & allowed irresponsible personal sentiments to metastasise into wobbly vested interests, competing with what's best for a baby. Businesslike facts differ- existing impersonally beyond pernickety idiosyncrasies in perpetuity: transparently accessible, open to forensic interrogation & ascertained by engineers as neutral building blocks to manufacture bridges, facts are sustainable; evanescent feelings aren't. Our mutual dissatisfaction stems from realising our DNA & nuclear family baggage as inherently poisoned burdens we simply don't care for. People can alter legal systems governing inter-human relations, but can't conceal natural injustices, cupidity, megalomania, contempt, or the destructive effects self-pitying consumption has on the wider world.'

Disparagingly labelled a 'mistake', poor Fiona was no stranger to the scathing stigmatisation immanent in child abuse; she wore testimonial scars, having whilom borne the brunt of merciless physical assaults at reoccurring condemnatory junctures. Thrashing their daughter with the metal end of a dead dog's lead, in the thick of hysterical overreactions to purported misdemeanours, triggered a paroxysmal excitement in Fiona's incandescent folks that smacked of perversity. As she recalled, ostensibly, this corporal punishment was validated as strictly remedial; glibly described as tough love meted out in corrective responses to misbehaviour- yet random blows, accompanied by the waggish taunt 'that's for nothing, now do something', recounted a horror story of despotic intimidators gleaning exhilaration by inflicting pain & humiliation upon a minor. As years passed, her strong personality developed. Sorely challenged by Fiona's hormonal evolution, her bickering parents' moody egos muddled vituperative feelings; volcanic rage fused with brutality, scuttling any traces of equilibrium. *Post eventum*, once sated, by way of semi-apology, both oppressors euphemistically designated their countless paddling crimes as heat-of-the-moment misunderstandings, rash acts best forgiven, or elsewise forgotten- viz: acrid effluence under the bridge. Steadfastly, Fiona adjudicated retrospective obfuscation as an expedient smokescreen, fog-of-war excuses, cop-outs: 'Truth is- people feel differently about shared experiences & what's morally right.'

Shortly after fracturing Fiona's jaw with a disciplinary left hook, father vacated their miserable family's council home to shack up with a brace of low-maintenance Australian barmaids (superdad died of asthmatic complications catalysed by dogging around the Welsh Harp Reservoir a few years after- a painful, undignified expiration by all accounts). As soon as the tumultuous patriarchal epoch faded, an unnerving matriarchal decade commenced. Mother, debauched firstborn daughter to a respected village postmaster, gallantly described as 'a foxy boozer' by regulars from The Old Spotted Dog on Willesden High Road, hosted a series of interchangeable boyfriends with whom she enjoyed protracted, enthusiastic sexual romps within a two-bedroom unit. *Ab ovo*, Jeanie deemed Fiona's unwanted nativity to have ruined her gloriously ribald youth; an ill-conceived manifestation, sparking concatenations of unforgivable episodes before annoyingly developing into a haughty quine. Minaciously transformed to natural competition in Mrs F's stingy green eyes- unbearably, a coquettish ingénue, perved on through the wide-angle beer goggles worn by mothers' unscrupulous saloon bar paramours. Tactically, Jeanie expelled Fiona, ridding herself of a treacherously intelligent teenage female dependent, whilst begrudgingly retaining an ill-tricket, bedwetting wee loon. In short, Mrs Findlay suffered her offspring as the anachronistic token ephemera of shambolic aleatory juvenile misadventures; investing no energy or imagination in developing substantive relationships with either.

Reverend George Oakley, a malverse parish vicar, visited Leopold Primary School to, *inter alia*, touch up Urquhart & other nominated prey. Although scarce unrolled from Leopold's infants, Urquhart resolutely informed the relevant authority. Jeanie's sole concern was withholding revelations from her estranged, delinquent husband- marking an exclusive moment when an unloved youngster learned to accept that in addition to adjunctive privations, he couldn't rely on maternal protection to ward off predatory paedophilia. On the contrary, she swore her son to solemn secrecy, warning that involving big daddy would purely serve to make matters worse; a lack of husbandry, plus reprehensible oversights, resulted in sustained exposure to indecency, multiplying Urquhart's fall from grace (regardless, each parent carried on cruising, heedlessly blind to unsparing criminal interferences conducted at their son's expense). Oakley serendipitously met freshly sundered Mrs Findlay at a church fête; praising her fortitude for struggling against debilitating maladies attributable to post-polio syndrome. Easily flattered & groomed, despite Urquhart's whistleblowing, Mrs F was convinced both she & her son would benefit from him staying on after Sunday school for extra-curricular tuition. Her boy needed a 'man's hand'. Whatever covenants Urquhart charily formed with Jesus or the Black Madonna shattered within the incensed bounds of St Mary, Our Lady of Willesden. Tumescent beneath the formal disguise of vicar's vestments, sporting a thick, unkempt auburn beard, during hazy dog days of summer, under clouds of frankincense & myrrh, Oakley belligerently thrust sordid designs upon the assembled innocents left in his care. Shepherding a carefully selected Boys' Brigade into the crypt to better marshal a fear of God, he employed theophilosophical orthodoxy to instil gullibility & total obedience into quaking rascals. Dissenters were separated from the flock, locked captive in an airing cupboard & released only upon asseverating fealty to a trin-ity: the Lord God, Her Majesty the Queen & their venerable vicarage. Antics continued unabated (however, the numbers of waifs decreased by degrees- half the original group stopped frequenting church altogether) until a pinnacle was reached come All Hallows' Eve; a seminal event, in which associates of Oakley enjoyed private audiences with hardcore remnants-forlorn proto-Ganymedes whose parents were too stupid or distracted to sense what was coming down. Suffering ghoulish 'purity' examinations, this sorry handful of kiddies was rough-ly fiddled by horny tormentors masquerading as self-styled senators, with Oakley assuming the starring role of pontifex maximus. *Malgré* the passing years, Urquhart couldn't forget those aroused catarrhine faces, & how they randily bent his puny armature like a pipe-cleaner in their salacious pursuit of happiness. Names & actions that autumnal evening spelt desolation for each defenceless target. Halloween was this doomed cohort's most intrusive encounter of all, the goriest of their ordeals; they'd never be pure again. Urquhart grew perpetually wary thereafter of powerful chauvinistic men in uniform, harbouring a justifiably jaundiced view of posh-spoken la-di-dah authority figures, the dissembling institutional types, never caught or convicted for atrocities perpetrated against humankind.

Partly on account of his dad's interminable shifts working as a *chef de partie* in St George's Hospital on Hyde Park Corner, Urquhart hardly knew his biological father, other than as a brooding figure prone to violent bouts of anger. Signally a culpable straw man, stuffed with chicanery, whose multifaceted failings & extramundane trespasses were gravely recanted by Urquhart's decadent, lower middle-class mother- how Doddie frequently beat her like a piñata, bullying her to pose in the artistic altogether, callously painting all manner of disgraceful trompe-l'œil representations of her atrophied body across cheapskate calico canvasses. Taking the piss, Dod joked that Jeanie's interior Rubenesque beauty wast veiled by vicissitudes of a backsliding nature: in lieu of celebrating her milky white femininity, Gaia had fabricated pitiful distortions to cover an inner belle- facsimiles of which Doddie unashamedly hawked to 'discerning trade' for £3 a pop at Church Street market. He was a mercurial legend in his own bathroom, his duped missus a scatterbrained alcoholic who rued the day she'd been ensnared by Doddie's extraordinary personal magnetism. A complex issue of working-class Scots fisher-folk, he'd seduced Jeanie as a whispering suitor, promising an all-consuming

106

sybaritism; notional pleasures that decomposed as Doddie reneged on his side of the compact. Sensitive heavy petting, foreplay to consensual lovemaking, descended into intra-marital bondage as a smarting period of squalid coercive coitus erupted. Reduced to a hard-drinking artist's dummy, unable to decipher straws in the wind, or imagine gratifying alternatives to the untenable positions he forced her into, Jeanie abandoned any hope for their dysfunctional relationship. Resigned to infamy, she'd endured disappointment with support from assorted placebos, & by publicly plying fakeries as delineations of adequacy. Her sham frame of stabilising references trundled along until, irrevocably, its wheels fell off, sabotaged by Doddie's antipodean tryst; without warning, she snapped: unilaterally denouncing Clan Findlay's patrilineality to her children as a dead host of damned souls, & her despicable bad seed spouse as a supernaturally spawned replicant- jaundiced, vain & dangerous to mortals. In a fit of pique & unprecedented panache, Jeanie alleged that Doddie, notoriously sired out of wedlock by Findlay63, was in fact the sixty-second arcane clone of an original sinner, Findlay the Farsighted. Talking slowly & distinctly on account of her medically wired mandible, feisty Fiona had rejected this swivel-eyed canard as deep-dyed tosh, but Mrs F persevered, archly embroidering for the benefit of her impressionable laddie (a molecular oddity who couldn't quite twig). He sat cross-legged, in elasticised plastic panties, anxiously captivated as mother blethered on- describing her scandalous ex-husband as a thug, scoundrel & errant egoist, infamous the length–breadth of Brent for never going on so much as a trip to the laundrette without thirty-six versions of his own selves in tight proximity (each a year apart, presenting the good citizens of the borough with alarming spectacles of his entire personage in sequence).

Gilding silly lilies and residual gospels, mother's liberated tongue articulated to Urquhart histories that escaped via so many interstices, leaving only farkakte myth & ruptured nonsense (evaporating beyond reach into Scotch mist). Mrs Findlay, incapable of cohabiting with her consort, mothering her adolescent daughter, or keeping faith with her nominal heritage, instead adopted full-on inebriation as a distilled form of freedom; unlike whisky, she didn't age well with passing years. Jeanie's debilitating condition worsened; peaking & pining by her two-bar electric fire with a pronounced physical disability, confronted by grammatically incorrect spastic-baiting graffiti, habitually illuminating the porch & external walls of their ground-floor wheelchair-accessible maisonette. From what increasingly resembled an absurd museum dedicated to devastated carnal ambitions & Green Shield Stamps, a subdued Urquhart graduated to torpid secondary state school education without complaint. Forcibly repressed by reduced mobility & self-inflicted ill-health, his mother intermittently detained him from classrooms on drookit Mondays, if a need to flex her dwindling strength reared its ugly head.any contrived reason sufficed: 'I regret to inform you that I shall be withdrawing Urquhart from school, as he refuses to act in a manner suitable to a child attending a decent educational establishment. I shall be placing him in a municipal borstal where he can continue to adopt the manners of a lout & skulk doltishly amongst a whoop of incarcerated lowland gorillas.'

If Urquhart hadn't already retreated into woolly theoretical safe-places, her autocratic behaviour would've mortified him. But all now proceeded as if a bad dream. That her boy was impassive didn't irk Jeanie, howbeit the prissy prefectorial tone of his school's administrator's letters in return offended her grandiose sense of superiority. This grievance compounded the number of occasions each term she'd unilaterally suspend Urquhart; sporadic gripes stemming from her constant need for attention, casual xenophobia & increasingly pronounced anti-clericalism. Through her dour final years, a bonkers-in-the-nut, querulous Mrs Findlay enacted demented, fruitless performances to, in principle, support her son's studies. Ranting at political-correctness gone mental for demeaning true sprigs of 'tree Britannica' to study at underfunded, leaking post-war prefabs- whilst church, mosque, Rastafarian, Vulcan or synagogue schools flourished, undergirded as they were by vast quantities of theological sausage & mash. Her discretional invalid's right to private audiences at school governors meetings was officially revoked on account of her insatiable, bigoted need to loudly expatiate downsides of diversity- attacking sovereign-state expenditure frittered to meet the requirements of mass immigration & damning subsequent drains on her local authority's educational resources presented by eighty-five per cent of Willesden's comprehensive schoolchildren burbling English as a second language: 'If anyone's peculiarly special needs, it's me! They need Confucian or Islamic tuition? I've heard enough about we *et seq* being net beneficiaries of immigration. Who are "we"? It's a big ask, isn't it? "We" are constituted of winners or losers- so, which am I? Well, I don't employ cheap imported labour, nor can I afford fancy foreign carry-outs, as I'm not in the forty per cent tax bracket. I'm but a poor lapsed Presbyterian, no longer able to communicate effectively with her exotic neighbours; one whose only son is the last indigenous Briton in his class- for shame! Tell me: just how am I a net beneficiary? And pray sir; inform me, in those middle-class schools of rural Surrey, what precisely is the percentage of English spoken as mother tongue in their ivy-muffled halls? The bloody system's failing me!'

By the time she finally shut-up & expired (following an aneurism), Urquhart had left school without qualifications; primed for failure, he wasn't unduly concerned. Moreover, he wasted none of his unquenchable grief mourning mommy dearest- still, he was loath to leave the maisonette. In the witching hour Urquhart spent staring intently at Jeanie's nude, goose-pimpled cadaver, he felt only apprehensive numbness attributable to emotional paralysis; far more frightening was a hell of strangers gaining forced entry. Coroners, police constables, undertakers, motley crews of pastoral care merchants seeking to tamp an orphan's void, & sundry bailiff repossessions re: missed household payments. These latter intrusions sparked a gnawing concern that amassing arrears that would culminate in an unwanted eviction by enforcement officers. Peculiarly, Urquhart was psychologically wed to home settings, which at worst represented a prison of sorts, at best a hidey-hole from outlandish perils lurking in vast tracts of shifting sands. The tenancy provided a multipurpose bolthole in which to sit

110

tight, wallowing amidst a Serbonian Bog of shame, pertur-
bation & purdah. Left to his own devices, Urquhart pandered
to jumbled hallucinatory phenomena, repetition compulsions, traumatic daydreams, et al. Compelled by a recurring
sense of resentment, he circled back around dead & buried
circumstantial situations; re-engaging incidents with beautiful hindsight, posing distorted 'what ifs' to evoke illusory
ramifications. Thus motivated, he convinced social workers
of his determined ability to make a decent fist of remaining
in situ & living solo. A trial period was agreed, commenc-
ing with pecuniary support to cover rents, plus living costs;
timetabled weekly telephone calls & supplementary monthly
check-ups chronicled predominantly optimistic assessments.
In the light of cuts in public spending, unprecedented in the
previous generation (which now voted en masse in support of
political decisions to purge Britain's welfare state), Urquhart's
immoderate agoraphobia, gauged purely as a cost estimation,
was projected as a significant boon, vis-à-vis departmental
cash-flow. Crucially, this assisted in securing managerial approval for scheduled handouts, as recommended by his case
workers; unwittingly, Urquhart participated in a libertarian
quest to curtail haemorrhaging expenditure from Brent social
services' shrinking budget. Accordingly, established as a qua-
si-independent lessee, he wasn't evicted following diagnoses of
ongoing mental health issues (primarily hypervigilance slash
severe anxiety) which prevented him venturing forth to acquire
gainful employment. Rather, this predicament was offset by
authorised entitlement to incapacity allowances- paving the
way for a peaceful furlough of empirical reflection.

Alone in a jinxed childhood home, emancipated from parasitic malfunctioning adults exploiting his vulnerability, Urquhart investigated his godawful patrimony. Dysfunctional relation-ships, abominable deeds, vile people fed foul offal diets; fetid intestinal feasts, cresting in a banquet of grisly consequences. Chaotic role models, mixed messages, no money, pride, status, or useful contacts- coupled with a congenitally sub-average personality. All elements considered, Urquhart was in a pick-le; a casualty from a hostile, insolvent menagerie- socialisa-tion that would appal a flange of baboons. Neither kith, kin, tribe nor religion to snuggle up with. Worse, disgracefully besmirched by the wretched stigma of belonging to an ut-terly pointless ethnic minority- white British working-class (aka wiggers anonymous), with over 1,000 coarse years of subjugation, murder, rape, persecution, incest, deportation, press-ganging, conscription, compulsory social-cum-indus-trial upheaval, contempt & self-loathing in their locker since its feral ancestors, alas, arrived upon this island- rolling-up at exactly the right times to intercept miscellaneous generative female victims. Throughout history, forefathers had leapt unathletically ashore from Hebridean rowing-boats, Norse longships, Saxon galleys, Dutch schuyts, Portuguese naus, Irish coracles- off the backs of solid iron penny-farthings or Number 52 Routemasters, to convey startlingly bad news to accursed women sufficiently optionless to take delivery of it, thereby taking another monster leap towards creating Urquhart H Findlay, the topmost chimney-pot, if you will, on the derelict & haunted House of Urquhart. It could have been different. He needn't necessarily have to become stuck in the mud, in the excrement, each meaningful decision scarily indistinguishable from its shitty predecessor- it's an ongoing visceral struggle to avoid supplementary calamity. Beyond the cruel chaos desultorily created by his immediate progenitors, Urquhart grew up in a modernising capital city of filth & fury, still inhabited by the ghosts of suffragettes, still inspired by the optimistic principles of Attleean reforms & encouraged by earnest campaigning from trades unions to reduce crass class privilege; still serenaded by lyrical pop music from apparently regular kids that afforded illusory access to education & a potential release from wage-slave drudgery. Adding as a caveat, that lucky industrial-estate-escapees represented an enviable minority of the post-war generation's stating the bleeding obvious. Nevertheless, sweet dreams are made of this.

In an unanticipated return, revenant Fiona instituted pragmatic rationality, swagger & a capacity to make Urquhart guffaw; her creative skills converted fantastical threats into risible cartoons, which buckled under the abdominal pressure of sustained belly laughs. None of this aplomb or levity was achieved easily. When she re-appeared out-of-the-blue, stood at the jet-black front door of her girlhood home, years after their mother's demise, her degenerated brother didn't recognise her, requesting she go away & leave him alone. So, for starters, she'd aggressively forced entry, beat him up badly with a cudgel drawn from her utility belt, & bound him with electrical wire. Thinking quickly, she kept him heavily sedated: a bedbound captive. No one was alarmed. Conveniently, social services had set-up standing orders for household bills & stopped monthly assessments (over time Urquhart had proved able to live alone with financial support). A bona fide survivor, Fiona capably kept him physically healthy & a roof over her own head- preferable to sleeping rough, a prospect that loomed large after being ejected by her latest sugar daddy. A month or so's drug-induced floccillation followed. Fiona had gained a fair degree of contrastive, experience-based knowledge in the clinical use of specific drugs. She applied these mixed insights adeptly to switch Urquhart off at the mains, prior to slowly easing his induced coma by reducing dosages in tandem with administering an economic quota of mercy-wanks to allay his ephialtes (carefully curtailing this emergency physiotherapeutic measure afore Urquhart regained consciousness). Darkness passed as coshed amnesia cleared. Cognisant of being nursed, only multitudinous months later did Urquhart accept that this nurturing succubus was his long-lost sister. As strange to a reclusive mind were murmurings- crosstalk, heated debates & opinions emanating from Fiona's snappy handheld radio. His parents hadn't rented televisions, nor even purchased record players, & whilst he conceded such devices operated abroad, he'd pretty much forgotten about them. Before Fiona induced him to awake, unravel, pay attention & tackle his inner demons, left to his own solitary artifices, Urquhart had diligently disengaged in matters beyond quiet meandering introspection; adamantly taking steps to bypass odd school-mates without acknowledgement, treating any unscheduled encounter as a surreal danse macabre with a stranger, ignoring street clamour & keeping necessary dialogues to a bare minimum. His customised self-defence regime had been quite a cerebral achievement. Now this perfect isolation melted at glacial speed. It took the flabbiest part of an annus horribilis before he recognised & recalled aspects of a cheeky lassie that bore witness to the opening scenes of his bleak minority

& shared contusions in proportion to its austerity. Despite a seven-year age difference, no one better understood his historical wounding than his sister. Graphically depicting dramatic scenes was her forte; flashbacks caught his attention as she reminisced over jarring experiences they shared until she was banished. Fiona recited a comprehensive backstory. She assiduously plugged memory gaps from times before his arrival, through his pre-consciousness, up to & including his sketchy grasp on information apropos the dawning of their parent's devil-may-care union; how interfamily disputes spawned inflammable material, posing a risk of detonation prior to his manifestation, then, how as a suspect neonate, Urquhart lit a fuse that caused a cataclysmic explosion. Inculcated to embrace guilt, he floundered in the jolting wreckage of family feuds that were not of his making. Luckily for him, Fiona was all he dreamed of emulating. Having jumped without a parachute & survived the landing, she'd struggled back to her feet, working out stages of grief on her way up. She was smart, an autodidact; despite her travails she'd retained a happy-go-lucky approach. Her counsel helped mitigate his angst-fuelled timidity. She coached him to permit anger, channelling it via therapeutic humour towards an alternative mindfulness, where he demanded more of himself, reoriented patterns of behaviour & expected different outcomes. Incrementally, Urquhart advanced his emotional settings from petrified, to wearily depressed. For the first time, he conceived autonomy & envisioned taking small steps towards protruding willpower. He was impelled by her company, & for a while it suited Fiona to doss down rent-free with her amenable, yet harrowingly bizarre, little brother.

115

Securing work in a private residential care home presented Fiona opportunities to steal drugs & build a nest egg by selling them to addicts in Roundwood Park. As part of a loose plan to stir Urquhart's integration into society, she started to take him with her, especially after dark, as mascot-cum-decoy-of-last-resort: 'Stay close to me, Urquhart. There are mad dogs out there. Vying interest groups, as evidenced throughout recorded history, can't sensibly negotiate differences in peace. Honestly, it's impossible for individual sensitivities & universal facts to rub along together without friction; mitigation's measured by narrow gradation, it's never absolute. Street trading revolves around limited resources, entrepreneurial spirit, bottom lines, endeavour; it's a relentless, pitiless, desire-driven exercise. Not for the timid!' Working with big sister was an eye-opener. Urquhart's incipient self-confidence burgeoned. Astonishing them both, he put the frighteners on a crackbrained twerp who'd forced his hands down Fiona's knickers whilst disputing her spot price for diazepam- pinning him down &, in a fit of inspired improvisation, ramming dog muck up his nostrils with a lollipop stick. Emboldened, Urquhart contrived further situations to display his new-found strength. Overpowering an eumelanin-skinned customer, who looked foreign & Muslim, he exuberantly rendered an emergency baptism- an act that brought an instant agricultural rebuke from Fiona: 'Get the fuck off him, you stupid twat!' She took control & calmed things down. At ground level, business was particularly risky. There & then she taciturnly marked Urquhart's card- planning to migrate whenever her money was right. She'd done her bit to help, but he was always going to be a liability. Urquhart, shocked by his actions rather than Fiona's reactions, felt it was mum's spectre possessing him. Walking home at end of trade, Urquhart distressfully recalled their mother's intransigent sense of supremacy, her lack of platonic friendships, her ethnic prejudice & aggressive intolerance toward any variation she distrusted; virulent characteristics that persisted in him, he concluded.

Arriving home, Fiona spared time to clarify, whilst skinning up & using language her brother could comprehend, that should he ever queer her pitch again, she'd smash his filbert in with a dustbin lid. With the radio on & joint half smoked, her manner relaxed. Rabbiting on a tad, she recounted a letter she'd received in response to a mail order purchase: 'Dear Ms Findlay, we thank you for your recent order; you asked for the large red vibrator pictured in our wall display. Please reselect, as this item is actually a fire extinguisher.' Stoned, Fiona insisted this communication was hilarious. Urquhart didn't comprehend her bawdy sense of humour that night; allowing his imagination to drift, he offered in return a few cunning stunts he could try out on unsuspecting community members: impersonating state-registered nurses, wasting police time (Fiona retorted, the filth could just as easily do that themselves), alarming educationally subnormal OAPs with false UFO sightings, & enacting racially aggravated citizen's arrests for littering, dog-fouling or- funniest of all- jay walking. Fiona replied 'whatever'- adding that so long as he didn't involve her in any of those buggered-up plans, she couldn't give a cunt. That said, before passing out for the night, she

117

covertly counted up her savings relative to a cash target & monkeyed-up a surmised date in the not-too-distant future when she'd once again bale from this fucking nut house.

One morning, Fiona was gone. No goodbye. No kiss-my-arse. Nothing, bar a transistor radio emitting siren voices sparking intrigue rather than intimidation; allured, Urquhart made a significant effort cogently to engage with his neighbourhood. Plucking up courage, he successfully sought work in a midsized convenience store across the road. Managers kept him well away from retail spaces, demanding that he stay out-back, unloading orders off the back of delivery lorries, methodically trolleying tinned-cum-vacuum packaged foodstuffs from service road to stockroom. Muttering monotonously about Judgment Day, Hell & damnation, he posed a terrifying cardiovascular experience for elderly customers, but most drivers found him highly amusing & were sorry to see him go. His employment terminated prior to completing his three-month trial period on account of his erratic attendance record. Some gregarious members of staff, who were reasonably well-disposed toward their special-needs colleague, did cross the busy road to knock on his door & shout at him through his scuzzy windows, beckoning him to join their working day. Urquhart wouldn't respond- every few days he'd simply not be in the mood to. Eventually a handwritten note was pushed through his letterbox: 'I've been informed that you didn't attend work today due to depression. Please be aware that on average the amount of time you've taken off during the past couple of months is greatly out of kilter with the rest of our core team. If

118

there's some underlying problem or condition that you've not hitherto mentioned that the rest of us need to know about, I'll happily set aside quality time to discuss it man-to-man. Please understand that I need to have a winning team which I can depend upon, especially in our busy time, ie now. I want you to be an integral part of my team. Ergo, I fully expect you to be here on time tomorrow, as per your shift agreement with Happy Shopper plc.'

Urquhart didn't return & made no effort to deflect & divert, distract from, or deny his emphatic failure to thole short-term low-impact patterns of local, part-time, unskilled minimum-wage employment; instead preferring unalloyed transcendental coherence sought through longer-term personal research into his subconscious mind. Fiona's portable radio, central to his rumination, provided a cocksure sounding board from which to equitably fathom how abnormal he was &, as an unforeseen bonus, hearkening segued to appraising in wonder what sophisticated commentators on his favourite talk radio programme (BBC Radio 4's *Today*) described as neoliberal individualism. Another channel, LBC, simultaneously aired callers arguing testily, which was exciting. Many decried immigration, lionising instead glorious British isolationism; disembodied voices warned listeners of the figurative opium anchoring us to a debt-laden global economy. Urquhart initially loved all of this self-satisfied-adulatory media dope. His heart skipped as contending voices metaphorically recoiled from each other in faux shock, projecting an instantaneous toxic admixture of feculent hatred. It was so slick, as if it were rehearsed. He listened intently & learned for days on end. The *Today* programme: evidently dictated by smug creatures with small brains, short–blurry vision & maximal contagion. Akin to being a vassal to fever- eavesdropping Urquhart was hooked. Narrators prattled on informatively. Audible Brahmin from far-flung neo-Varna dreamworlds, crammed with opulence; egocentric silver-spoons reared on abundant ancestral nourishment- producing super-confident personalities, ravenous to consume smorgasbords of absorbing materials & intellectual titbits, yet more committed to espousing how these hedonistic experiences made them feel in minute detail- ad nauseam. Braggadocious performances- getting uncomfortable ideas off a few chests- ventilated as an educational service. Even Urquhart's humble comprehension alerted him to just how much government licensed radio verbiage was opinionated propaganda. Its principal purpose, selling ideas aimed at convincing listeners that irrelevant psychobabble was perfectly normal, business as usual; a life less ordinary, spent in a cosy silk-stocking world but affording cursory nods to non-gripping peripheral aspects (levies on cargoes, freight transport, tenant farmers, *The Archers*, shipping forecasts, disadvantaged backgrounds, etc).

A familiar British Airways captain, recently retired, entertainingly bemoaned how a pilot's life was no longer a merry one: 'Work became a trial of avoiding irritating administrators, eager to thwart one's best efforts & show their usefulness: soul-destroying-stuff. Time was when pilots-in-command were left alone to safely manage flying from A to B, from wife to girlfriend, via a stopover with concubines. Nowadays, one hands over one's home telephone number or dog's name at one's peril, & to top it all, they allocated us one of these new-fangled mobile telephones free. Their choice of that word "free" being particularly nauseating as we were, as a result, less free than ever- in a matter of minutes, hideous voices of cretins-who-know-nothing-about-flying sounded-off over the god-damned device, no doubt wagging semen-encrusted fingers in admonishment at some transaction costing the business 50p. As regular listeners can imagine, moving house cost me a pretty penny- but it was worth it to hear the last supervisor complaining that my home number had stopped working!' Most callers were supportive of overworked aircrew (in the interest of passenger safety), albeit to comply with demands for what passed as middling diversity, one fired-up manifestation of certifiable nationalism fulminated that the mere thought of impropriety from British Airways was disloyal- whatever the actualité. Mr Algernon Seymour of Hungershall Park, Royal Tunbridge Wells, stressed: 'Certain people, thankfully small in number, never grasp that however regrettable, certain actions are best left unremarked, far less pursued. Surely our tireless leaders are allowed a measure of indiscretion! Who among them hasn't at some point overstretched their estimable remit? Baron Marshall of Knightsbridge knows something of paramount importance: the interests of Britain's state élites are concurrent with those of its ordinary people- lamentably, commoners often fail to grasp this truism, busy as they are with worrying about paying bills & associated menial matters.'

Airtime afforded to debating political viewpoints antithetical to the standard mantras routinely advanced by mainstream media was prejudicially skewed to entrap duck soup transgressors. Urquhart heard well-meaning champions of ethical divergence awkwardly couched as ultra-radicals, patronisingly referred to as quixotic, quirky, error-prone personalities discombobulated by conspiracy theories; implying that the aberrant hypotheses proposed by such credulous dissenters were offset by said proponents' innate gullibility. He obliquely recollected authentic, critically thinking acquaintances from auld lang syne: scant replicas were broadcast on-air. Some pundits shed a flickering light on fundamental faults in government policies, challenging fellow citizens to strive harder to foster changes urgently needed to stave off ecological destruction- but even these earnest guests, when studied, turned out to be incumbents of posts with, and hence funded by, institutions integral to prevailing orthodoxies. Psychonosologists could characterise the chattering classes as a cancerous group afflicted by an oxymoronically slavish eleuthromania, personality differences being questions of degree, not kind.

A verbose family-friendly BBC producer, confessed to being happily domiciled in a securely gated community area of north London he'd described as 'excruciatingly suburban' thirty-five years previously; his middle-aged contentment coming as a result of chaperoning his goodly wife there, as part of a catchment area relocation, from her mortgage-free, grace-&-favour townhouse off Highbury Fields. Now a solid family unit, they contrived to throw 'surprise' themed parties, during which invitees performed spangled acts supposable as footloose amusement (improvisations translated as trite by Urquhart). Featuring faux dismay- pretend horror- pie crust enlightenment: 'It's hilarious interpreting extemporisations whilst we carouse!' To Urquhart's lugs it enounced a load of pretentious bollocks. Parlour games a-go-go featuring a wacky series of scrupulously collected personality types, formally approved & attired in rented fancy-dress. Artfully staged, with devotees orating heartfelt pedestrian panegyrics, trumpeting how their prestigious hosts were *bons oeufs*, perfectly splendid role-models, & exemplary characters, prime cuts above peasants, plebs and podiatrists. Apparently, quality me-time & tons of money heals misgivings *au milieu*. Who knew? Feigning a hesitant apprenticeship, he embarrassingly recalled a callow, conscientious, socially conscious correspondent; claiming all he'd wanted was to live centrally, report breaking news in the public interest & play for a Hoxton-based ANC-affiliated soccer team. Fortuitously, he'd hooked up with a high society party gel, smoking Sobranie Cocktail cigarettes as she protested at an all-night vigil outside the South African embassy on Trafalgar Square. Pursuing fashionable champagne socialism, Missy publicly disagreed with her knighted father's politics-spurred by his conflicting interests to her worthy charitable work, she seized opportunities to release ad hominem press statements & wed morganatically. Liquid capital was no obstacle. The gushing journo paused to reiterate how grateful he was that this left-wing public school firebrand married him in the humble setting of St Mary Undercroft Chapel. By the sounds of it, his wife's ancestral riches stemmed from her mater's lineage (pater, Conservative MP for the Royal Borough of Kensington & Chelsea, earmarked & hitched low-hanging bequeathed wealth). It wasn't clarified by what means her family's magnificent prosperity was accumulated, but given those South African connections & his mother-in-law's stellar Caribbean pad in Aruba, Urquhart took provisional guesses. Summing up this romantic *Woman's Hour* piece, a diamond-encrusted & debt-free newshound repeated with genuine satisfaction: 'Life's been good!'

Urquhart felt bullish financial market analysts on Radio 4's money programmes astonishing. Entitlement by definition avoids those bromides inherent in meritocracies. A post-Big Bang breed of promissory money-makers & offshore fiscal refuseniks increasingly sounded like hereditary mediaeval kleptocrats toying with unlimited tensile human resources. Pontifications about free markets were lies. Rigged decks created false signals, ensuring pimped MTM valuations; auditors rinsed their hands. Unwilling to compete (they didn't have to), such interdependent cantillionaires resented the nuisance value of unredacted brass tacks, which if publicised, would reflect badly on their crimes *contre l'humanité*. These charlatans pretended, misinterpreting & falsifying equations to suit the ordinary working person's addiction to fairy tales- & of course, it's easier to fib from a comfort zone decorated with plush playthings (more difficult to fake it if dreams fester into nightmares). Concomitantly, a vexing cross-section of vulture capitalists, tax-avoiding rogues & media whores broadcast pet interests. Urquhart imagined restrained commentators lacking in vim, mildly inhibited, possessed of short, stumpy leathery wings capable of impressive, if limited, leaps of faith.

124

Contrastingly, armed with flawless conviction, booming opinion formers were apotheosised into BBC demigods, enjoying faculties unaccountable to external scrutiny. State-funded government-sanctioned doctrines & weasel words aplenty from the uppermost echelons atop our Great Chain of Being-spokespeople for an ultimate pan-Earthly cartel (C-of-E values, purpose-built for the foremost); unpleasantnesses enforced by laws merely warranted inconveniences- inconsequential memories of colonial pasts. Historical events to recount at swanky fondue parties- each new generation living royally off of flesh & blood collateral; descendants of mining investors, compensated plantation owners & usurers were paid from all-party government deficits- the National Debt was on tap for QE, stock conversion, equity release, asset inflation & securing international playboy lifestyles underwritten by an ignorant-oppressed ninety-plus per cent. Recited in full, it's a hell of a concept, making the Mỹ Lai massacre resemble post-luncheon high jinks. Melancholic cycles mourned by an ersatz morality sermonised over by intergenerational bad actors, with all their liabilities legally removed, herding folk with impunity, inexorably retrograde, towards neofeudalism. Whilst unsure who specifically constituted this cabal, Urquhart assumed them to be the smallest of interest groups. But these types can't get enough. As long as there's more than one standing, there's a conflict of interests. Ultimately, unavoidably, the nature of the beast draws our species too close to the sun. Even if divisions of power didn't mutually assure destruction by relentless economic-cum-martial conflicts- a monopoly would ravage our biosphere. Humanity's hardwired to soar, crash & burn. Enjoy it while you can: ravish one's kicks before this whole shit-house goes up in flames. In conclusion, Urquhart reinforced his working theory that life, born out of chaos in a cross-fire hurricane, flourished thanks to stability: continuing to transmogrify, precariously, balanced upon repercussive ebbs & flows of fortune- the impact of these grew to apocalyptic significance as humans evolved into the planet's apex predator. With nothing bar themselves left to destroy, their malevolence turned inwards- savagely. Devoid of unclaimed Lebensraum for manoeuvre, our terrene was fucked. Urquhart suspicioned an End of Days to be unfolding & meekly hiding inside a hum-drum maisonette only guaranteed his unspectacular oblivion.

Through dirty old sash windows, he tentatively appraised attributes of sempiternal street folk. Today, despite being part of a standard working-week, saw the usual suspects: quadru-pedal knuckle-shuffling vagrants, pushers, *souteneurs* & their jezebels- single black baby-mammas skanking around by the score. Promiscuous assemblies loitering with red-blooded intent, mature women in idle patois chit-chats- more nubile models taking minxish liberties; pungent pot-shots aimed at creature comforts: rum, collie weed, cunnilingus, a rub-a-dub down with Palmer's Cocoa Butter. Large-limbed ebony women, blaming everybody bar themselves for a patent collective lack of civilised achievement or self-respect. Urquhart felt a kindred spirit- in awe of what he saw as a fastidious, clannish hatred of their environment. Hectoring mobs, overripe with leucorrhoea & preposterous oral traditions, railing against impoverish-ing über-blandness, abetted by innumerable mix-&-match progeny. Spraying neighbourhoods with crude tribal tags of a type ethnologists call 'sign stimuli', projecting vibrant, atten-

126

tion-seeking 'what the fuck-are-you-looking-at' demeanours, heaps of colourful big-brand litter, spunky-funky sound-system noise pollution, plus grotesque anti-social outbursts. Urquhart wondered about feckless haphazard men, in'n'out of their lives, picturing headstrong unreliable baby-fathers, historically illiterate and unable to sustain much beyond an erection or a bad mood (medical fraternities as yet offered no cure or diagnostic test to mensurate exactly how badder it gets). Still, he was attracted to the sluttish appearance of these shunpike Magdalenes, whom he imagined doggedly claiming varieties of imaginative state-benefits: chronic debilitations ranging through RSI, non-specific back pain, fibromyalgia, to highly irritable bowel syndromes. In hordes they flirted, preened, & braced fat-smelly-soggy-tightly-thonged-buttocks against razor-sharp December winds, blissfully unaware their voluptuous bodies were ogled, dissed & frantically masturbated over. Urquhart desired to schtup black mamas, craven fat wog whores. Sat bolt upright by his kitchen-sink, halitosis steaming cracked glass windows, rhythmically jerking pelvic contractions- eyes closed- envisioning lewd images of rippling prepubescent negro girls, strutting provocatively to beating riddims. In mind deeply encunted, he gripped a throbbing, rubbery, uncircumcised chipolata with the primal urgency of a wild animal.

Raging love bulge relieved, a salty detumescent voyeur all dappered up in his best clobber, he sallied forth to embrace death or glory (keeping folding money in his pockets but forgetting to carry a precautionary umbrella). True to form,

127

outside on NW10's forsaken insanitary streets Urquhart was micturated upon from on high by driving gelid sleet. He entered a vacant telephone box, braving pronounced scents of urine, to avoid a torrential soaking. Vox populi was scrawled across every available surface; more intriguingly, a plethora of multi-coloured calling cards decorated its atmospheric interior. 'Biggest, baddest, blackest nipples in Neasden', claimed one. It was a catholic church, albeit a very small one, providing diversions for all cummers, inc Rebbe Melnick: an arsehole so tight it squeaks as he walks. This brash bottom boast appealed to Urquhart. Recalling Oakley, speculating as to what physical, mental, emotional or spiritual solutions Melnick's derrière might hold for his peculiar rage—a prevailing plutocracy, or plastic contaminants poisoning Earth's biosphere? Outside, a dishevelled, disconcerted Afro-Caribbean in desiccated footwear paced the public highway. Stopping several yards further on, struggling to think his way out of a wet paper bag, shouting: 'Ain't nobody gonna tell us to do what we don' wanna do, we be British citizens & free people. We know our rights!'- Before disappearing into a bookmaker's. Urquhart placed his bet. Inexperienced in these matters, he wasn't unduly surprised that the number listed was screened by a professional call centre. A virtual receptionist skimmed salient points, including the length & girth of Melnick's manhood, concluding with a bottom-line SP yielding two and a half per cent discount on cash transactions. A £25 tariff, applied as an entrance fee, included hand-relief; extras to be negotiated upon arrival. Everything appeared kosher.

Urquhart stoutly trotted to a run-of-the-mill address in New-
man Close, just off Brondesbury Park. Rebbe Melnick was
short, dark, hairy & aggressive. No sooner had Urquhart
crossed the threshold into his grim ground-floor maisonette,
than Rebbe barked: 'Get it out.' Taken aback, Urquhart stood
still, unsure how best to proceed. 'Get it out FFS!' Melnick
screamed apoplectically. Startled, Urquhart unzipped, producing a flaccid penis for this funny old man's scrutiny. 'No, the
money, you schmuck.' Clumsily, Urquhart provided Melnick
with the prerequisite pony before negotiations commenced
as to the proposed nature & fathomable extent of their union. Our protagonist was amazed how fiendishly complex a
dialogue this bespectacled Rebbe eked out of a basic back-of-
the-envelope subject. Hunched at a messy bureau, Melnick
poured over reams of preprepared contractual documentation,
painstakingly cross-referring- insisting Urquhart countersign
complicated, legally binding, commercial pre-conditions. Just
as a spurious deal was to about be struck, issues- eccentric
correlations between star signs, moon phases, or uniquely
unorthodox interpretations of the mystical Kabala- stymied
hopes of a mutually beneficial conclusion. In a truly rapturous
burlesque performance, master-craftsman Melnick strove to
seize an upper hand. Wearing rancid scaly skin, house slip-
pers & threadbare Tottenham Hotspur FC-branded wincyette
bedclothes; he winked a dodgy mince pie. 'Don't you mind,
my boy, it's all worthwhile. Rebbe Melnick puts the Jew into
jouissance. Coupled with my fabled studiousness, I'll show you
a crisp-thinking yiddishe kop, swift riposte, twinkling eyes &
dainty dancing feet.' Urquhart suppressed a giggle. Finally, a
priapic party started. Coughing, Melnick arose to his feet with
a twitch, hoarsely promising his client a sexual awakening of

Biblical proportions (already furnished with Melnick's vital statistics, Urquhart doubted this). Rebbe enquired if Mr Findlay desired deluxe golden showers before grinding intimacy (ablutions subject to a £9.99 surcharge). Urquhart dismissed unhygienic urinatory formalities, entreating Melnick (who insisted on being addressed as 'master') to use his Christian name. Melnick declined to acknowledge this request, pausing, weighing up his customer whilst itching furiously. 'You wait a moment.' He entered an adjoining room (where a decidedly unmade single bed was noticeable); barely out of view Melnick stripped-off before re-appearing stark-bollock-naked, with just a stripy tasselled shawl draped across stooped shoulders. 'Nice shawl,' complimented Urquhart. Master smiled flirtatiously, retreating backwards into his caliginous bedroom- its bed resembled classic installation art, the career pinnacle of an assemblagist. Urquhart cast a gaze, observing items this raving inbred patriarch played with when not publicly masquerading as reasoned tradition. Alongside discarded moccasins, official club merchandise pyjamas, lay smegma-smeared Y-Fronts, non-vibrating dildos, half-drunk bottles of Supermalt, handcuffs, a gartel, crushed packets of Rothmans, a shtreimel, scatological bed-sheets, masoretic texts, sleeping-pills, painkillers, Vaseline & used condoms. 'Please, relax,' announced a naked master, who'd thus far embodied a sterling incarnation of the least chilled out chap in Willesden. Urquhart sat down upon the borough's singlest most dirty mattress, considering how now to develop this strange tryst. 'Would you care to pillow fight?'

'Okay, so you like to flirt with your master?' Urquhart said nothing, but rose to carefully undress; neatly folding second-hand Levis, Harrington jacket & Ben Sherman shirt out of harm's way beside his choice charity shop oxblood Martens. Mute, mano a mano, they collided as two vectors of fate. A flurry of love-bites preceded a dirty five-fingered goosing session, before his bearded elder beckoned Urquhart under thin polyester sheets; there Melnick manhandled his client licentiously &, with a miraculous fart, retched up enteric gases from decaying bowels in a closely confined Dutch oven. Piteous groans accompanied master's descent into bestiality as he grappled a spry, stronger man. 'What big strong arms you've got. Have you been hanging from the branches of a tree?' Sweat glistened on the vendor's torso, prompting his dodgy customer to nip masters' hirsute chest, pinning him down to tongue recently shaven armpits. 'No fuckee no buttee with no rubber on,' gasped Melnick. Putrid claustrophobia threatened to spoil their mood, prompting Urquhart to toss off the frayed sheets, deftly positioning himself to take Melnick's schmeckle down his throat. 'Wait! Not so fast.' Master stretched to reach his sacred tefillin. Urquhart patiently stalled whilst Hasidic Rebbe dexterously inserted cubic black leather boxes attached to long leather straps deep up inside his sweaty rectum. 'Suck now, bubbeleh!' Urquhart agape, the beardy-weirdy geezer's rabbinical bollocks on his faithless chin, craned his neck back to drink reverently from this font of wisdom. At an optimum moment of ontological serenity, Melnick tightly grasped his pink patent leather straps; sharply tugging, wrenching them out from his lubed anus with a God-fearing shriek, enjoining, 'Eat my load!'

Seemingly becalmed after releasing 2.5cc of horribly tortured man lust on behalf of this sperm-gobbling punter, master condescended to cradle Urquhart in his eczematous arms for a short session of pro-bono pillow talk. A garrulous unsolicited confession persuaded Urquhart that Melnick wasn't in fact a religious icon, but rather a very naughty boy. Actually named Spivack, he was the special son of pharmaceutical retailers; academic failure in chemistry was followed by rustication from a yeshiva in suburban Gateshead & (the final straw in his relatives' eyes) a botched apprenticeship made of him a humble shochet. He now scarcely coped on a meagre family stipend of £20k per annum; what rough trade passed his way hardly covered his bargain-basement call-centre costs. A sideline singing falsetto in a klezmer band aborted as he was identified as a nonce by WUPJ audience members whilst entertaining a bar mitzvah. On top of it all, a few shitty schwartzers upstairs had started to menace him for monies. *Under Mi Sensi* could be heard above: 'Babylon come an tell mi dat naw right'- always some slag imposing their ill will on you, figured Urquhart. Rested & revitalised, Spivack started biting frenziedly at the nape of his youthful vendee's neck, aiming enlightened oaths at a damned yok; hissing all types of theofascistisc opprobrium- abruptly pivoting from tender whispers to 'Dirty goy scum. Helot. Exegesis now!' Apparently the main avodah of his generation was a final war of the golus to conquer & pacify gentiles in pursuit of cheap, docile labour, but Spivack was so highly strung- no wonder he'd struggled to establish a repeat customer base. Urquhart perceived that the very drawing of breath to answer some platitudinous comment from a cretinous vaginard shopkeeper would be- for this mentor of anxiety- an act of torture, of magnificent, mythic futility. Clearly, this incorrigible character's highest value aimed loyally to a greater cause, formulating a worshipful coterie, domination for eternity over everyone else & all means to this climactic end were imbued with spiritual justification. Unfortunately for Spivack, Urquhart wasn't keen to accompany him as pet knob-jockey on this deranged journey- so, it inevitably ended that evening; but prior to wanton destruction, there was tormenting fun.

Overpowering Spivack, Urquhart punched him percussively on the jaw until he limped out. Improvising with a sturdy leather belt & frivolous consecrated garments, Urquhart tightly bound his captive, ransacking his greasy kitchen for implements. Options disappointed; nothing surgical, far less sensitively scientific, or able to detect a frozen tardigrade fart in the vastness of space. He'd have to make do, avert a mental health crisis & gather together devilish domestic cutting devices into a tidy toolkit. Stylishly designed, lightweight, ergonomic, Urquhart put high quality Japanese steel to an ultimate test. The pain of being butchered alive soon brought his former master back from unconsciousness: gagged & tongue-tied, only capable of sustained low moans, akin to slaughterhouse cows. Urquhart pondered. A little bit of give in the tethers to adjustable footboard-supports bestowed his subject matter a modicum of room in which to struggle, but for the most part, as fey tormentor, Urquhart was able to lacerate, slash & stab to his heart's content. Having gouged out & cut off all of

Spivack's soft bits, Urquhart was at bit of loss. He was making it up as he went along. He'd been substrate for all & sundry to spit on, talk down to, beat-up as a whipping boy to fuel their petty self-centred interests & he was so over it. Now he was biting back. He considered saying grace, but was unsure whom to. Spivack, reduced to a helpless ichor &/or blood-covered homunculus, might be able to weigh him in, but he'd probably scream shrilly for his temporal life if this mouth was freed. A blow-torch & needle nosed pliers could persuade him to write out answers- but if not now, when? When would Urquhart permanently cut out the middleman?

In an act of impulsive humanity, he slit Spivack's throat. Wouldn't it be cool to converse with a colossal trading God, mused Urquhart; maybe he'd be galvanised to remove a temporal lobe tumour? Create a makeshift golem from ectoplasm? The notion of beseeching a butch fairy in the sky, striking manly covenants that should one day bring him to predominance in Brent by peddling lies, or by hawking consumer commodities, seemed really far out. He might be praised by the prime minister. He'd heard her on the radio talking about Jimmy Savile, OBE: 'Jimmy's truly a great Briton, a stunning example of opportunity Britain, a dynamic example of enterprise Britain & an inspiring example of responsible Britain.' Dolefully, Urquhart accepted he wasn't destined to be such an ornamental national hero, adorned with medals & allocated BBC tour buses in which to sensually entertain an admiring public. Despondently noticing his delicate hennaed hands were bloodstained, he took time out to wash. Re-scoping

Spivack's oily kitchen, he noticed it was pitch-dark outside, preventing him scavenging for psychoactive hallucinogens from the garden; liberty-caps grew in wild profusion amidst the unbagged dog faeces that covered the shrublands beside the Welsh Harp- there'd probably be loads out back, too. Shame- they'd have purveyed psychedelic fun. He could've stuffed a few hundred down the humourless throat of archangel Spivack. Too late for that, but it crossed his febrile mind that whoever dwelt upstairs may be interested in joining the craic if they were tripping on mushrooms.

Without magic mantras or hallucinatory drugs to lively up a bland Monday evening, it just seemed pointless. There's no mileage in sober veracity, whole truth & nothing but. Pop culture isn't comfortable minus celebrities, with just quotidian verities revealed via elementary experiences- stripped of théâtre, props, metalanguages, fancy assumptions; prognosticated, contemporary, or historical pie-in-the-sky is indispensable. Patriarchs in venerated garments, majestically mouthing hushed tones, trooping across palm leaves, announcing divinities, denouncing imperial authorities to uncircumcised citizens residing in cities wearing dawns like gowns; forming bases for pristine truths, novel new management founding institutional schisms, to grow rich & revered on imaginatively edited versions of ancient teachings. All he'd ever been taught was baseless fantasy, lumped on, & now it'd come on top, to end an anti-divine tragicomedy- farewell to divided conquered rabbles worldwide, people at the mercy of corporate raiders, who hated themselves/each other. Cultural appropriation, a

135

pyrrhic victory for product marketers: everyone, everything, each bias, every single perception, was objectified, atomised, revalued, resold in guzzle-size parts, lavishly reassigned for mass-market consumption.

If Urquhart deciphered Melvyn Bragg's affected plummy comments correctly (transmitted from BBC Radio 4's thrilling live-to-air discussion series *In Our Time* in congress with a proportionate trio of absolutely top-class academics), until 70,000 years ago there was an impecunious absence of domination throughout humanity by any elaborate social structure identifiable as tyrannical- precious little by way of subjugating heritage or creatively intimidating spirituality. For millennia, by necessity, anatomically modern humans shallow-mined functional flint for blades or spear-tips & fired unembellished clay utility pots- otherwise roaming, pragmatically content, around rude hetaeristic squatting places; fishing termites with twigs to supplement omnivorous seasonal diets. Visitant conspiracy theorists from Area 51 jived with ancient astronaut hypotheses; opining conviction anent immemorial extra-terrestrial–human contiguity triggering a cognitive revolution. Homo-sapiens perceived mind-blowing hitherto inconceivable knowledge & gossiped about it; ominously armed with a unique futuristic language- genetically mutating into dreadful life-forms on a mission, deploying self-representative symbols to empower rich impromptu concepts that they crafted into awe-inspiring extortive masterpieces. Thus organised, our lowbrow ancestors purposely destroyed sibling Homos. Urquhart wasn't destined for a fortunate, favoured,

or ingenious existence. Back in his jolly remedial DT classes
(all sharp &/or pointy objects excluded), sir had had no truck
with his primitive philistine attitude: 'Homework! A word to
the wise Findlay: You say Monday, my diary says Wednesday;
therein lays a communication breakdown- breakdown being
the operative word. Scrutinising how your passionate impulses
are cramped, I fear for your sanity. I see you boy. Suppressed,
modified, impalpably camouflaged in order to adapt to im-
mersion beneath the terrible pressures of puberty. You know
it; I know it- don't try & fight it!' During classes, playtime or
at home, freaked-out schmendricks dished-up grief under
the traditional guise of vague points of principle, typically
accompanied by moral homilies. Do as I say, not as I do. A
genuflecting response, repressed mortal inertia- adopted a
full-on, horrified retreat toward automatic lip-service, arrest-
ed development-cum-imperilled psychological degradation;
hitherto condemned to live a mouldering life of cognitive
dissonance. Fate brought him here. Everything happens for a
reason. It is what it is: an assemblage of disparate components
in search of a blueprint, spin doctors, credible narrative.

Urquhart, without understanding or explanation, had nothing
to offer save clues to posterity- should anyone deem it necessary to investigate this crime scene (aka his discordant torch
song). Swallowing all available analgesics & sleepy-time pills,
he doused himself & his coagulating 'ex' with lighter-fuel.
Spivack- formerly a repository of esoteric paraphernalia &
electrifying delusions of grandeur- perhaps would serve as a
burnt offering? Even kuckuck Spivack had shown the wisdom

& will power to mould himself an ample ethos by purporting to understand exhortatory articles referring to an aggrandised ontological status (circumcised members only). He'd demonstrably accrued a raft of foolish accoutrements to rig-out his pope in Rome. No matter- protracted analysis only served to inhibit; Fiona's fortitude, based on decisive purposefulness, proved she was right to eschew it. Urquhart & his sister were damaged goods, discarded loners in abjection- unimportant to anyone but themselves. That certainty was an indisputable matter of fact; feeling depressed about it altered nada. He accepted that as an antagoniser- Fiona survived *ferae naturae*, whilst as an agoniser, he ached unceasingly. It was his hamartia; continued lame ambivalence merely engendered more extend-&-pretend- fashioning further gnomic episodes of pusillanimous failure. Insufficient durability, deficient animal spirit & relentless suffering springing from an inability to overcome adverse childhood experiences hexed Urquhart to self-identify as a flightless albatross; allergic to ideological power structures, forever trudging austere treadmills of post-traumatic stress disorders. His demeaning cognitive impairment threatened newfangled Kafkaesque chapters of noxious stress. He couldn't trust himself to embrace positive changes by way of relinquishing ingrained negative discriminatory perspectives, or validate & adopt the right profile, far less clear up this gory mess. Without a ceremonious coda, or any significant others to kiss farewell, Urquhart cuddled-up to Spivack's lukewarm corpse, adrift in phantasmagoria, sedatives & proleptic rigor mortis. Burning final sparks of energy in a spasm, he arose to strike a book of matches before falling back onto a four-legged Uranian pyre. Recumbent upon this pocket-sprung altar to tribal memorabilia & reusable sex toys,

Urquhart exhibited a portentous sibilant rictus as he ignited; artistically cleansing multifarious subjective horrors, sprawled atop & under Spivack's faygeleh bed- an eerie medley of concepts that, along with his bemused rebellious mind, burst into a devastating blaze of trouble-free extinction.

In the distance, a figure approaching. Coming closer, footsteps louder. Closer, right up to the screen. The man in the pale suit

The Message | Mark Keane

The receptionist informed him he was two hours early for his meeting.

'If you're looking for something to do while you're waiting,' she added, 'I can recommend an art gallery that's nearby.'

Donal half-listened, too busy thinking about the message on his voicemail. His name had been suggested for a new ad campaign. They liked what they'd seen of his work and wanted to meet him. He got the address right but must have misheard the time.

Donal Lysaght: freelance copywriter, author of promotional bumf, leaflets and brochures. Tedious stuff that paid the bills. Speculative fiction was his true calling—where the familiar intersected the strange, and the incredible could be found in the ordinary. But instead of exploring his imagination, he churned out banal sales pap.

He had two hours to kill in a part of town he didn't know. He walked from the building, and stopped. His neck muscles tensed. Someone was watching him. He'd had the same sense earlier but now it was much stronger. He turned around—

there was nobody there, or no one he could see. A sign on a lamppost read: Art Gallery Next Left. The receptionist had mentioned something about an art gallery.

A second sign directed him to a three-storey building, the paintwork cracked and peeling. No name above the door or anything that suggested an art gallery. The entrance led into a small foyer dominated by a painting of a bearded man in a tweed suit, two wolfhounds at his feet. Donal read the inscription: *Sir Hugo Drouet, founder of the gallery, and his beloved hunting dogs.*

A thin woman with grey spikey hair stood behind a counter. She handed him a visitor's guide. He entered the first room. Smallish squares hung on the walls, non-figurative panels. A philistine might say a four year old could do better, but Donal was no philistine. He appreciated the artistic vision in all its forms.

Here were recognised artists, their work chosen for display. What had he to show? Three stories in obscure e-zines that garnered faint praise from a few editors and nothing from readers. No matter the response, he was compelled to express life as seen through his lens.

He stopped at one of the abstractions, smudged grey with a thin red diagonal line. The entry in the guide read: *View from the Bridge: CG, 1949-2008.* How strange, he thought—only the artist's initials were given.

Walking farther into the gallery, he came to a room with a collection by a single painter. He paused to read the guide.

The artist, WV, was a troubled soul who hanged himself, aged thirty-four. WV tried to capture the effect produced by pinching both eyes between thumb and index finger. The light that is seen though no light enters the eye, what WV termed 'the memory of light'. *He represented this as an excess of black cut through with daubs and dribbles of white. By repeatedly squeezing his eyes, WV damaged his sight and he could no longer paint. This brought to an end his depiction of light without light. WV put a noose around his neck and shut out the light for good.*

Donal inspected the monochrome paintings, searching for meaning and puzzled by the dismissive commentary in the guide. He continued on, taking his time over portraits with lollipop heads, misshapen and angular bodies, smeared and fragmented images. Larger rooms housed installations. Papier-mâché cubes and oblongs, murals with strobe lighting and dialogue playing on tape recorders, interspersed with cries and screams. Hanging breezeblocks, mounds of grass and ugly weeds, a child's paddling pool filled with razor blades. The few visitors he passed looked away. It was a strange art collection, off-kilter in a way that appealed to Donal.

Another room contained work by an artist whose name was given in full—Max Plunkett, born in 1941. A single painting commanded one wall: *Picture of Winifred*. A striking portrait of a young woman: alluring smile, jet black hair lying in ringlets on her shoulders. Close up, every blemish, every pore in her skin was revealed in magnified photographic detail. Donal moved closer to examine the crusty mucus in the corner of one eye, each flake of rheum painstakingly rendered.

Two smaller canvases, layers of sombre colours with grainy splotches, were titled *Picture of Gwyneth* and *Picture of Isobel*. Donal checked the guide.

Portraits by the young Plunkett were lauded for their attention to detail. The artist renounced this work as mere copying with no creative merit. Instead, he paid more attention to the background than the sitter. In subsequent work, the figure was absent and painted over with background. Plunkett claimed he imbued the background with the spirit of the subject. Gwyneth and Isobel were understandably outraged when they saw themselves represented by muddy greys and browns. Plunkett soon returned to realism, producing portraits that flattered the subject.

At the end of a corridor, Donal came to a digital sign with scrolling text: *New Acquisition Straight Ahead.* A table under the sign was piled with envelopes. He took one, put it in his pocket and followed a sequence of arrows on the floor, through an archway and into a room illuminated by light from a screen. He sat on a bench.

A black and white film was playing. A man appeared— clean cut, hair short and parted on one side. He wore a pale suit, thin dark tie, trousers tight at the ankles. Looking left and right, he walked down a street with houses on both sides. There was the sound of footsteps. The camera lost focus, then picked out arbitrary views. The gable end of a factory. A close-up of the underside of a bridge. An Indian take-away with an ambulance parked outside. A laundromat, someone seated at the window. Another street with different houses. In the distance, a figure approaching. Coming closer, footsteps louder. Closer, right up to the screen. The man in the pale suit.

A change of view, the camera trained on a house with a small garden. The man in the pale suit unlocked the front door. A shift to the interior. He placed a briefcase on a table, opened it with a loud click and took out some pages. He left the room and returned with an envelope, folded one of the pages and put it in the envelope.

The screen went cloudy. The noise of traffic, tyres on tar-mac. Then, the view of a street corner. The man in the pale suit

144

appeared and walked towards a building. Donal recognised the front of the gallery. Black screen, white letters appearing, one by one: *The Message: A Film by Sidney Katz.*

The screen turned bright again. The same man with his neat haircut and pale suit going down a street. The sound of footsteps. The film ran in a loop. Donal stood up and searched for the exit. How long had he been there? He would be late for his meeting.

He arrived, sweating and out of breath. The client apologised profusely but the meeting had had to be postponed. Some confusion over missing documents and conflicting deadlines. They agreed to reschedule it for the following week. Before Donal left, the client handed him a business card.

Out on the street, he watched traffic whoosh past and brooded. Another wasted day chasing unfulfilling work to eke out a living. How he longed for the freedom and peace of mind to write and release his imagination. Some evenings, he would open one of his stories on the computer and read passages. A sentence or phrase brought a rush of enthusiasm, the words singing in his ear.

The sky clouded over and an easterly wind nipped his cheeks. He buttoned his coat and felt something in his pocket—the envelope he had taken from the gallery. He opened it and removed a page bearing a single typed sentence.

'Leave this behind *The Collected Stories of Jorge Luis Borges* on the second floor of the George Street public library.'

He folded the page and put it back in the envelope. The library was on his way home. He would do it—out of frustration, the need to do something, however irrational. He didn't want to be rational. But it was also the name, Borges, an author Donal admired, a writer of fantastical tales.

Two kids playing with their phones blocked the entrance to the library. Donal glared at them but they took no notice. He went up the stairs to the second floor, then along the bookcases, past Joyce and Grabiński, past Dostoevsky and Bradbury. He spotted the Borges book, pulled it out and placed the envelope against the back wall. Before returning the book, he leafed through the pages and wondered what it would be like seeing his own work in a library or a bookshop. *The Collected Stories of Donal Lysaght.* He scanned the books on the shelves and imagined his book among them.

The following day, he worked on advertising copy for water filters. It was a referral from an earlier job, promoting photo-copiers and office supplies. He drafted and redrafted slogans to convey the client's mission to personalise customers' needs and sell filters. *Water that tastes the way water should taste. Don't you deserve purity?*

He thought about the art gallery and the film. The man in the suit, putting a page in an envelope, then going to the gallery. It bothered Donal, the way he'd followed the instruction so blindly. There may have been something on the page that he missed, a possible explanation.

He returned to the library. The envelope wasn't there. He tried the information desk.

'I left it behind the Borges short stories,' he said.

The librarian, red-cheeked with spectacles hanging from a chain, had no idea what he was talking about. Donal didn't want to create a scene and left. He decided to go back to the gallery—a quick visit before the rescheduled meeting.

Sir Hugo Drouet and his dogs were there to greet him. The spiky-haired woman handed him the visitor's guide. He walked past the abstract panels without a second look and through the room with the blind suicide's paintings. Rushing past one installation, he almost knocked over some bowls of rice arranged in a row. He slowed down and looked around. It was then he realised the gallery didn't have any guards. He checked the guide. The commentary was as he remembered—critical and disparaging. Paintings were lifeless. Installations lacked structure. One artist had no discipline or feeling for line or form, another had ability but was misguided.

The digital sign still directed visitors to a new acquisition but there was no table with envelopes. In the screening room he watched images flick on and off; not the same sequence as the week before. A view down a street with parked cars. Then, the front of the gallery. The sound of footsteps, growing louder. A figure came into view. The camera zoomed in. Donal's face filled the screen.

A shift in perspective—Donal walking away from the camera. Two kids standing in the entrance to the library. Then, a view of bookshelves framing a narrow walkway. Donal bending down, taking a book from the shelf. *The Collected Stories of Jorge Luis Borges*. A close-up of his face, his yearning to see his own book on those shelves captured on the screen. White words against a black background: *The Message: A Film by Sidney Katz*. The room hummed in the eerie light.

He approached the spiky-haired woman behind the counter.

147

'What are you playing at in this gallery?'

She looked up from her display of guides. 'How can I help you?'

'What's the meaning of that film? Who is responsible?'

She handed him a guide, which he pushed away.

'Who made that film? Who is Sidney Katz?'

'Everything is explained in the guide,' she said.

Outside, he checked the gallery entrance and adjoining buildings, lampposts and the buildings across the street. Nothing anywhere that looked like a camera. Surely it was against the law, an infringement of his privacy. Somehow, Donal had known; his instinct had told him he was being watched. He walked away from the gallery, in no particular direction. The feeling of being watched wouldn't go away. He crossed a street and went under a bridge, passing shops and parked cars. His thoughts were chaotic, one ambiguity after another unravelling in his brain. He sidestepped shoppers and tripped on loose paving. A man in a suit inspected the menu outside a restaurant. The meeting—it had slipped his mind, and it was too late to show up now.

Donal lay awake that night, replaying scenes from the film. In the morning, his face appeared gaunt in the bathroom mirror. Not able to write another word about water filters, he Googled the name Sidney Katz. The first entry was a Wikipedia page for Sid Katz. Born in Philadelphia, son of Ukrainian immigrants, educated at Temple University. An actor, typecast as a heavy in TV westerns. A history of depression. Katz died in 1962 after jumping from a bridge in San Diego. That ruled him out.

Another entry, Sidney B Katz of Cook County Illinois, designer of hoods worn by prisoners in solitary confinement. The page included sinister images of calico head covers with square eye-holes. Donal clicked on links. Katz Deli, the best kielbasa sausage in Brooklyn. *Katz Plumbing, call the best and flush the rest. Katz Music in Marylebone for rare classical recordings.* Hundreds of other entries, an impossible search, but Donal needed answers.

That afternoon, he watched the gallery from across the street. He couldn't face going inside. No one entered or left. Ten minutes, thirty minutes, an hour passed. Finally, a heavyset man in a sheepskin coat came out and made his way to a car parked near the entrance. Donal crossed the road in a running walk to intercept him.

'Excuse me,' he called, 'can I ask what you were doing in there?'

The man fumbled with his keys, almost dropping them in his rush to open the car door. He kept his face averted, lunged into the seat and started the engine. Donal watched the car speed away.

Over the next hour, he accosted a younger man and an elderly couple leaving the building, but they refused to answer his questions. This wasn't getting him anywhere. He found a pub nearby where he could plan his next move. Four o'clock, the bar was empty. Was he being filmed at this moment? The barman paid him no heed as he stacked glasses on the shelves. Searching his pockets for a pen and paper, Donal pulled out a card. It had an embossed logo, a quill and ink-pot with the words, *Realising your Ambition.* In the corner, a name: *Sidney Katz.*

The client had given him the card when they rescheduled the meeting. Why hadn't he noticed the name before? Donal tried to remember what the client had looked like. He'd worn a suit, but all the clients wore suits. Hair—yes, he'd had hair—short and parted at one side. Tallish, no glasses. That described the man from the first film. Is that who he'd met? Donal turned over the card. Printed on the back was a telephone number.

He made the call when he got home. The telephone was answered on the first ring.

'Who is Sidney Katz?' Donal asked.

His question was met with silence.

'Why did you make that film?'

'It's better we discuss this in person,' came the reply. 'We will contact you.'

Donal started to give his number.

'We have your details.'

A week passed. Donal stayed in his flat, only going out for food. He put in some desultory work on the water filter brochure. At last, he received a text, setting up a meeting at an address on the outskirts of town.

He arrived on time and recognised the receptionist as the attendant from the gallery. Gone were the grey spikes; her hair was coiffed and hennaed. She acted as though she had never seen him before and took his name. In the waiting room, Donal checked for anything that might be a camera.

What was he doing there? What did he hope to achieve? He had no answers—helpless, not deciding his own actions, like a character in a story following a script. He had crossed an invisible line, watching events unfold and being watched.

The receptionist brought him into an office with bare white walls. A man sat behind a desk; pale suit, narrow lapels and thin dark tie. His hair was parted on one side.

'What can I do for you, Mr Lysaght?'

'You seem to know a lot about me but I know nothing about you.'

'I serve the interests of the Drouet Organisation.'

Donal knew that name. Sir Hugo, the painting in the gallery with the wolfhounds.

'Are you Sidney Katz?'

'If that's what you want.'

'I don't want any of this, and I don't want to be part of that film.'

'You mean *The Message*?'

'I want to be removed from it.'

'It's not quite that simple.' Katz leaned back in his chair.

'You've done this without my approval. It's unacceptable. It has to be illegal. I demand the film be destroyed.'

'There are cameras everywhere,' Katz said. 'Video surveillance is part of modern life. Why does it bother you so much?'

'I refuse to be used like this.'

Katz pursed his lips.

'What do you want from me?' Donal asked, dismayed by how pathetic he sounded.

'You shouldn't upset yourself. Let's forget the film for now. The important thing is that we have your attention.'

'What do you want?'

'You feel undermined and undervalued. We understand your plight.' Katz brushed some fluff from his sleeve. 'You wish to be a writer and have your writing acknowledged as unique, compelling and thought-provoking. Your work has come to our attention and we see a great deal of promise.' Katz paused. 'We can provide you with an admiring readership. Work with us and realise your ambition. A mutually beneficial collaboration. All that's required is your cooperation. Only then can the film be removed and no others shown. If not, it will be there as a record of your failure.' Katz leaned forward, his elbows resting on the desk. 'We are here to help you, Mr Lysaght. Rest assured, you're not alone.'

Donal took the lift to the ground floor and dawdled at the entrance, going over everything Katz had said. The film, a record of his failure. Not just one film; Katz had implied there were more. He didn't notice the woman until she stood in front of him. Middle-aged, tousled black hair flecked with grey, her face seemed familiar but he couldn't place it.

'I must speak to you.' She turned abruptly as though hearing an unexpected sound. 'But not here; follow me.'

She crossed the road and went down a side street, Donal two steps behind. They entered a park and continued along a path, past a fountain and play area with swings. She sat on a bench by a pond, hands plunged deep in the pockets of her raincoat. Donal sat beside her.

'Who did you meet in that building?' she asked.

'A man named Sidney Katz.'

'Did he mention my husband?'

Her questions had an urgency that didn't give Donal time to think.

'I don't know your husband.'

'He's an artist: Max Plunkett.'

Now Donal recognised her; when Plunkett had painted her she'd been much younger.

'You're Winifred.'

She turned to face him. 'Have we met before?'

'Your portrait is in the art gallery.'

She looked away, a nervous tic causing her mouth to twitch. 'What do you know about the gallery?'

'Absolutely nothing.'

'It's a vile purgatory. Don't do what my husband did. They destroyed him.' She shifted in her seat. 'They killed Willie Vine.'

'What do you mean, "killed"?'

'The poor man took his own life but they were responsible. He went blind because of them.'

Donal recalled the painting in the gallery, 'the memory of light'. 'Willie Vine—you mean WV.'

'The artists who refuse to compromise are reduced to initials. They're only given the skeleton of an identity and their work is mocked. The gallery is a punishment and a warning to others. The ones who cooperate are rewarded with success. Their work doesn't appear in the gallery.' She took her hand from her pocket and squeezed his arm. 'You must have nothing to do with them.'

Confused and moved by Winifred's earnest warning, all Donal had were questions. 'Why me? How did they find me?'

'Are you an artist?'

The question made him uncomfortable but Katz must have read his e-zine stories. 'I write.'

'My husband surrendered but it wasn't enough. They gave him back his name but he's still paying the price.'

Donal remembered the room dedicated to Plunkett's work. 'His paintings are on display.'

'I told you, the gallery is a punishment. They own everything and control the artists. It's too difficult to explain here.'

153

'Who's behind this?' He moved closer, their legs touching. 'What are they looking for?'

'They pander to popular taste, exploiting talented artists to give the public what it wants.' She raised her hand to brush away some stray hair. 'They abort art that is difficult and uncomfortable. The public doesn't want to be threatened or feel insecure. They punish any defiance. The artists who don't compromise are destroyed.'

Donal struggled for a response, not wanting to appear incredulous. She turned suddenly and he followed her gaze. A man stood on the other side of the pond, dark suit, trousers tight at the ankles.

'I must go,' she whispered.

He watched her rush away. The man in the suit followed her out of the park.

Donal remained sitting. Everything Winifred had said seemed far-fetched but he wanted to believe her. All that effort, the film in the gallery, the meetings and the message, just to get his attention. It meant someone saw something in what he wrote. There was Katz's threat, but was it a threat and not a ploy? Part of the negotiation—unconventional, but so much the better.

Katz had offered him readers. What was the good of writing that went unread? A collaboration, Katz had said. Donal came to a decision. No more brochures selling water filters and no more excuses. He would write a story about an unfulfilled protagonist, his visit to an art gallery and what he found there. A story to disturb and disorientate. He would give it to Katz to read. A test, not a compromise. Donal refused to compromise.

❖　　❖　　❖

Three months later, he sat across from Katz in his office.

'Much more work is required to knock this into shape.'

Katz shook his head at the pages, which were covered in red ink with comments and question marks. Words, lines, entire paragraphs crossed out. The sixth draft and Katz still demanded wholesale changes.

'The reader doesn't like being told everything. Show more and tell less.'

He leafed through the pages before pushing them across the table to Donal.

'One more iteration.' Katz smiled.

Donal straightened the pages. He had a dedicated reader now, but Katz was never satisfied, and seemed to take pleasure in finding fault.

'Have you been to the Drouet Gallery recently?'

Katz was referring to the latest acquisition. The film showing Donal walking down different streets, past shops and houses and under bridges. Donal sitting at a computer, his words on the screen, the cursor stationary. Then, a view of Katz from behind, reading pages of text, crossing out lines, shaking his head and sighing loudly. In the final scene, the camera panned from shelves lined with books to Donal, staring at the pages.

'Are the films necessary?'

'I'm afraid so, but we still recognise your potential.' Katz examined his fingernails, in no apparent hurry. Normally he ended the meeting once he had returned his corrections.

'Potential based on three e-zine pieces?' It was the first time Donal had mentioned his stories.

'Not those.' Katz waved his hand. 'What really impressed us was your commercial work. Anyone who can bring to life something as lifeless as photocopiers and stationery has talent worth investing in.'

Donal felt his guts shrivel at this casual disregard—his stories had meant nothing to Katz.

'What you call speculative fiction is just reporting life as it is. All that business about disquiet and hidden threats. It's indulgent. What's more, it's lazy. Those brochures, now there we could see your powers of imagination.' Katz tapped the desk for emphasis. 'Where's the creativity in your stories? There's nothing to grip the reader and raise him from the humdrum of his daily routine. No, it certainly wasn't those e-zine pieces.'

Katz laughed. Donal had never heard him laugh before.

'Why waste your talent writing about what is? Write about what could be. Utilise your imagination, don't limit yourself to drab brown and grey. Dip your brush into a palette of vibrant colours. Feed the readers' hunger for exotic worlds, heroes and villains, good overcoming evil. Do that and you'll find an appreciative readership.'

Katz opened a notebook and began writing.

'I believe we've made real progress today. Do you know what I suggest?' Katz didn't wait for a reply. 'First of all, a sizeable advance that will give you the freedom to create. A contract that protects your interests. Then, a deadline—nothing too pressing, say six months. How does that sound?'

Donal looked down at the pages covered in red ink. He thought of the gallery and Willie Vine and Max Plunkett and Winifred.

'Time to unleash your creativity. Your audience is out there, waiting for you.'

Audience. The word danced in Donal's head. He felt Katz watching him, waiting for an answer.

The older woman hissed, 'Serrez encore' at Carlotta. Carlotta tightened the buckle around her throat another notch.
'Et encore un peu'

Room of their Own | SK Mongrl

'She in her room?'

   'Suplika!'

   'I'll find her.'

   'Suplika!'

   'Don't worry.'

   'She's probably at the neighbours, the de Maistres, across the courtyard, number seven. I'll call them.'

   'No, no. I'll go over there. Where should I put these?'

   'Gifts?'

   'Christmas presents, for Suplika.'

   'Christmas is weeks away.'

   'But you're off to Canada soon.'

   'Thank you,' she said, looking at the name embossed on the golden ribbons. 'From Harrods?'

   'Was in London last week.'

   'You're not staying here for Christmas, are you?'

   'No. No. I'll go visit my mother in Madrid for a couple days. That's all I can take. Then a meditation retreat in Sri Lanka for a week and a half'—which she pronounced 'Three Lanka', one of the occasional lapses in her nearly flawless English.

'It'll be good for you.'

'First holiday in over a year.'

'How's your mother?'

'Still wheels herself to church every morning. But it now takes her twenty minutes instead of five.'

'Why don't you get her an electric wheelchair?'

'She absolutely refuses. I bought her a lightweight wheelchair last year and had to take it back.'

'Can't be easy,' said Caroline. Clasping both Carlotta's hands, she leaned back and looked her up and down. 'The picture of elegance. As ever. How do you do it?'

'If there was more light, you'd see how worn I look.'

'Tell me—this might be the only chance we get this evening—how're things at work?'

'All good at work.'

'Did the extra funding from Gates come through?'

'Yes, it did finally.'

'How much?'

'Thirty million, in total.'

'Thirty million.'

'Yes, the twenty million I got earlier this year, and then this extra ten.'

'Unearmarked, too?'

'No, the ten is earmarked.'

'For?'

'Prevention of stunting in the first 1,000 days. For the same five-year period.'

'Started hiring yet?'

'Yes, just started.'

'Congratulations, Carlotta. So glad it's all working out.'

'I am reaping what you have sowed. Is that not the expression?'

'Sown. Not sowed.' And Caroline added, mumbling, 'Be not deceived; God is not mocked: for whatsoever a man soweth that shall he also reap.'

'And whatsoever a woman soweth?'

'A legacy operating system, I guess.'

'A relic. In your mind.'

'A relic in my mind?'

'I just continued with the funding strategy you had developed,' said Carlotta.

'Putting in eighty hours a week to make it work.'

'I'm so grateful to you, Caroline. For helping me get the job and, especially, for all the advice—precious advice—you've given me this past year. Thank you.'

'Just glad that what I started is in safe hands.'

'The two clowns have now filed an official complaint against me.'

'They probably can't abide the thought of being sidelined.'

'Major headache. Wouldn't be surprised if Mario hires a private detective to dig up dirt on me.'

'Wouldn't put it past him.'

'Really? I thought I was just being paranoid.'

'When have we had time to generate dirt?'

'Work, work, work, work and more work for the past twenty years,' said Carlotta looking out, through the open door, into the darkened courtyard. Here and there the cobblestones, shiny from the mist that had drifted in, reflected the lights from the windows opposite. She wondered if the hired hand—or Mario himself—would know how to hack into her computer. Images from earlier that day flickered through her mind. She

161

heard Caroline say, 'But it's all paying off.' She felt herself nod.

A full-length mirror opposite her bed. A large screen next to it. Heating in her room turned up. On the screen, an older couple, on a sofa. Naked, except for black and gold filigree Venetian masks. His head bald and shiny. Hers with pale yellow hair slicked back. Strangers she had connected with online a few weeks before. Both their bodies thin with loose, leathery, tanned hides. Her hand, a faded ichthys tattoo on one of her phalanges, wrapped around his semi-erect penis, glans poking out of foreskin. In the mirror, leaning back into red velvet pillows, Carlotta could see herself. Her face hidden in a full leather mask fastened around her throat with a silver buckle. Her jaw forced open by a black ball gag, secured by a strap behind her neck. Saliva dribbled out of the corners of her mouth, down the sides of her chin, and onto her breasts, which were bound tight with rope and beginning to darken. 'Plus fort,' the woman ordered from the screen. Carlotta pulled harder on the clamps attached to her nipples with one hand, while the other played with the multicoloured clothespins pinching her labia. She stared at the camera as the man's grunts intensified. The older woman hissed, 'Serrez encore' at Carlotta. Carlotta tightened the buckle around her throat another notch. 'Et encore un peu.' Another notch.

Later—camera off, blackout curtains drawn, bedroom door shut, phone recharging in the living room—she was, for once, for a few brief minutes, cut off from the world. She had removed the mask, gag, clamps, clothespins and ropes and packed them away in the split-handled doctor's bag she had inherited from her grandfather. Spread-eagled naked on the bed, body moist, head thrown back, sinews limp, soul slack, she felt swaddled by the warmth of the room. Her upside-down gaze roamed idly around. Chandelier. White ceiling rose and cornice work. Yellow wall below. The top of a black picture frame and garish pinks, oranges and apple greens—the upper section of the painting she had recently spent half a year's salary on, without telling anybody. She listened to the clanging sound travel through the old heating pipes. She felt the internal pressure, almost pain, of a gas build-up in her gut. It worked its way down. She pushed and a felt a sense of release as the gas escaped from her. She sniffed the air. Nothing. She waited for the smell to diffuse through the air and sniffed again. This time she detected the smell of putrefaction from her innards. She sniffed again, more deeply, and then she must have dozed off.

'Yes, yes, it seems,' Carlotta finally replied to Caroline, blinking, her finger touching, through the fabric of her scarf, the tender mark on the side of her throat. Too far, I let it go too far, she heard herself think.

'You okay?' asked Caroline. 'You just blanked out on me.'

'Sorry, utterly exhausted. But you better get back to your guests and I better go find Supli.'

'Glad we were able to talk a bit.'

'Me too. Your support means so much to me.'

Caroline's gaze followed Carlotta as she walked out the entrance door, high heels making her hips sway. Once in the courtyard, she slowed down. She walked as if afraid her heels might slip on the fog-slicked cobblestones or catch in the cracks between them. Her strict diet of fish and green vegetables had, it appeared, turned her body back into that of a skinny teenager. She was forty-eight. They were both forty-eight. Born five months apart. The scaly patches of eczema that had spread across her trunk and the chronic inflammation of her bowels had, she claimed, completely vanished.

163

Carlotta heard Caroline walk back into the apartment, leaving the front door open. Carlotta stopped and peered through the mist, searching for number seven. When she was half way across the *Cour du Cherche-Midi*, a door opened, lit up the courtyard, and closed again. Suplika ran towards Carlotta, calling out her name, which echoed back and forth across the courtyard. The English phrase 'like swooping bats' came to Carlotta's mind. She squatted down and spread out her arms. She pulled the little body against her chest. She felt its warmth seep into her. Carlotta whispered hello through Suplika's blond hair, into her ear. Suplika giggled, squeezed her tight, and wriggled free again. Holding hands, they walked back into the apartment. Carlotta swung the door too hard and it slammed behind them.

'I want to show you something,' said Suplika, tugging on Carlotta's hand.

'Let me go say hello to everyone first.'

'No, no, come.'

Carlotta pried the little fingers off her leg.

She swept into the dining room, purple coat billowing, scarf looped around her throat, flowing. Behind the long countertop, Caroline and Carmela, Caroline's Filipina maid, were finishing preparations for the meal. Seated at the table were two couples: Abe and Paula, Jürgen and Josephine—Abe and Jo, colleagues from work. She kissed Abe, Jo and their spouses on their cheeks.

'How was Dhaka?' Carlotta asked Abe.

'Back this morning. Productive meeting at the ICDDR,' said Abe and turning to the others added, 'the International Centre for Diarrhoeal Disease Research.'

'We'll debrief on Monday,' said Carlotta.

'Karishma from Gates was there. Seemed impressed with our work. Know her?' persisted Abe.

'Met her once,' said Carlotta turning her back on Abe as she strode around the counter. She gave Carmela a hug and asked her to put her coat away. She kept her scarf on, carefully looping it around her neck one more time.

'Carlotta! Come. You've now said hello to everyone. Come,' said the little girl, raising her voice. Everyone laughed.

'Carlotta!'

'Okay, *mi corazon*. Show me,' said Carlotta as Suplika led her out.

Caroline stared at the coat Carlotta had thrust into Carmela's hands.

'Same coat I used to have,' said Caroline softly, walking up to Carmela and touching it.

'That you gave me,' whispered Carmela.

'Yes, which you passed on to your sister because it was too big for you, no?'

'She was wearing last weekend.'

Suplika's room, in an alcove through an arched entrance, was adjacent to her mother's, with no door separating them. To reach it, they walked through Caroline's bedroom—terra cotta floor tiles, four-poster bed, white bedspread pulled tight over it, and an old mahogany wardrobe. 'Lúgubre,' Carlotta thought. An image of herself lying on her maternal grandparents' bed in their Salamanca apartment came to mind. The same heavy furniture. Like a magnifying glass, tiny chinks in the shutters concentrated rays of the already fierce summer sunlight into hotspots on the cool floor tiles. She had burned the sole of her bare foot on one of them making her way to the bed. The occasional creak from the shock-absorbers of a scooter bouncing over the cobblestones rose from the street below to disturb her midday doze.

'Lúgubre,' she mumbled.

'What?' asked Supli.

'Will your grandparents be coming to stay with you again this spring?'

Suplika shrugged her shoulders.

Carlotta followed Suplika into her room, ducking under the arch. She couldn't help examining the room to check if anything—even the slightest detail—had changed. Blue curtains, yellow duvet, small red chair and desk under the loft bed, and big, shiny hexagonal tiles covering the central area of the floor in matching blue, yellow and red. 'The parents of all other colours,' Suplika had explained, parroting, Carlotta had assumed, something her mother had said. 'From them,' Suplika had added, 'you can create whatever you like.'

Carlotta felt relieved. Other than the toys and clothes scattered around, nothing had changed. But her shoulders, back and gut began to tense up. The clothes. It won't be complete until it has a copy of Suplika's entire wardrobe. I'll slip back in later, take pictures of the clothes, of the labels, brands and sizes. Dread seeped into her body. The old compulsions were back. Had been back a while. But she had failed to recognise them. Back in a guise she would never have suspected. The compulsions she thought she—with the help of psychiatrists—had eradicated from herself years ago.

'What are you staring at?'

'What do you want to show me, Supli?'

166

'Look,' she said, pointing at her large doll's house. Its roof reached the top of Carlotta's chest.

'Where?'

'There! There, Carlotta! Can't you see? There!' she said, stabbing her plump little forefinger at a room on the right-hand side of the second floor of the doll's house.

Carlotta bent down to look more closely.

'Yes, I see. It's a replica of this room.'

'What's a replica?'

'A copy.'

'No, not like at your place. It's smaller.'

'A miniaturised replica.'

'Look who's in it.'

'Did your mother help you make it?' asked Carlotta, trying to conceal her growing alarm.

'No. Carmela. Look! On the bed.'

'What is it?'

'A baby.'

'No, no, it's a … what do you say? A gusano,' said Carlotta, about to poke it with her nail.

'A maggot. But it's dead.'

'What did your mother say?'

'She laughed.'

'At the maggot?'

'I didn't show her the maggot.'

'We better go back to the dining room now,' said Carlotta. When she straightened up, she felt unsteady on her feet. Her hands, forearms, feet and shins has started to go numb. She thought of the clorazepate in her handbag. She had already taken two today, and lost count of how many she'd swallowed the day before.

As they were crossing Caroline's room again, they heard footsteps approaching.

'Please bring your violin, Eleanor dear,' said Caroline.

'No. I don't want to play.'

'Eleanor?'

Carlotta left mother and daughter alone and returned to the dining room. Caroline closed the door to her bedroom.

'I don't want to.'

'You play so beautifully, my dear.'

'No. I don't want to.'

'And the sooner you get used to playing in front of others, the better.'

'Why?'

'That way you'll learn to be less nervous when you have to perform.'

'No.'

'One of the pieces we practised together this afternoon. Just one,' said Caroline, opening up Eleanor's little violin case and handing her the instrument.

She refused to take it. Caroline pushed it against her hands. Eleanor crossed her arms tight.

'You play the piano with me,' she said.

'It's better that you play alone, dear.'

'Why?'

'I just told you.'

'Which one?'

'You choose.'

Everyone sitting at the dining table turned around. Caroline and Carlotta leaned against the counter, while Carmela continued to cook, humming to herself.

'Which oven should I use for this?' asked Carmela.

'Steam oven I've pre-heated it,' said Caroline. 'What are you going to play, Eleanor?'

'Eleanor?' whispered Jürgen to his wife.

'That's her real name,' Jo whispered back. 'Suplika is a nickname Carmela gave her. *Spitzname*,' she added. He nodded, looking over at Carmela, who was sliding a dish into the steam oven.

'*Ave Maria,*' said Suplika.

'By?'

'Fran Subert'

'Franz Schubert.'

Suplika jerked the arch back and forth across the strings, her body moving from side to side mechanically. She looked up at the ceiling as she played a speeded up, choppy, but technically correct rendition of the song

They started clapping before Suplika had quite finished and, while they were still clapping, she started to play the piece again.

'No, no, Eleanor. Thank you. That's enough. Please go put your violin away now,' said Caroline.

The little girl continued to play and, face scrunched up and tongue sticking out, marched slowly towards her room.

'Côte Rotie 2015 from Domaine Jamet. Tell me what you think,' said Abe, pouring her a glass.

Caroline swirled the wine around, tipped the glass away from herself and sniffed it, freckled nostrils twitching above the rim.

'If you want, I'll add you a case to our order.'

169

She poured some into her mouth, swished it around, brow furrowing, eyes half-closing in concentration.

'Yes, maybe.'

'Nick, Sanjay and I have each ordered two cases. Not cheap though.'

'No?'

'But at least you'll have a few good bottles for the new wine fridge.'

'Okay, one case.'

'Did you finally go for the dual-zone refrigerator?'

'Yes, that's what you suggested. And, as I recall, you said it was best to store at the upper end of the recommended temperature ranges. Sixteen to eighteen degrees for reds, and ten to twelve for whites.'

'Well, rule of thumb. Depends on the wine; you see Côtes-du-Rhônes should ...'

'Abe!' said his wife, cutting him off.

'Saw you and Carlotta out running at lunch the other day,' said Jo. 'Training for the marathon again?'

'Not till April,' said Abe.

'Yes, we just started training again. Want to join us, Jo?' asked Caroline.

'Never ran a marathon, but—' She was cut short by Abe again.

'Marathon running is not necessarily—'

'Abe!' said Paula.

'I'm sorry, Jo,' said Abe.

'No, it's okay. Please.'

'You see,' said Abe, turning to his wife before continuing, 'I was saying that marathon running is not necessarily good for your health. Did you see that new systematic review of reviews on the effects of running on longevity?'

'What does it say?' asked Caroline.

'Complex picture, but the gist is that ninety-150 minutes of running per week will add three extra years to your life, on average. More than any other form of exercise. But more than 150 minutes a week may be detrimental.'

'Send it to me.'

'I will. Lee, *et al*, 2017,' said Abe, taking out his phone.

'Thanks. Better put the little one to bed now,' said Caroline, getting up.

'Paper sent!' said Abe as Caroline left the room, and turning towards Carlotta, he added: 'Congratulations, Carlotta, for turning our department into the star of the organisation.'

'Thank you Abr-r-r-aham,' said Carlotta, with a Spanish rolling of the r. 'But you've all contributed.'

'How much bigger do you think we'll become?'

'We're planning to double in size this year and grow even more next year.'

'And they're promoting you?'

'I have to apply for it. Spent the afternoon working on the application.'

'Why?' asked Jürgen.

'They have to open all such promotions up for competition,' said Abe. 'Waste of everyone's time.'

'And the deadline is less than a week after they first advertised it,' said Carlotta.

'It'll be a formality for you. But how about the rest of us? Will we all be keeping the same positions?' asked Abe.

'Nobody is going to lose their jobs or be relocated. You

know that. But, please, let's not talk about such work matters now. We are here to socialise,' she said, and looked around at everyone. But Abe could not help himself.

'You've been our director a year now and I've been dying to ask you: did Caroline hand you a poisoned chalice?'

'Abr-r-r-aham R-r-r-ragin!' Carlotta said, using his full name, 'the job is fantastic, simply fantastic. And such a fabulous team. Much better than doing research and being a professor. And yes, yes, before you correct me, I know it's Abr-r-ram and not Abr-r-r-aham. Sorry.'

'Full professor by the age of thirty-eight with 250 papers to her name,' Abe said to his wife, Paula.

'I'm so grateful to Caro for talking me into taking the job.'

'You put in awfully long hours.'

Paula laid her hand on her husband's forearm.

'Longer than Caroline did?' Carlotta's asked.

Abe and Jo looked at each other.

'Caro now has Supli and a job as adviser to the under-secretary-general. And me, I have her former job. Enough now,' said Carlotta. She lowered her head and threw back her mane of curly dark hair in one sweeping movement. The scarf around her neck came loose. Carlotta saw Paula's eyes lock onto the side of her throat. Carlotta pulled the scarf over the mark which was now exposed. Paula looked away.

'Carlotta,' said Caroline, coming back into the dining room, 'she won't go to sleep until you've read her a story. Would you mind?'

'No, of course not.'

'Don't be too long though; we'll be eating in fifteen minutes.'

'Okay.'

'Thank you.'

'Shall I let her choose the story?'

'No, we're working our way through Hans Christian Andersen's tales. Let me check,' said Caroline picking up her iPad.

Carlotta leaned over and saw that Caroline had pulled up a spreadsheet.

'*The Little Match-Seller*. Here,' said Carolina, handing Carlotta the iPad, which slipped from Carlotta's fingers and, with a thud, fell onto the thick wool rug.

'Oh no. I'm sorry,' Carlotta said, bending down and picking it up.

'Soft landing. Is *The Little Match-Seller* still there?'

'No one imagined,' read Carlotta, finishing the story, 'what beautiful things she had seen, nor into what glory she had entered with her grandmother on New-year's day.'

Carlotta, with Suplika nestled against her, put the iPad down.

'Stupid story,' said Suplika.

'Why?'

'*La petite fille aux allumettes* it's called in French. We read it in school.'

'But why didn't you like it?'

'She died for no reason.'

'Well, she was so afraid her father would beat her if she went home without any money that she stayed out all night trying to sell matches.'

'My father came from the internet,' Suplika stated, sitting up in bed.

'Who told you that?'

'Tonton Nibombé.'

'Who?'

'Carmela's husband.'

'What did you call him?'

'Tonton Nibombé.'

'When did he say your father came from the internet?'

'In the car once.'

'What did he say?'

'I asked him if he knew who my father was.'

'What did he say?'

'*Aucune idée*.'

'I see.'

'My father is a conductor and he lives in San Francisco.'

'Is that true?'

'He gave his sperm to Caroline as a gift so she could have me.'

'Who told you that?'

'Caroline.'

'Okay.'

'I asked Tonton where my mother had met my father.'

'What did he say?'

She shrugged her shoulders, pulled down the corners of her mouth, and then blew a raspberry. After a moment, she whispered, 'He said maybe he came from the internet.'

'Is that what your mother told you?'

'No.'

'What has she told you?'

'That she's never met him. But when I'm eighteen I can, if I want.'

'Do you think you will?'

'He gave his sperm to many ladies. I'm probably not very

special to him.'

'You're very special to me,' said Carlotta, kissing her forehead, 'and to your mother.'

Suplika looked up at Carlotta and frowned.

'Go to sleep now, *mi corazon*, you've had a long day,' said Carlotta, climbing down from the loft bed.

'Boring day.'

'A boring day?'

'I had to watch cartoons all afternoon.'

'Because your mother was cooking?'

'No, Carmela cooked.'

'What was your mother doing?'

'I'm not supposed to say.'

'Then I won't ask again.'

'Don't you want to know?'

'Not if you're not supposed to say.'

'Good night,' said Carlotta, now standing with her face at Suplika's level. She kissed her cheek.

'Job application,' Suplika whispered, and grabbed Carlotta around the neck, pressing on the mark under her scarf, pretending she wanted to pull Carlotta back up into the bed.

The little girl's words sent a cold jolt through Carlotta. Almost certainly *her* job.

'Good night,' Carlotta repeated.

'Don't say, okay?'

'Our little secret.' And that's quite a few too many, Carlotta thought.

Trying to grab her handbag from the floor, Carlotta knocked it over. Her suede make-up case, keys, spare sanitary pads and two blister packs of pills spilled out. Suplika stared down as Carlotta stuffed everything back.

'Are you ill?'

'Those are just in case I get a headache. Good night now.'

Carlotta closed the door to Caroline's room and stood still. Her legs were shaking and the hand clutching her handbag was slippery with sweat. Instead of going back into the dining room, she slipped into Caroline's private bathroom, rather than the one next to the dining room that Caroline insisted guests use. She had to defecate.

She lowered herself onto the toilet seat. Her eyes wandered around the bathroom. It was white—fixtures, tiles and towels all white, except for two green plants. On the floor beside her stood an orange and green shopping bag. She had felt a swelling and ripples of pain in her belly for a few days now. Her periods, so regular for decades, had, these last months, become sporadic. The beginning of perimenopausal syndrome, she had concluded. And these last days, she had been constipated again. She winced and arched her back in pain. She pictured faeces like clusters of hazelnuts glued together twisting around, poking into and stretching the inflamed walls of her colon. Her anal sphincter clenched shut. But the urge to defecate, in spite of the pain, in spite of the locking of her sphincter, kept increasing. She took a deep breath and pushed hard, making herself dizzy a moment. She felt the stool—hard from being stuck in her colon too long and having had all the water sucked out it—forcing its way out, her sphincter resisting. She wiped herself and inspected the white toilet paper for blood. Nothing. But when she bent over the toilet bowl and examined the over-sized, dark, lumpy stool she had forced out of herself, droplets of blood stood out on the white porcelain. Had a haemorrhoid burst again, or had her period finally appeared? She wiped her vagina and her anus separately. Still no trace of blood on the toilet paper. She took a sanitary pad out her handbag attached it to her underwear and pulled up her jeans. She flushed, lowered the lid of the toilet and sat down on it. The pain had vanished. In its place, she felt a deep sense of relaxation and well-being—poo-phoria was, she remembered, how the phenomenon was sometimes referred to.

She leaned down towards the shopping bag and removed threadbare towels from the top of it. Under lay a garbage bag with its drawstrings tightly knotted. She undid the knot and pulled the bag open. Sex toys. A collection of them. She rummaged through, handling each in turn. She recognised the ones that had come in and out of fashion over the past twenty-five years—the Rampant Rabbit, the Bullet, the Hitachi Magic Wand and the G-spot Vibrator. But the one she handled the longest was a large pink dildo—a long, fat, soft and slightly sticky translucent worm. It suddenly occurred to her that Caroline had probably not disinfected them before consigning them to this bag. Her hand recoiled. She got up, opened the tap, and pressed several large globs of Caroline's liquid soap into her palm. She rubbed her hands together, spreading the soap over front and back, interlocked her fingers, lathered up her wrists and forearms methodically, and then rinsed carefully. Scrubbing up, she thought, like during my brief career as a paediatric surgeon. Now that Supli is old enough to search around and ask questions, Caroline appears to have decided to throw out these replicas of the human insemination tube, she thought. Just before switching off the light, she saw that the garbage bag was still open with drawstrings loose. Let her try to guess who it was.

'A few more wine glasses and then the table's clear,' said Carlotta, setting down dirty dessert plates and turning around to head back to the dining table.

On her way back to the sink, one of the wine glasses pinched between her fingers slipped free. It hit the corner of the counter and broke into pieces. The pieces fell onto the slate floor tiles and smashed into a galaxy of shards and splinters.

'*Dios mío.*'

'Crystal,' said Carmela, and headed for the dustpan and brush.

'Let me do it,' said Carlotta.

'No, I think you need a rest,' said Caroline, looking up as she texted on her phone.

Caroline's phone rang.

'My sister.'

'Hi Jesse.'

'Hi there.'

'Say hi to Carlotta and Carmela,' said Caroline holding out the phone so they could all see each other.

'Hi Jesse!' said Carmela and Carlotta, waving.

'Hi there,' replied Jesse, 'and this is Mary, Eleanor's cousin in Vancouver.'

'Hi Mary,' they said, each at a slightly different time.

Caroline went into her study and closed the door.

'See that?' whispered Carmela.

'What?' asked Carlotta.

'Same coloured tiles on the floor.'

'Must have been Mary's room.'

❖

'Sorry about that. Latest instalment in Jesse's divorce saga,' said Caroline coming back into the kitchen.

'I think we've finished. All clean,' said Carmela, surveying the kitchen and dining area.

'Spick and span. Fantastic job. Thank you.'

'I better get going now,' said Carlotta. 'Will call a taxi. Shall I drop you off on the way back, Carmela?'

'Plan was for me to spend the night here,' said Carmela looking at Caroline.

'Now the kitchen is all cleaned up, you're free to go if you want,' said Caroline.

'Okay. Thank you.'

'But before you go, ladies, are we clear about the plan for next week when I'm in Nairobi?'

'I think so,' said Carlotta; Carmela nodded.

'Carmela will,' said Caroline, addressing Carlotta, 'pick Eleanor up from school Monday afternoon, come back here and pack up her things, and then bring her to your place around 7pm.'

'And on Friday, after she's done the cleaning at Carlotta's, Carmela will collect Eleanor's belongings, pick her up from school, bring her back here and then stay till I get back round 9pm. Okay?'

'Yes, ma'am,' said Carmela .

'Ma'am?' asked Caroline.

Carmela covered her mouth with her hand.

'And, Carlotta, I will drop by your office tomorrow and give you a set of keys to this place, just in case.'

'Hi Nathalie.'

'Hi Caroline,' said Carlotta's personal assistant, who till a year ago had been Caroline's.

'Is she in a meeting?'

'No, no. She's alone in there.'

Caroline knocked on the door and walked into her former place of business, one of the most prized in the building: a large corner office on the top floor, with floor-to-ceiling windows along the length of two walls and a panoramic view of the botanical gardens, the river and the mountains beyond.

Carlotta was on the phone. She motioned Caroline to sit down. The doors of a cupboard at the bottom of the white bookshelves that lined one of the two walls were half open. Inside Caroline should see a rolled-up futon, a pillow, a toothbrush and toothpaste in a mug, and toiletries.

'Sorry,' said Carlotta hanging up. 'Was the procurator maximus.'

'Is that what you call him?'

'It's what we called the principal at la Señora del Recuerdo.'

'I think I'll spare Eleanor the kinds of educational institutions we both had to endure.'

'Sorry, but I have a conference call in a couple minutes.'

'No problem. Here're the keys.'

'Okay. Thanks.'

'Sorry, to impose this on you.'

'Please, having Eleanor over is a pleasure. And Carmela is around to help.'

'I couldn't discuss it the other night, with everyone there.'

'What?'

'There's a problem with Carmela. Well not so much with Carmela as with her husband, Jean-Marie.'

A bugle call sounded.

'Your video conference?'

'Yes, but tell me. It can wait.'

'Well, I don't know what to think about Jean-Marie?'

'Tonton something, rather?'

'She's told you about him?'

'The other night, after I read her the story.'

The bugle call sounded again. Carlotta ignored it.

'Did she say anything? Caroline asked.

'No, no; nothing of any significance.'

'He's fat, diabetic, almost eighty and walks with crutches.'

'Almost eighty?'

'Thirty years older than Carmela.'

'Still could be a paedophile, I suppose.'

'Emigrated here and became naturalised years ago. From Togo originally.'

'She married him for the passport?'

'Used to own several bars. Carmela worked in one of them when she first got here.'

'Bars?'

'Last time I picked Eleanor up from their place, while I was chatting with Carmela, I saw how Jean-Marie interacted with Eleanor.'

'In front you of?'

'Too familiar, much too physical.'

'How?'

'He was sitting in his armchair, giving her a ride on his knee, then she crawled around his lap and up and over his big belly, and she wrapped her arms around his neck and kissed

181

him—on the cheek, on the forehead.'

'Oh.'

'She kept on saying, 'Tonton Nibombé' and he chuckled, enjoying every minute of it.'

'Well, I …'

'Before you say it all sounds pretty innocent, I have to tell you …'

'What?'

'But I'm not sure.'

'Still, tell me.'

'I think he might have had an erection.'

'An erection?'

'I think there was a bulge in his trousers. I think. But I'm not sure. He wears loose trousers. So, it might have been a fold in the material. And the room was not well lit.'

'At his age? In his state of health?'

'But it's not only that.'

'You sure?'

'Jean-Marie can hardly walk, but he still drives. Eleanor told me—and Carmela has kept very quiet about this—that sometimes, instead of Carmela picking her up from school, Jean-Marie picks her up and they go for drives through the countryside. Just the two of them.'

'Where do they go?'

'And I don't think he puts Eleanor in the booster seat I bought especially for their car. He lets her sit in the front, in the passenger seat. Not even sure he puts the seatbelt on her.'

'You sure?'

'And he smokes in the car. His stinking cigarillos.'

'With Eleanor there?'

'She says he opens the window.'

'Where do they go?'

'To collect chestnuts. She wasn't sure where. Up the mountains, to see the first snowfall.'

'Did she bring back any chestnuts?'

'*Flâneries motorisées*, he taught Eleanor to call these excursions. I had to look up *flâneries*. Dawdling, sauntering.'

'*Flâneries*. Yes. *Paseos.*'

'I'll have to talk with Carmela about this. When I get back.'

Caroline looked down, put her phone away in her handbag, and said, 'They finally advertised your post, I saw.'

'Yes, deadline is Wednesday. Still have to finish my application.' As she said these words, rage surged up in Carlotta. The edge of her vision blurred. She glared at Caroline. She was on the verge of lashing out. She felt her forearm stiffen and her right hand open up. Caroline sat in the orange armchair, fiddling with her handbag. Carlotta continued to glare, struggling to contain her fury. Caroline cast a glance her way and, as if blinded, looked away immediately. Carlotta forced herself to breathe deeply, once, twice.

The bugle call sounded again.

'You better join that video conference.'

'Suplika will be okay. Don't worry,' Carlotta said, voice breaking. Her eyes filled with tears the moment Caroline closed the door behind her.

'Carmela?'

'Who's this?'

'Me, Carlotta.'

'Oh, hello Carlotta.'

'Hi.'

'Everything okay? Suplika good?'

'Yes, yes, she's fine. But I need your help. As soon as possible.'

'Something happened?'

'Caroline called and said she will only arrive tomorrow morning.'

'Missed flight?'

'She's going to have to take a later flight out of Nairobi and will almost certainly miss the last connection from Amsterdam.'

'Missed flight.'

'And she wants to pick the child up here after she lands'

'The room,' said Carmela.

'Yes, the room.'

Till now, although Carmela regularly went in the room to clean it, they had pretended in didn't exist.

'Shops still open a few hours,' said Carmela.

'I'll pay you. How much?'

'Jean-Marie will have to drive.'

'€250?'

'No, not enough.'

'€500. Plus the expenses.'

'Okay. Will take a few hours. First to Ikea, then your place, then change everything in the room.'

'€500 plus expenses.'

'New curtains, duvet, desk and chair, and rug to cover floor.'

'Yes. And you'll help me move the doll's house.'

'Loft bed?' asked Carmela. 'She will notice.'

'I think it's okay to have one thing that's the same. We'll put it in another position.'

184

Carlotta, Carmela, and Suplika stood together in the middle of the replica of Suplika's room, on the shiny coloured tiles.

'Better start,' said Carlotta.

'Let's first take Suplika back into the kitchen and make sure Jean-Marie is comfortable,' said Carmela.

His two underarm crutches leaning against the wall, Jean-Marie sat at Carlotta's kitchen table, legs stretched out in from of him, pants hitched half-way over his large belly by a pair of red suspenders.

'*Un verre d'eau? Une bière?*' Carlotta asked Jean-Marie.

'Beer please,' said Jean-Marie. His gaze travelled up the window that rose to the high ceiling and down again over the copper cookware ranged along the wall. Then he noticed, on a plinth fixed above the door, a statuette of the Virgin Mary, in a light blue cape, holding the Christ child. He crossed himself— quickly, discreetly. Carlotta shut her eyes and bowed her head.

'Fancy place you have here,' said Jean-Marie.

'Thank you.'

'Huge apartment in the fanciest arrondissement.'

'Not that big.'

'More than you can afford, even on your salary.'

'I inherited when my father died.'

'Not a bad investment.'

'Supli, *s'il te plaît*, take off my shoes and socks,' said Jean-Marie. And addressing Carlotta: 'I can no longer bend over.'

Supli sat cross-legged at Jean-Marie's feet. One foot at a time, she undid his shoelace, tugged off his shoe, pulled off his sock, rolled it up and stuffed it in the shoe, and gave each

185

foot a brief massage. She had, Carlotta thought, done this many times before.

'Take yours off too,' said Jean-Marie to the little girl massaging his feet. 'You'll be more comfortable.'

She arranged her little blue shoes neatly next to Jean-Marie's large black, polished shoes.

'Carmela,' he said, lowering the bottle of beer from his mouth and wiggling his toes, 'also treats Bernie's room in our house like a shrine.'

'And, just like Suplika's room here, no one is supposed to know,' Carmela laughed.

'But your daughter comes to visit now and then?' Carlotta asked.

'Once a year,' said Jean-Marie. 'The rest of the time, the room must be kept absolutely immaculate, and no one can sleep in it.'

'She'll be moving here next year, when she finishes college in Manila,' said Carmela.

'Tonton Nibombé,' said Suplika now standing behind him with her fingers pushed deep into his frosted, frizzy hair, 'you must get a haircut. It sticks out too much.'

'He looks like Don King,' said Carmela.

'I don't think our friends here follow boxing,' said Jean-Marie.

'Let's go do the room, Carlotta,' said Carmela

Jean-Marie took a long, worn wooden box out of his satchel, unclasped it, and opened it up. He rearranged the pebbles so that there were four in each of the two rows of six pits carved into the long pieces of rectangular wood on each side of the hinges.

'You two go finish transforming the room. Mademoiselle

and I are going to play a bit of adito,' said Jean-Marie, '*N'est-ce pas, mademoiselle?*'

Suplika pulled out a chair, climbed onto it, and sat opposite Jean-Marie—ready to play.

'I don't understand,' said Suplika.

'What?' asked Jean-Marie.

'Why they don't want Caroline to see my room here.'

'Is it exactly the same?'

'Except that it has a door.'

'No door at home?'

'No. That way Caroline and I can talk at night.'

The video intercom rang. Jean-Marie and Suplika looked at each other.

Carlotta came down the hallway, back hunched, knees flexed, holding her finger over her mouth, followed by Carmela.

'What if Caroline made the connection after all?' said Carlotta.

Suplika ran over to the small screen next to the entrance door and, stretching up on her toes, peered into it.

'Not her,' said Suplika, shaking her head.

'Hola?' said Carlotta into the receiver.

'Where do we put all this stuff and the dolls' house?' asked Carmela, in English.

'In the cellar.'

'All the way down in the basement?'

'You're getting €500.'

'For my silence, mainly,' said Carmela, laughing and giving

Carlotta's shoulder a squeeze.

'Let's put it in the hallway for the moment and finish up in here.'

The new curtains and bedspread were grey. The coloured floor tiles were now covered by a fuchsia rug. Under the loft bed, the red chair and desk had been replaced by two trestles, a plexiglass table top and a black stool.

'No longer a child's room.'

'No. Thank you Carmela. You chose well,' said Carlotta.

The creases on Carlotta's forehead were leaking sweat and the bleached down on her upper lip had spawned miniature pearls of perspiration.

'You're nervous,' said Carmela.

Carlotta let her head fall forward and slowly shook her head from side to side.

'I will leave the room like this now. Next time you come, we will tear the coloured tiles up from the floor,' she said.

'Was much prettier before. And good for you.'

'Good for you,' echoed Suplika, who had walked up in her bare feet and had been standing in the doorway, listening.

She put a hand on his thigh and leaned in. With her other hand she pulled his tie to bring his head forward. He felt her lips against his ear. 'Thing is, Hywel, you're never going to get another chance.'

Norfolk | David Rogers

1

Stevie Wonder was playing on the pub PA. Hywel lowered his menu a smidge, risked another glance. Lovely as a summer's day. Strange eyes, though. What colour would you call that? Teal? No, not teal. One of those Farrow & Ball shades. The one Jocasta had picked out for the nursery. He looked away. Stanton was sprawled on the Chesterfield, scratching his nose with a stick of celery. A nudge and a nod? Nah. She seemed absorbed, but you could never tell. Besides, he wanted her to himself a few moments longer.

Stanton put his celery back in his glass and turned to his agent. 'See that sexy redhead in the LBD?' he asked, with a little eye-swivel.

'What about her?'

'She's reading *Another Shore*.'

Hywel darted a glance. 'So she is. I didn't notice. She's got good taste.'

'Maybe she has. And maybe we'll find out what it is, too. Now, be a poppet and get the grub in. I'll have the usual.'

He meant the Gruyère burger. It was part of his Saturday system: four double-shot espressos, a Bloody Mary, a G-burger, a cheeky snort on the baby-changer and a cab into town for cocktails at Bourne & Hollingsworth, or somewhere much like it.

By now—getting on for two-thirty—the Queen's had filled beyond its seating capacity and the drinkers, clumped in the track between bar and tables, were shouting at each other over Donna Summer. Hywel had to wait ten minutes to place his order. When he pushed back through, wooden spoon in hand, Stanton was already deep in conversation with the girl. He was making big gestures, like an opera singer performing an aria. Hywel stood by as the writer and broadcaster took her hand and raised it briefly to his mouth. Neither acknowledged his existence. He moved Stanton's camel-hair coat from his side of the sofa, snatched *The Guardian*'s motoring section off the pine dining table and stared angrily at BMW's plans to produce an electric five-door hatchback that was sportier than one might expect.

Oooooooooh, falling free, falling free, falling free, falling free … Falling free …

A waiter came over, plates balanced on his arms.

'Who's the burger?'

'That would be him,' said Hywel, nodding towards Stanton.

'You're the lamb, yeah?'

'I'm the lamb.'

He was introduced an hour later, in the taxi. Her name was Emma. On the Greys Inn Road, Stanton stopped talking long

192

enough to answer a text, and Hywel had the chance to impress his new acquaintance with his command of wit and repartee. He listened, appalled, as one godawful question after another emerged from his mouth. You've just moved to London? Where are you living before? Oh, right. Where are you staying now? Oh, Tottenham—what's that like these days? Haven't been up there since … On Chancery Lane, Stanton put his phone away and got the conversation back on track with a buttock-clenching speech about how he owed his success in life to this little chap here—his peerless understanding of the media market, his skill in negotiation, his meticulous line-editing, his blah, blah, blah.

They got out at the Marquis in Fitzrovia, where they met up with other members of the writer and broadcaster's camarilla. This Saturday, there was Keith the divorced BBC producer, Paul the City fixer, and Rory, who was presently appearing as Dr Astrov in the Almeida's *Vanya*. And, for one night only, there was Matt, the *Sunday Telegraph* hack Hywel had lined up to write a feature interview after Stanton's long meditated masterwork, *Carceral Continuum*, came out in the summer.

They knocked back a couple of rounds, then headed south in the February drizzle. Emma tagged along at the rear. Hywel tried walking alongside, but she kept her attention on the pavement. He fell back and watched her. How elegant she was. How self-contained.

First port of call was the Groucho, where Bloomsbury were launching a novel set in Helmand, written by a former captain in the Royal Marines. The main point, however, was to touch base with Armand, the showrunner on Canal Plus' production of *Sans Abrit* (as *Another Shore* had been retitled for the French market). They sat together on a bright orange sofa, and Hywel discovered his contact to be a quietly-spoken, serious-minded young man. But all the while they were discussing Frankfurt and Modiano, and how the Hackney/Norfolk scenes in the book translated to the Saint-Denis/Brittany locations chosen for the series, he was distractingly conscious of the girl. At first, she stood by herself, not talking to anyone, or drinking from her flute of prosecco. But then Keith sidled up, followed shortly after by Matt. On the way to Ronnie Scott's, the two journalists walked either side of her, talking in both ears at once, personalities dialled to eleven.

At the first interval, Hywel introduced Stanton to Armand and tried, with limited success, to get his client to focus on the changes that would have to be made to reflect French social work practices. By the time the Canal Plus man left, around eleven, Keith and Matt were talking Arsenal midfield options and Hywel had been buttonholed by Rory, who wanted to pitch a crime novel written by a young man of his acquaintance. Emma, meanwhile, had got Stanton on his own at the bar. As Hywel pretended to listen to Rory, he watched her fingers rise to the writer's cheek and his fall to her haunch. Their faces were the colour of low-oxygen blood in the crimson jazzlight. The girl had dropped her air of extra-terrestrial reserve and was talking freely, laughing, her head uptilted, moving from foot to foot. Stanton was pretending to fend her off, but then she undid one of his waistcoat buttons, slipped a hand into the gap and, Hywel presumed, stimulated an authorial nipple. When they kissed, he felt himself lifted by a wave of nausea. He apologised to Rory, lurched to his feet, waved at the pundits without expecting or receiving acknowledgement, and walked out, leaving his coat uncollected in the cloak room.

2

Hywel didn't ask Stanton how the evening had ended and Stanton didn't tell him. But that day and that night, distilled to certain images, remained with him as the weeks passed. And as they passed, he noticed his attitude to the world had hardened. He dropped one of his readers for copying him in on a jokey email. He took to jangling the change in his pocket when he walked past *Big Issue* sellers, and voted for Tory candidates in the May elections. His home life was changing, too. Jocasta's bossiness, her habit of affectionately undermining his manhood and competence, began to grate, and ovulation-night intercourse came to feel like a faintly resented duty, on a par with putting out the bins, or filling in a tax return. He began making sarcastic ripostes to her under his breath, and smoked secret garden cigarettes on evenings when she was out. Even his Saturday chevauchées with Stanton, formerly the highlight of his week, happened less often, and when they did, there were silences …

In the end, it was the author and broadcaster who initiated the looming relationship convo. This occurred one evening in early June, after they'd been to the Lyttelton to see Rory as Arnolphe in *The School for Wives*, and were walking back together along the South Bank.

'Hywel, old chum. This might just be in my head, but is something the matter?'

'What do you mean?'

Stanton put on his Joan Crawford voice. 'You've been so cold and distant lately. Was it something I said? Something I did? I can't bear it, I really can't. *Tell* me, darling; *tell* me.'

Hywel smiled, shook his head and suppressed an urge to hit his friend in the face. 'Sorry—been a bit distracted. One thing and another.'

'This'll make you laugh: I was thinking it might be something to do with that girl.'

'What girl?'

'You know, that Emma whatshername.'

Hywel was overcome by a squall of emotions. Some of them must have registered in his face, because the next thing he knew, Stanton's heavy arm was around his shoulders. 'Ah, come on. We can't let a mere *woman* come between us. Not after all these years. Give me a kiss and I'll buy you dinner.'

Hywel submitted to the embrace, which continued until he tapped the author's back to signal that it had been completed satisfactorily.

'Excellent. Now, let's get comfortable and I'll tell you why you shouldn't get so worked up over these things.'

They caught the lift to the seventh floor of the Oxo Tower. 'Truth be told, you dodged a bullet there,' Stanton boomed on. 'She was a couple of stamps short of a coffee, that girl. Take it from one who knows: if you're thinking about committing adultery, you've got to pick the right pony. Take up references.'

'How are you a writer?' Hywel asked as they walked down the corridor to the restaurant. 'You just mixed seventeen different metaphors.'

'I wasn't writing; I was talking. Other standards apply. You didn't need the "different" just then, did you?'

'And you didn't need the "just" just then.'

The conversation fell into abeyance until they'd been greeted and seated, and each had a gin and tonic in hand.

'So, what happened?' Hywel asked, forcing himself to add:

196

'With the girl— with Emma.'

'Much as you might expect. Don't flinch, I'm not going to give you a blow-by-blow account … Just the main thrust.'

'Yeah, okay. Not sure I want to hear about any of it, to tell the truth.'

'Yes, you do. You asked, didn't you? Well, thing is, it wasn't entirely fate's inscrutable design we ran into her that afternoon in the Queen's.'

'How d'you mean?'

Stanton leant in. 'She'd been stalking me.'

Hywel stared—and suddenly felt himself unburdened, as though he'd just taken a large, emotionally satisfying dump. He smiled a natural smile and leaned forward too. 'What? She's a *bunny boiler*?'

Stanton nodded. 'That's exactly what she is.'

'How do you know?'

Stanton lowered his voice to a conspiratorial whisper. 'We'd got to the après stage and I was trying say my farewells before Vickie started hitting redial and she just came out with it.'

'And told you what, exactly?'

'That she'd been scouring Harringay for me. Been searching pubs along the route of the W7. Since before Christmas.'

Hywel finished his drink and looked for a waiter. It seemed he was feeling fine. More than fine. 'Bloody hell. The W7? What's that got to do with anything?'

'Saw me getting on one at Finsbury Park, recognised me from the dust jacket.'

'But, why …?'

'She's obsessed with *Another Shore*. No idea why, but she is.'

Hywel laughed. 'Jesus. Book like that.' He shook his head. 'How many groupies do you think Thomas Hardy had?'

'What can I tell you? There's no end to female perversity. Anyway, I was out of there like a ferret on fire, I can tell you.'

They took a drink at the same time, and Stanton gazed at the serrated outline of the Right Bank, silhouetted against indigo sky and framed by the restaurant's picture window. 'We went back to her place,' he continued. 'She's got a room on the third floor of a boarding house on the Ladder. There're no stair carpets, five bikes and a pram in the hall, people coming and going all night. When I'm making my getaway, she insists on walking me all the way to the front doorstep, still dripping, spaghetti-bollocks-naked, holding my arm and giggling as though she was three years old. Thought for one grim moment she was going to get in the Uber with me.'

'God. So, I guess that was that?'

'Er—yes. That is where the story ended. So, my dear, dear friend and delicious business partner, the moral of the story is: be careful what you wish for … unless it's written on a menu. Starters, farters, I fancy the lobster soufflé. You can deal with the wine.'

3

The next time Hywel saw Emma was at the launch of *Carceral* at the Kensington Roof Gardens. She turned up at about nine, as most of the other guests were leaving for their second engagement of the evening.

He was out on the decking having a post-match fag by a potted osteospermum when he saw her. For a moment, it didn't click. Her pre-Raphaelite tresses had been dyed a lustreless black, and she was wearing a miniskirt, fishnets and a scuffed leather jacket. She looked around herself in some confusion, spotted him and came staggering over.

'You're Howl, aren't you?'

'Emma. Goodness. Hello again.'

'Can I have a cigarette?'

'Sure.' He took a pack of Marlboro Lights out of the side pocket of his pinstripe suit. 'Didn't know you smoked.'

'Prefer rollies.'

She took one, and Hywel lit it for her.

'What are you doing here?' he asked. 'I didn't see your name on the list. If you've come for the do, I'm afraid it's done.'

'I came to see Gerald.'

'Sorry: you've missed him.'

'He's gone?'

'Went off with Will Self about ten minutes ago. You should've come earlier.'

'I was celebrating.' She looked at him a moment. 'Do *you* want to get a drink?'

Hywel knew, of course, that the correct answer to this was, 'er—maybe another time', but he was experiencing a rush of turbid emotions and was unable, for the moment, to say what he wanted.

She crossed her arms and shivered. 'Oh, alright then. Don't have any money anyway.'

'No, that's okay. They're clearing up in here but there's that place.' He nodded towards a glass box overlooking the river.

She glanced over and shivered again. He put an arm around her shoulder and shepherded her along the terrace. They found a couple of stools at the bar—she mounted hers on the second attempt—and he ordered two glasses of Pouilly-Fuissé.

While he was waiting for them to be poured, he took a closer look. Her make-up looked as though it had been applied by a distracted mortician: lipstick smeared, mascara clotted, liner thick and uneven, an underlay of beige that failed to conceal the pits beneath her eyes. The effect was ghastly. And there was a brittleness about her—the crossed arms, the hunched shoulders, the jerk of her motions. A sense of impacted misery.

The wine glasses were placed on scalloped paper doilies; he slid hers over, she drank half with a couple of gulps, set the glass down and began looking around again.

He waited until she turned back to him. 'Emma …' he said slowly, 'tell me to fuck off if you want, but I can't help but be a little bit curious.'

'About what?'

'About what's happened to you. You're like a different person.'

'Yeah, okay. Fuck off, Howl.'

Hywel laughed good humouredly. 'Fair enough.'

She looked at him in a blank way, then laughed too. 'You know, I'm sorry about that other time.'

He smiled a puzzled smile. 'How do you mean?'

'You wanted to talk to me—when we were walking to that club. I was a bit mean to you.'

'I didn't really notice.'

'Yeah, you did. You forgive me, right?'

A molten sweetness ran down Hywel's spine, and he searched his mind for the most magnanimous statement it would be possible for him to make, eventually settling on: 'Don't worry about it.'

She looked around again, and he decided on a conversational initiative. 'So, I gather you're a fan of Gerald's first novel— *Another Shore*?'

She snorted. 'Fan?'

'You know what I mean.'

'Let's just say I have a connection with it.'

'Oh, okay … Anyway, you haven't told me what you're celebrating.'

She picked up her glass and looked at it. 'Is this any good?'

'Twelve quid for 175 centilitres, so someone must think so.'

'Okay, well here's to my launch.' They clinked and drank. 'Gerald had a book out; I had a foetus.'

This statement—once he was satisfied that he'd heard it correctly over the laughter and chat filling the box—had the same effect on Hywel as if the girl—Emma—had bent over and retched a partly digested mouse onto the stone countertop.

'A-an abortion?'

She nodded.

'I'm sorry,' he said. 'That must have been horrible. Are you okay?'

'Better out than in. That's a quote from the father, by the way.'

'He did tell me a little bit about what happened,' Hywel ventured cautiously. 'It was just bad luck, I guess.'

'How do you mean?'

'Well … you just did it that once.'

She gave a shrill laugh. 'Is that what he told you? Is that really what he told you?'

Hywel looked at his watch. 'Look, I'm going to have to make a move.'

'Oh, so you are fucking off.'

'Well …' He sighed an I'm-afraid-so sigh, but at once felt a stab of proleptic regret, and added: 'Do you want to get a

201

cab north? We can talk about it on the way.'

'Are you sure?'

'Why not? If you want … It's only a cab.'

'Oh, I get it. You're thinking maybe you'll get the chance to give me another one. You might want to wait for the bleeding to die down a bit.'

'God, why would you say that?' Hywel demanded, flushing with bruised rectitude. 'All I said was, do you want to get a cab.'

She laughed, showing slightly incurved teeth. 'Come on, Howl, show some spunk. Faint heart never won fair maid.'

Aiming at stern admonition, he hit querulous complaint: 'Yeah, there's really no need to have a go at *me*. I'm not your enemy.'

Her face relaxed into an expression of contrition. 'Okay. Sorry. Bit drunk.'

'No, that's … I understand.'

She shook her head wonderingly. 'You think that's a good excuse? For anything?'

Wrong footed again, Hywel ran a hand down his face. He was beginning to feel as though he were being arraigned for another's crimes, and was at a loss as to which emotion he ought to display in response. Anger? Resentment? Sympathy? Something more imaginative? All he authentically felt was excited, confused and a bit frightened, as though he were a child strapped into the chair of a roller-coaster and it was too late to get off.

'I thought you were a tough negotiator,' she went on in the same mocking tone.

'Yes, well I am, actually. If I were selling a book you'd written, I'd be a lion.'

For a moment, their gazes locked.

'What if I said yes?' she asked.

'What?'

'What if I said, "yes, let's get a cab".'

'What do you mean?'

'What do you mean, you mean. It was your idea, wasn't it?'

'I'm sorry, we're talking hypotheticals, are we? I don't think you're—'

'No, we're not.' She leaned a little towards him and her voice fell to a murmur. 'We could go somewhere quieter, I could tell you what happened to me, you could nod along, buy me some more drinks, share a fag or two. Who knows what might happen? Anyway, it's only a cab.'

'Well … I don't …' He picked up his glass, but it seemed to be empty.

She put a hand on his thigh and leaned in, face raised. With her other hand she pulled his tie to bring his head forward, and he felt her lips against his ear. 'Thing is, Hywel: you're never going to get another chance.'

Hywel now felt himself in the position of a man trying to weigh up the pros and cons of open-heart surgery while a firehose played over his face. At that moment his phone buzzed. He took it out and saw on the lock screen, over his companion's leathery shoulder, the name Jocasta and the word 'Bingo', followed by seven exclamation marks.

4

Vickie Stanton heard the sound of heels clacking over the pine floorboards of the Queen's and looked up from her phone to find the imposing form of Jocasta Chabrier bearing down on her. Both women's blank expressions flicked to ecstatic delight, Vickie rose and hurried round, Jocasta retracted the handle of her suitcase and they embraced like long lost sisters.

'Sorry I'm late. Flight was on time but the bloody trains are up the spout.'

Vickie put a hand on her Jocasta's belly. 'They're not the only one.'

'I know. Isn't it dreadful? No booze for a gazillion years.'

'You haven't got a bump. How far are you along?'

'Making a start on the second trimester.'

'Congratulations.'

'Yes, well, I'd like to thank my agent for all his hard work.'

They hugged again. 'Don't want to rub it in, but I was just about to get another. I guess you're on the barley water.'

'Can I just have a chamomile tea? I've developed a bit of an addiction to kombucha, but I'm pretty sure they won't do it here.'

She was wrong about that. Vickie came back with a K-spritz and a bottle of Entre-Deux-Mers, after which they settled down for a natter about antenatal classes, epidurals, birthplans, stretch marks, Muswell Hill nurseries, pelvic floor exercises, au pair nationalities, breast pumps, maternity wear, doulas, gender reveal parties and, in various contexts, fannies. Having thus covered the subject of Jocasta's pregnancy, they moved on to her busy week. Turned out she'd just flown back from Seville via Geneva, after successfully arranging the sale of an eighteenth-century Moorish dining table to an American banker.

'*How* much?' Vickie asked.

'With cost, insurance and freight? I charged him €126,570.'

'What did he say to that?'

'Well, if I could quote my client's exact words, "When I saw the pictures, I liked it; when I heard the price, *I was in love*".

This anecdote, which Jocasta told with some relish and a comical New York accent, did not get the reaction she was hoping for, and it occurred to her that, beneath her surface manner, Vickie wasn't quite her sweet, good-natured self. After a pause, during which they both looked around the bustling pub, the conversation shifted register.

'How's that husband of yours?' Jocasta asked, throwing an arm over the back of the sofa. 'I can't remember the last time I saw him.'

'You know what he's like … Thing is he seems to be getting more like what he's like as the days go by. Anyway, I don't want to talk about him. Tell me about the proud father.'

'That's a horse of a very similar colour.'

'You said he seemed a bit detached … Is he still?'

'Oh, no: he's much worse.'

'How do you mean? You mean he's not around, or …'

'No, it's not that. Well, it's partly that, but even when he's there, he's somewhere else. I have to keep snapping my fingers under his nose to get him to focus. Something's going on with him. I wanted to ask if Gerald had let anything slip.'

Vickie hooked her hair behind her ears. 'Not that I know of. He's pretty distracted too, these days.'

'Because of the reviews, you mean?'

'They were pretty horrible.'

Jocasta laid a consoling hand on Vickie's denimed knee. 'How did he take it?'

'About as well as *King Lear*. You know he'd been working on that book for ten years.'

'I saw the one Will Self wrote, "The stripper that never takes off any clothes". Bastard.'

Vickie poured herself another glass. 'He can talk. Did you read it? *Carceral Continuum*, I mean.'

'Oh, you know—most of Gerry's stuff goes right over my head. What did you make of it?'

'I didn't think it was any worse than his short story collection.'

'Oh, yes. *The Rubaiyat of Harold Shipman*. That's a ringing endorsement if ever I heard one.'

'Some of it was a bit … self-indulgent, perhaps.'

'Why does he have to be such an intellectual all the time? I keep hoping he's going to write something like *Another Shore.*'

Vickie gave an eye roll. 'I don't think that's likely to happen.'

'Why not? Is he worried that people might enjoy reading it?'

'Not exactly.'

'What Will Self said was right, you know,' Jocasta went on. 'He never comes out with anything he really believes. He just criticises things other people believe. That's why *Another Shore* was such a hit—he really seemed to be saying something. You know … communicating.'

Vickie nodded mutely, reached for the bottle to pour another glass, and, as she did so, gave Jocasta a speaking look.

'What? What? Come on, girl: spit it out.'

'I've always hated that book.'

'Really?' She considered this statement. 'That's quite a strong word.'

Vickie looked at the glass in her hand, shrugged, and her thoughts seemed to jump track. 'They do get away with a lot, don't they?'

'Who do? Men, you mean?'

'The thing about my husband …' she began, then hooked her hair behind her ears again.

206

Jocasta allowed the silence to lengthen before prompting. 'Yes? What?'

'You know what *really* annoys me about him? It's not the calls he never returns, the anniversaries he never remembers; all the wine stains on the sofa and the crumbs in the bed and the drinking and the lying and the boasting and the "I can't help it, I'm bipolar" bullshit. It's not even the assumption that none of my views on any subject ever need to be taken seriously. The instant withdrawal of affection whenever I fail to do exactly what he wants. That's par for the course, probably. It's his sense of justification. He'll never change because he doesn't see any reason why he should. He's a forty-year-old child. Most of us grow up because we've got no choice. Not Gerald Antony Stanton. He just assumes that everyone will let him get away with whatever he does. And he's right, they do. They always have. The rules don't apply.'

'Because he's on the telly?'

'Because of that *fucking* book.'

In the twenty years she'd know her, Jocasta had never—or almost never—witnessed Vickie lose her temper, use the 'f' word, or glug an entire bottle of wine by herself. Yet here she was, performing all three feats in the same evening. This was getting quite interesting.

'I don't get what a novel he wrote ten years ago has to do with anything that's happening now ...' she said, then stopped and stared at Vickie, who deflected her gaze and bit her bottom lip. 'Has anything happened?' she asked, carefully, like a doctor tweezing debris from a blast wound. 'Has he done something?'

Vickie cracked. 'Nothing he hasn't done plenty of times before. It's me: I've done something.'

'Don't tell me you've started an affair?'

207

'I've asked him to move out.'

'No way,' Jocasta breathed, and raised a hand to her mouth.

'I can handle difficult people quite well—I'm a social worker, after all—but I'm starting to feel as though they've got me surrounded. You just get to a certain point and you think, you know what? I can't be bothered with this. There are other things I could be doing. Other people I could be doing them with.'

'Oh my god. Don't tell me I'm going to go home and find him lying on my couch like a huge, homeless … labrador. When did all this happen?'

'Tuesday. He went out for lunch at the Gay Hussar and he came back in the small hours pissed out of his mind throwing things around the kitchen.'

'Why the kitchen?'

'He was making profiteroles—don't ask, because I don't know. I think he just wanted to eat some. He kept saying he'd been betrayed. I mean, it was very *King Lear*. Except with more flour. With flour everywhere. And cream. It was like he'd ejaculated over the entire room.'

'Oh my god. I'm sorry, I shouldn't laugh. It's just, I can picture the scene. What are you going to do now? I mean, how do you feel about it all?'

'I don't feel anything, really. Apart from relief.'

Suppressing giggles, Jocasta hugged her friend. As if expelled by the pressure, she felt the pit, pat, pit of tears on the left shoulder of her Issey Miyake blouse.

When Jocasta got home, it was her husband she found asleep on the couch, cut-crystal whisky glass cradled in the crook of an arm, mobile phone gripped in a hand. A copy of 'that fucking book' lay open on the coffee table; the TV showed the frozen image of a moonlit sea.

She took her suitcase to the utility room, threw her clothes in the washing machine, noted with pursed lip the number of bottles in the recycling, made herself a cup of tea and returned to find he'd begun to snore. Tender as a bomb disposal expert in love, she took his glass, and was just easing the mobile out of his hand when he came awake. His sulky expression changed to alarm, and he yanked the phone out of her grip.

She laughed. 'Alright, calm down. I'm not the big bad wolf.'

He blinked bloodshot eyes. 'I was going to take you for a curry.'

'Oh, sweet. I had a hot date. Did tell you.' She sat beside him, nodded toward the TV. 'Netflix?'

'Oh, no. They sent me the first three episodes of *Sans Abrit*—Canal Plus did.'

'*Sans Abrit*? Oh, *Another Shore*. Can't get away from it today. Do you remember—when you couldn't get on the Tube without seeing three people reading it?'

Hywel grunted. 'That's when people still read books.'

'What's it like? Any good?'

'They found a good actress for Molly.'

'You're supposed to call them "actors". How about you? Your face is red.'

'I'm fine. Missed you.'

'Aw. You've heard the news about your favourite client, I take it? Vickie's finally kicked him out.'

'I know.'

'I never thought she'd do it. Even doormats have feelings, it seems.'

Hywel sat up, hunched. 'That's a bit unfair.'

'How's he taking his eviction?'

'About as well as you'd expect. She was your date, was she, Vickie?'

'I just had this really weird conversation with her. Why are you looking so …'

'No, nothing. What was the conversation about? Why was it weird?'

'I don't know.' Moments from the evening appeared and disappeared in Jocasta's mind. 'I got the feeling there was something she wasn't telling me,' she said, speaking more to herself than her husband. 'Do you know why she kicked him out? Did he say anything to you?'

'No, nothing.' Hywel said, and swallowed.

'You look as though you've been crying. It was that good was it?' She nodded towards the TV.

'No, really, I'm fine.'

'It's okay. I always cry at the end. Everybody does.'

'I wasn't. Anyway, I'm not even sure he is my client any-more.'

'You haven't fallen out with him too?'

'He's gone a bit … haywire.'

'Because of the reviews?'

Hywel nodded. 'Thing is, I granted access to a *Telegraph* journalist to write a piece on him, and when it came out it was all about how he'd lost his audience, you know? Comparing him with Martin Amis. Obviously, they just went for the best news angle, but for some reason, that was my fault. So, the long and the short of it is—I'm fired.'

He rose and walked to the mantelpiece, picked up a bottle of Glenmorangie and half filled his glass.

Jocasta watched him with an expression somewhere between puzzled and troubled. 'You literary types: you're like a bunch of autistic toddlers. Messy play, every day. And that's why he said he'd been betrayed? He was betrayed by *you*?'

'*Me*? No, of course not. Why are you having a go at me? What did *I* do?'

'I'm not. Hywel … what's *wrong* with you?'

'Why? What do you mean?'

'Now I'm getting the feeling there's something you're not telling me.'

'Why are you having a go at me?' he asked again. He drank half the glass in a couple of gulps. 'Jesus. You're not five minutes in the door and you're already starting a row.'

'I'm not doing anything of the sort; I just find it frustrating—when people aren't straight with me.'

'What do you want me to say?'

'What do you want to tell me? I get the feeling there might be something.'

A spasm of exasperation passed over his face, and Jocasta had the premonition that he was about to throw his glass at the wall. 'All I've ever done is try to help,' he said in a strangled voice. 'Why does everything *always* have to be my fault?'

'You know what? I've had enough of this.' She rose from the sofa. 'I'm going to bed. Maybe when I wake up things will start making sense again. You, dear husband, can have the spare room—assuming you can find it, state you'll be in after you finish that.'

5

'Why do you *always* knock? Why do you never use your key?'

'Happy Christmas to you too, Lady Scrooge,' he said, taking off his shoes. 'Should I put this in the fridge?'

'Put what in the fridge?'

'Champagne.'

'Put it where you like.'

'What's wrong? What did I do now?'

'Seriously: use your key.'

'I'm sorry. You were in the shower, were you?'

'I was having a bath. With your laptop.'

'*Your* laptop. I bought it for you.' He went into the kitchen/living room and put the bottle in the freezer. As she didn't follow, he re-entered the hall, where she was still standing, dripping angrily. 'Why were you having a bath with a computer?' he asked. 'Isn't that rather dangerous?'

'I was doing some editing.'

'But it's all been proofed. They won't thank you for making changes now.'

'Tough,' she said, walking into the bedroom. 'Anyway, everything's tracked,' she added, through the closing door.

Hywel went into the living room and stood a while by the window, watching cars pass below on Stroud Green Road. *No sex tonight, then*, he thought. Why was she such a bitch? No matter what he did for her; no matter how he helped her, she treated him with the same irritated indifference. Why had he done this? Why had he laboured so diligently, so passionately and so successfully at the task of making himself miserable? He looked around the barely furnished room, the blank walls. When he'd picked the flat, he'd imagined they would travel round European galleries together, choosing paintings, discussing art. Ha! What would she do if he picked up his coat, now, this moment, and walked out? Would she care? Would she notice? Eventually, perhaps—when the agency phoned about the rent. And then his thoughts fell into a well-worn groove. Her personal world, he reminded himself, was hard for someone like him to understand. He had to be sensitive to that. All the things she'd been through. Broken homes break children; broken children break homes.

Her copy of *Another Shore* was on the coffee table; he picked it up and began reading the page where it parted—

of the ambulance are open and the front door of the house is, too. There's nobody around, so I go into the hall, but then I hear boots on the stairs and duck into the living room. Looking through the front window, I see them take mum out. She's strapped to a stretcher with a red blanket over her. Colin's alongside, in his jogging bottoms and his don't say motherfucker t-shirt. I duck behind the curtain, and I wonder whether I can run up to the room without being noticed.

'Hang on a minute, she's in here.' He knocks on the central pane of the bay window with his knuckles. 'Come out here, you.'

There's an ambulance man on the front doorstep wearing a shiny green and yellow uniform. He comes into the hall. 'Could you just tell us if you know about any pills your mum had she might have taken?'

I look down, shake my head. What did that even mean?

Colin broke in: 'You better have her, cos I'm going out.' Understandably, he's irritated that mum's suicide has occurred on his quiz night.

As I walk past, he says in an undertone: 'She's a silly bitch, your mother. Why did she do that, eh? There was no need to do that.'

'Are you her partner?' the ambulance man asks Colin, over his shoulder, as he's shutting the back.

'Partner? I'm her landlord. Was.'

They keep the blue light on and sound the siren at roundabouts. The streets tilt and blur and flash on and off. I hang onto the strap of my seatbelt, and I'm thinking, if anything happens to mum, I'll have no family and no home. She was the last hand holding me. And she'd let go.

When we get to the hospital, they wheel her through A&E into a brightly lit room with a couple of metal beds and plastic chairs and telescopic things attached to the ceiling. Triage Room 1, the sign says. There are two doctors and two nurses. One of the doctors talks to mum, pats her cheeks and shines a light into her eyes. Then he says something about taking her to the theatre. It's a moment before I realise, he means the operating theatre.

One of the nurses notices me and comes hurrying over. 'This way, darling. Through here.'

When we're outside she crouches a little, puts a hand on my shoulder. 'What's your name, darling?'

I tell her.

'Are you that lady's daughter, Molly?'

I nod.

'Is anyone looking after you? Is there anyone I can call for you?'

These questions stump me, because there isn't, really. Then I remember Caroline's card. I'd put it in that plastic wallet they give you with your Oyster. I hand it to the nurse

214

and she takes me back to the waiting room.

People come and go. A lot of them are wearing coats over their pyjamas, dressing gowns, dinner jackets, going-out clothes, weird combinations of things they'd grabbed from the wardrobe or the washing basket. There was a Chinese couple with a little girl in a fluffy pink rabbit suit. It occurs to me that I could stay here, in this hospital. I could sleep in the waiting room, get food from the bins. The idea appeals to me. There are so many beds here.

Caroline turns up a little after midnight, wearing jeans, a velvet jacket and high heels. She bends down to say hello, rub my arm. She's got make-up on her face and her breath smells of alcohol and cigarettes. She talks to the nurse about EPOs and Section 46 orders, then she leads me out to her taxi.

It takes us to a basement flat on one of those streets off Graham Road. Once we're inside, she ushers me into the living room and goes out. I want to turn on the television, but I'm not sure if I'm allowed. I look at Caroline's books instead. I don't understand what most of them are about. But it's nice, here. There are plants, and pictures on the walls.

She comes back with a mug of cocoa and sits beside me on the couch. 'Okay, Molly? I bet you'd like to go to bed, wouldn't you? When you finish your drink, I'll show you your room, then I'll come and talk to you. Alright?'

I nod. 'Can I stay here with you?' I ask, but I already know the answer.

'Well, we'll have a think about that when we know how your mum is.'

She leads me to a little study with a bed and a desk and a filing cabinet and she gives me a pair of pyjamas. I change

215

and get into the bed. She talks to someone on the phone for a while, then I hear a shower going. After about half an hour, she taps on the door and comes in with a glass of water. She's wearing sweatpants and a T-shirt. She sits on the bed, quite close to me. She smells of toothpaste and shampoo now.

'I'll phone up the hospital tomorrow morning, see how your mum's doing,' she says. 'I'm sure she'll be feeling better. How about school? I'll call in for you, if you like.'

I drink the water and shake my head. 'I'd rather go in,' I say. I don't want to be a burden.

'Okay. If you're sure.'

I nod.

'Molly, you know you can talk to me, don't you? Anything you want to say—I'll listen.'

I smile. It's a bit dangerous to make a promise like that.

'Molly?' She reached out a hand, touched my shoulder for a moment. 'Where did you and your mum go when you left Hyacinth House?'

'We went to live with Colin.'

'Colin. Is he a relation of yours?'

I shake my head. 'Mum said he'd let us stay without paying rent.'

'Oh, right. I see.' There's quite a long pause, then she says: 'I know you must be feeling a bit weird now, but I don't want you to worry. Whatever happens, we'll take care of you.'

I look at her. 'If you can, why didn't you?'

There's a long silence, during which I go back to studying the paisley pattern of the duvet and she thinks about what to say next. What she eventually comes out with is: 'I'm

216

sorry, Molly ... I don't know what to tell you.'

There are shapes like tears with circles inside them; red and yellow spirals. I trace round them with my eyes.

'What happened to your mum and Mandy—there really wasn't anything we could have done, not after the bank sold on the mortgage. Once upon a time, we might have found you a council house, but there aren't many of those left. You know there's been a bit of a financial crash, don't you? There are so many people in emergency accommodation now—we have to find other ways to rehouse them. That's why we put you in Hyacinth. I know it's not a very nice place to live ...'

I look at the backs of my hands. I should stop biting my nails.

'The thing is, Molly, the world can be a heartless place ... Sometimes ... I don't know ... '

She leans forwards and put her arms around me. She wants me to comfort her. She stops when she sees my arms are dangling by my sides, then she sits back, sniffs and wipes her eyes quickly on the heels of her hands. 'Okay, well, we both better try to get some sleep, eh? I'm just next door. Knock if you wake up in the night and you want to talk.'

When she's gone, I turn the light off and lie in the dark, listening to sirens in the street and looking at the headlights sweeping across the ceiling. Every so often a train goes by on the North London Line.

I think about what Caroline said. I think about that day me and Mandy sat in the Holiday Inn reception. I think about taking Mandy for a walk on the beach and sharing out the last of our Wotsits. I think about Mandy's pink puffer and

217

the white trainers mum bought her. I think about the peanut butter sandwich and the Twix mum put into her Princess Picky lunchbox. I think about mum strapping her into the booster seat in the back of Caroline's car.

And I think about me.

I should say—I do know there's something wrong with me. I don't understand why people do most of the things they do. I don't know why they want to drink alcohol, or watch football games, or have a job, or be part of a country. I don't know why they want to have sex, and that seems like the biggest part of a lot of people's lives.

And I don't know what's going to happen to me now.

It must be hard to understand what it feels like, if you've never been in this position. If you've never been outside and alone, looking through windows at everybody else. It's like walking backwards into the sea, watching the land as it recedes and trying to stay afloat for as long as you can, because despite everything, you can't rid yourself of the hope that one day, you might reach another shore.

Hywel's phone buzzed. His first impulse was to reject the call, but he took a deep breath, looked at the ceiling, held the phone sternly to his ear. 'Hi, Gerald,' he said coldly. 'What can I do for you?'

He heard Stanton's voice, evidently talking to someone else. Then: 'Hywel? Sorry, amigo, just assumed you wouldn't answer. Listen, quick call: d'you know what year Marilyn Monroe died?'

'Marilyn Monroe? Not really. Sometime in the fifties, wasn't it? Why?'

'Some time in the fifties? Are you accusing the thirty-fifth

218

president of the United States of being a corpse rapist?'

'Oh, well the sixties then. I don't think you can rape a corpse, can you?'

'Course you can. Can't give informed consent, can they?'

'No, but they don't they have legal rights.'

'Yes they do. Necrophilia's a crime, isn't it? They have the right to rest in peace, don't they? You can't go around digging one up every time you fancy a spot of erotic desecration.'

'So—you called to discuss corpse raping, did you? Where are you anyway?'

'I'm at the Marquis, having a pint with Paul Moorhouse. They've asked me to go on that new corpse-raping show—sorry, that renaissance in BBC arts programming—that threatens to bring back the glory days of *Omnibus* and *Arena* and … whatever the other one was. Hence my interest. I'm on with Keith Sommerville. Remember him? Sweaty jowls? Christmas pullovers? Talks about the Byzantine Empire a lot? They've just given him *Front Row*.'

'Yes, of course I know who he his. He's my client. I negotiated his package.'

'Yes, well. Lucky him … Talking about digging up dead bodies, have you spoken to my wife recently?'

'No, I haven't. Jo went to the Coq d'Argent with her the other night.'

'Yeah, I know. Listen, mate, I just wanted to give you a heads-up. You might want to put in a bit more time with your trouble-and-strife. Fascinate her with gefilte fish, comfort her with chopped liver, whatever it is you two get up to behind closed doors.'

'Thanks, but you might not be the best person to offer relationship advice right now. Where are you living?'

'Good question. Where do unaccommodated men live? In my case, Regent's Park, in the daytime. In the evenings, I stay with some dear friends I made at the Brunswick Square car park. Yes, thanks, same again.'

'I heard Camden.'

'I'm flat-sitting in Mornington Crescent, if you must know. Rory's in California. More to the point, where are you right now?'

'I'm at Emma's flat.'

'No, you're not. You're at *your* flat. The one you rented to stash her in.'

'Come on, Gerald. Let's not start that again. Jesus. Not everything belongs to you, you know.'

'It doesn't belong to anyone. Love isn't possession. You can't *keep* it. It doesn't last. It's just moments. It's just moments and the memories of those moments and in the end, you lose both.'

'Okay, well, look, I didn't realise you were composing an ode. I better let you get back to it.'

There was a burst of laughter. 'I am, as a matter of fact. *Ode to an Idiot*. Want to hear how it goes?' There was the sound of a throat being cleared. 'Cunt-struck, I gazed at her mysterious face—'

Hywel spoke quickly, his voice tight with anger. 'How do you do it? How do you manage to be so completely shitty, all the time? Look, Gerald—I'm with Emma because I want to be with her, because, just now, today, this evening, this moment, she's the most important thing in my life.'

There was nothing but the susurrus of a Fitzrovia pub in reply. Hywel turned away from the window to find Emma standing in the doorway, looking at him. A voice spoke into his ear. 'Listen to me, mate, get out now. I mean it. Pull your panties on, grab your coat and run for your wife. You don't know that girl. Trust me, she's going to eat you alive … Hywel? Are you listening to me?'

But Hywel couldn't listen, because Emma had taken the phone from him, thrown it backhand across the room, and was kissing him with the kisses of her mouth.

6

They lay together in the overheated bedroom, in the exhausted armistice that follows a pyrrhic victory. She stared at the candle, flickering on the night table, while he pressed his nose to the back of her narrow skull, breathing there the cut-grass odour of her shampoo.

Bits and pieces of thought drifted through his mind and slipped away behind sheets and streets and alleys and fields and the miles of wheels that lie concealed by nets of grass and curls of glass and the seashores she wore with foamwound frames of smokebound names and games and homes and drones and crones and the bird-thin bones of microphones and—a stumbletwist at ice and salt and a panicked grasp at the edge of

'Hywel? You spazzing out?'

'Uh? No. Sorry. Falling asleep.'

She bucked him in the stomach. 'Hey, not allowed.'

A siren played bent music in the street below.

'What time is it?'

There was no reply.

He gripped her waist, pulled her to him, moved a little to feel the slick of sweat between their bodies, rolled over to savour the chill of evaporation.

'Why did you never tell him?' he asked, after a while.

She turned, rested her forearms on his chest, posed her face on the backs of her hands. She looked like the Sphinx. 'Tell who what?'

'Tell Gerald that you were Molly. That you are Molly.'

'I'm not Molly; I'm me.'

'He told me once you were stalking him.'

'I was stalking him,' she said, and her pupils, dilated in the candleshadow, grew greater yet.

Psychobiochemical mechanisms spurted various fluids from various tubes, and as Hywel's stomach grew hot with bile, his heart expanded with longing for this missing woman … who grew more distant the nearer he approached; who was never more absent than when he held her in his arms. Her elbows dug into his ribs. Everything about her was painful.

'I love you so—'

'Shhhhh.' She laid a chewed finger on his lips. 'When does Jocasta expect you back?'

'Don't know. Sometime.'

She continued to regard him, thoughtfully.

He cleared his throat. 'I was reading *Another Shore* when he called. That bit where Molly goes back to Caroline's after her mum takes the antidepressants. Was that real? Is that what she actually said?'

She twitched one side of her mouth in that smile that is also a shrug. 'Why did he call you?'

'He was drunk.'

'Drinking and dialling; he wants you back.'

'Really?'

'Yes, really … You think he's jealous, don't you?'

'I try not to think about him at all.'

'Yes, well he is. But he's not jealous of you, Hywel; he's jealous of me.'

'What do you mean?'

'How long have you two known each other?'

'Since freshers' week.'

'And it's never occurred to you—you're his only friend?'

'Why do you say that?'

'Because it's what he told me.'

'Has he been calling you, too?'

She rolled away, gathered up tobacco and papers. She lit her cigarette on the candle and smoked for a while, staring at the ceiling. 'He never called me. Not once.' She held the smoke in her open mouth, sucked it back, released it in a grey plume. 'You remember the night we went to that jazz club? I lay in bed the whole of the next day with the phone in my hand, staring at it …'

'What am I supposed to do with that?'

'Sorry.'

He turned his head away. Rain began to tap at the un-curtained window. After a minute or so he turned back. 'I remember why he called,' he said. 'He's on television; that BBC thing about twentieth-century writers.'

'Is he? Do you want to watch?' Without waiting for an answer, she took the laptop from the night table, put it on her stomach, began tapping keys.

Hywel closed his eyes and tried to think about what was happening to him. He thought about Jocasta. He tried to bring her face into focus, recall some moment of connection they'd shared. He thought about the baby squirming inside her, the sensation of it moving against his back in the early morning.

He thought about what their friends and family would say, if it all came out. He thought about losing his home, his work, his reputation. Meh. It all felt a bit unreal. Then he thought about the way his life had somehow shrunk so small that it could be encompassed by this strange, dark dream. That seemed closer to the money.

He heard voices and opened his eyes to see a close-up of Stanton's pallid, sweating face on the screen of the laptop. He pushed himself up into a sitting position, put an arm around Emma's waist, hazarded the cupping of a breast, leaned forward. 'Jesus Christ,' he said. 'How did they let him out of make-up looking like that?'

The face spoke through tinny speakers: '—remarkable that she found the time to do the damage she did to the English novel, not to mention successive generations of British schoolchildren forced to read her maunderings at the point of a UCAS bayonet.'

The screen cut to a shot of Will Gompertz, the BBC's arts editor. 'Keith: it's true that Virginia Woolf has become a mainstay of the A-level curriculum. Some would say to the detriment of more recent voices who better reflect the more complex and cosmopolitan society we live in today. What do you say to that?'

'Yes, well I think that's true to a point, Will, but I also think that it is precisely because society has become more diverse, and in a way more incoherent, that it needs the firm cultural grounding, and to do that we need to explain what that ground is. That's really, I think, a big part of the contribution Virginia Woolf, and if I may make so bold, the BBC can make to—'

'Yeah, sorry, if I could just interject an objection—I think the most valuable contribution the BBC could make to defining

British identity would be to recognise the futility of the project.'

'If you hate the BBC so much, Gerald, why do you make programmes for it?'

'I don't *hate* it. I'm just willing to acknowledge that its primary purpose is the restriction of independent thought. That's its raison d'être—'

Will Gompertz cut in: 'That's quite an extreme position, isn't it, Gerald? How can you justify that?'

'Well, what I'm trying to describe to you is an extremist organisation.'

Incredulous laughter from the audience.

'Oh, god. It's a meltdown,' Hywel said. 'I can't watch.'

Emma could. Her eyes were like saucers, and she'd stopped blinking. Stanton, in tight close-up, was blinking a lot.

'I'm perfectly serious. Its purpose was and is ideological indoctrination. That role was more or less explicit right from the founding charter, right from Reith's educate and inform dicta. As soon as you make those verbs *transitive*, as soon as you ask what we're to be educated and informed *about*, the penny ought to drop. It's an organisation dedicated to instilling deference and servility, and a kind of herd immunity to critical inquiry.'

'Keith, do you want to come in there?'

'Yeah, okay, as far as I can comprehend what Gerald's point might be, I can't accept it. I know, you'd expect me to say that, but the fact is that the BBC strives to understand and respond to the views of its audience; that ethos absolutely saturates the whole organisation, from the DG right down to the people serving your coffee in the canteen. I think what you're really saying is, "I don't like that ethos", and of course you're entitled to your opinion, Gerald, even though most people would say

225

you're wrong, but I don't think—'

'Yes, Keith, but it's patently obvious that you don't respond to the views of the audience for the simple reason you've got no fucking clue what they might be. You're not interested. You tell them what their views are and then you report it back to them. The whole thing's circular. It's based on the fiction that there exists a single normative opinion held by a single entity called "the British public", which, I should add, is itself a way of limiting and controlling the parameters of debate. If you can't be honest enough—'

'I can't accept that. We're a public service broadcaster, and that's—'

'Or, put another way, a self-selected, self-serving oligarchy of talentless bureaucrats with your tongues so far up the culture secretary's arsehole you can taste her lunch before she does—'

'Come off it. Really. I'd've expected a bit more originality from you.'

'You've just proved my point.'

'As naught to what you've just proved, chum.'

'Oh, do fuck off, Keith.'

'Okay, thanks, guys, I think I'm going to have to wrap there. Well, if nothing else, I think we've shown why we're right to be afraid of Virginia Woolf. Next Friday—'

'If this is your pitch for another series, Gerald, I've got to tell you, mate, I'm refreshed by the originality of your approach.'

'It's more a declaration that I'm never making another.'

'Sorry, guys—you mind just letting me finish this bit?'

'By the way, well done for keeping Azhar out of the papers.'

'Thanks. Be sure and ask your solicitor to give my love to Vickie.'

'At least I didn't make her sign an NDA.'

'Yeah, you might regret that.'

Hywel watched, aghast, as Stanton muttered something he didn't catch, hauled himself upright and careered obliquely across the shot. Shortly after there came a loud crash and the camera panned to show the remains of a lighting rig on the floor.

Emma closed the laptop, got out of bed.

'Where are you going?'

'To have a piss,' she replied. 'Then I'm going open the champagne.'

7

Stanton strode down Little Portland Street in a state of fierce exultation. It was pissing it down, and he'd left his coat in the greenroom, but what of it? If he stripped naked and whipped himself with electrical flex, he imagined it would feel pretty good right now. At the Marquis, he breasted the closing time crush, two lagers held aloft. He handed one to Paul Moorhouse, who was smoking a Marlboro Red under cover of a Credit Suisse golfing umbrella.

'Cheers, Ger.' Paul flicked his fag into the road, accepted the pint, took a gulp. 'You had an interesting night, I see.'

'It's not over yet,' Stanton replied, downing half his in four swallows. 'Watch it?'

'Saw a clip on me phone. You're trending, mate: hashtag dofuckoffkeith. What was it all about?'

'Oh, you know, just trying my hand at social commentary.'

Paul raised his glass in salute. 'Well, you done that. Made television history by the sounds.' He took another drink. 'That's you finished at the Beeb, then. You got better offers? Netflix series in the works or summink?'

'What are they saying?'

'Quite a few things, actually. You'll be hearing from your agent about it, no doubt.'

'Hywel? Nah, we've parted ways.'

'Oh, really? Sorry to hear it. What d'you two fall out over?'

Stanton sighed. 'Long story.'

'Oh, well, tell me next time.' Paul finished his pint and set it on the windowsill. 'I got a rush job. You remember Barry the Cunt? Property geezer, done them conversions in Burnt Oak? Wears a homburg? He's got an orgy on at the Dorchester and they're running short.'

'Coke or Viagra?'

'Six of one, half-a-dozen of the other.'

'Right. Actually, Paul, I was going to ask you for five.'

'Jesus, Ger. I done you five last Friday.'

'Yeah, I know, I know. Busy week.'

'You should slow down a bit. Not good for the mentals, that rate of progress.'

'It's not for me; it's for my mum.'

'Oh, really?'

'It's her birthday tomorrow. I get her a cardigan usually, but as it's her seventieth I thought I'd try something a bit different.'

'I see. Well, I can do you three, but it'll have to be cash up front. And I can't give you a receipt, neither. Case she decides she'd rather have the cardigan.'

'Right … okay. I can give you fifty now. All I've got on me. I'm expecting a postal order.'

'Yeah, yeah, I believe you. Alright, motherfucka, but I'm going to need payment in full next time. Too much to keep track of. Mind how you go, yeah?'

Stanton suspected he'd gone too far when he began experiencing accelerating Mandelbrot zooms into the transdimensional abyss that had opened up behind his eyelids. Opening them, he found that the German sociologist, whom he'd assumed to be a figment of his imagination, was quite real, and still talking about Foucault. There was a martini on the LED-lit glass counter of whateverthefuck bar he was now in. Beside it, the screen of his mobile buzzed and lit up with antibritish broadcasting company ramming marxist propaganda down everyones throats to erase our culture and

'If we stay with the subject of *Discipline and Punish*, I recently co-authored a paper for the Max-Planck Gesellschaft on the very subject that you have explored in your novel, Cherald,' the German sociologist continued.

Bzzt. Strutting around like some latterday Voltaire instead of the cheap, pseudo intellectual hustler he is

'We are seeing already the cultural interpenetration of prison and street and already a blurring in the underlying relationships between the state as supporter and the state as regulator of civil society, so your mischievous dystopian fable is already not as far-fetched as you might have wished. In the field of *Sozialarbeit*, in particular, there is already a—'

Stanton looked at his hands. Was he wearing nail polish? Was that a *severed finger* in his martini?

Bzzt. He da MAAAAN. GA Stanton 10, state-employed propaganda unit 0

Bzzt. No fees! Microsoft, Amazon, Uber, Google. Invest in the world's largest companies and watch your

He closed his eyes again.

Like a circle in a spiral, like a wheel within a wheel, fractal involutions congregating in a creel, like a Spirographic mongoose on a date with David Icke, up the rectum of the rechtung with an echtung on a trike, like the nonsense that you vomit from your amputated face, like the pornotropic vectors of a magnified disgrace

Bzzt. Absolute state of him. Coked up to the gills

Bzzt. It is cold and wet so am going to make butternut squash soup with sage butter

Bzzt. Vanitas vanitatum omnia vanitas, innit

'Cherald? Are you feeling okay, old chap …? You have not spoken for a long time now.'

Stanton knew for sure he'd gone too far when Carmen Miranda broke his nose in the doorway of Randall & Aubin while a homeless man in a Santa hat played the intro to *Layla* on a kazoo. The homeless man was some species of dwarf. Ms Miranda was seven-feet tall, with an erect plume of gorgeous green feathers, a prominent Adam's apple, intercontinental ballistic breasts and a right hook that could, as it turned out, stun an amorous water buffalo. His face was wet with blood and rain and he didn't feel a thing until he felt the agenbite of wristrings courtesy of a young woman in a high-vis tabard who avoided his reproachful gaze while talking to her lapel radio about the whereabouts of Unit 46. He passed the time waiting for the removal van by sitting on the wet pavement and shouting vile sexual suggestions at a group of Chinese tourists who'd gathered round to view this splendid example of Hogarthian London street life.

Then: lurching, over toppling, falling nose-first from seat to corrugated steel. Convulsive spewing of the night's cocktail choices accompanied by a bucket of chunks in hot, creamy lager.

Then: the drunk tank induction. Asking the custody sergeant for a happy meal. Mouth swab, digital finger prints, belt and tie; cell. Blanketless, plastic mattress; seatless aluminium toilet. Signs on the ceiling (Tired of always feeling tired? Swap your dealer for ££££).

At four am, a doctor entered his cell and checked his blood-pressure. When she'd gone, he lay on his moulded bed and folded his arms against the chill. Little by little, he fell into a shallow doze and was tormented by a vision of Hywel as a cherubic, curly-haired, rosy-cheeked toddler, running blind as Cupid across cropped grass in confident expectation of a paternal lift-up-and-twirl-round while he ran after in jerky POV, sobbing with anguish, shouting into the anechoic void as the cliff edge grew nearer …

The eight am shift change brought an eye in the door and a hearty breakfast. This frosty winter morn, the carte de jour consisted of abattoir drain blockage in natural casings, snot-strings of egg in a tinned tomato jus and a corner of charred toast, all washed down with translucent half-a-teaspoon Nescafé, served chilled in a cylinder of Styrofoam.

'This interview is being recorded. I am DS Belfiore and with me is DC Dodds. The time is 11.29, 23rd December. Could you please state your full name?'

'Gerald Antony Stanton.'

'Thank you. And where are you living at present, Gerald?'

'No fixed abode.'

'Do you want a solicitor present?'

'No.'

'That's a no.'

'Yes.'

'You're waiving your right to a solicitor.'

'Yes.'

'So, if we understand you correctly, no solicitor. Okay, Gerald we've got a few things we'd like to ask you about what happened last night. The first thing we'd like to know a bit more about is what went on between you and Regina Surprise outside Madame Jo Jo's nightclub.'

'I have no idea what you're talking about.'

'Ms Surprise has made a statement alleging you bit her on the breast.'

'Did she?'

'That's what she says.'

'Well then, I don't really remember doing that … but if I did, I think it might have been something to do with nuclear disarmament.'

'Nuclear disarmament?'

'Yes.'

'So, you did do it?'

'No, I didn't. But if I had, that would have been why.'

'I think he's applying the subjunctive mood, sarge.'

'I see. The other thing we wanted to bring up is the cocaine we found in your wallet. Anything to say about how that got there?'

'No.'

'You knew it was there?'

'I had no idea.'

'So, you're telling us it wasn't your cocaine?'

'We should just let you, before you answer, the mouth swab did test positive for cocaine.'

'My drink must have been spiked.'

'Someone spiked your drink with cocaine? Was that before or after they slipped it into your wallet without your knowledge?'

'Could have been either.'

'Definitely don't want a solicitor?'

'No.'

'Thing is, Gerald, cocaine is a class A drug, and unlike some nicks I could mention—Lewisham springs to mind—we don't let you off with a caution. Not for three grams.'

'According to the latest Sentencing Council guidelines, the starting point for setting the tariff is eighteen months. Added to which we have to consider a charge of aggravated sexual assault occasioning actual bodily harm, and that could be quite a bit more.'

'I had every right to be aggravated.'

'The thing is, Gerald, the DPP might decide to class it as a hate crime. And it would also mean you'd be put on the Sex Offenders List ...'

'Gerald? Any response?'

'Take your time.'

'I want to see a solicitor.'

'Yeah, we thought you might.'

233

8

It was that time of the day known to the extra-national min-imum-wage service staff of the Queen's as 'the armpit'. This was the period after their lunchtime clientele had gone home for sofa siestas in front of *Homes under the Hammer* and *The Millionaires' Holiday Club*, and they could take a breath before setting up for the evening. As a result, the bar's bright and bustling marketplace atmosphere had tarnished to a rail-way station waiting room, filled with day-long drinkers, each awaiting a train that would never come, or had long since departed. At least, that's how it seemed to Hywel Robertson as he sat on his Chesterfield, a bottle of wine and two empty glasses before him, listening to Otis Redding singing *Dock of the Bay* and reading from his iPad, but breaking off every two minutes to check his phone, or else chew the inside of his mouth and stare vacantly through the transom at the grey sky above Broadway Parade.

He waved at Vickie as she made her entrance, bang on four, shaking water out of an umbrella and unzipping her German army parka. She came over, bent to kiss him on the cheek, unshouldered her backpack.

'Hello, stranger,' she said. 'Like the new look.'

'Oh, you mean the beard?'

'Yes. You look very grown up.'

'That's a backhand compliment if ever I heard one. You look exactly the same as you did at university.'

'You mean I still dress like a student?'

'You're the only person I know who wears mittens. Chianti?'

234

'Oh, go on then ... Haven't had a drink all week.'

He poured, she lifted the glass by the stem and gave it a bit of a swirl.

'Been somewhere?' he asked, nodding at her rucksack.

'Staying at my mum's,' she replied, and talked for a while about life in rural Hampshire—a monologue that drifted by degrees into her experience of dwelling alone in the Stantons' five-bed semi.

'Actually, I'm in the same position,' Hywel put in.

'How come?'

'Jo's decided she wants Jocelyn to have French citizenship, so she's moved in with her father until she arrives.'

'Oh, right.' Vickie wrinkled her nose and seemed a little taken aback. 'Makes sense, I suppose. But you'll be there for the big event, won't you, Huey?'

'Of course. I'm going down next week, probably. Eurostar to Paris, TGV to Lyon; set off at breakfast, you can be there for *l'heure de l'aparo.*'

'Let's hope she's punctual. Will be, knowing Jo. So, you're enjoying your last days of freedom?'

'Yeah.' Hywel paused to sip his wine, then went on: 'Talking about last days of freedom, I was wondering if you were planning on going to *Regina v Stanton.*'

Vickie shook her head. 'Haven't decided. Are you?'

'I suppose so. Old times' sake and all that.'

'Have you been keeping in touch?'

'Not really, but I ran into Paul Moorhouse the other day; he's been seeing him, off and on.'

'That doesn't surprise me. So, what's the story?'

'Apparently, he's now looking a bit like that guy.' Hywel nodded towards the picture of Jim Morrison on Vickie's T-shirt.

235

'In his later years.'

'You mean, what? Size of a bear? Ankle-length beard? Bottle of bourbon a day?'

'Not sure he can afford a whole bottle.'

'Oh, I see.'

'Yeah.'

Vickie sighed, hooked her hair. 'I'm sorry, Huey, I'm not going to do this.'

'Do what?'

'Get sucked in again. It's like, you know, those people who escape from a cult. You go through this period where you have to resocialise. I'm just starting to get my brain back … Isn't it the same for you?'

'Well, I was just his agent.'

'You were a bit more than that … What else did Paul say?'

'He said he was comparing himself with Alexander Solzhenitsyn.'

'What? Why?'

'He thinks they're going to send him to the gulag for crimes against Englishness. Paul said he was a bit … agitated. I mean, I don't think they will, will they? I can't see that drag act making too much of a fuss, given that she was the one who decked him.'

Vickie nodded, laughed, coughed.

'And as for the marching powder—the amount he had on him—he's not exactly El Chapo, is he?'

'I suppose so. In any case, well-educated white objects like him don't go to prison, do they? All those books? All those TV series? Honorary doctorate from the University of the West of England?'

'Unless the powers-that-be decide to make an example of him.'

236

Vickie shook her head, looked away. Hywel frowned. 'What did you mean when said I was more than an agent?'

She turned back. 'Come on, Huey, you know Gerald. You know what he's incapable of. He'd never have got anywhere without you.'

'Or you.' He refilled her glass. 'Now he hasn't got either of us.'

'I hope you're not trying to guilt-trip me, Mr Robertson.'

'Not at all. Honest.' He held up his hands, palms extended. 'I wasn't even going to bring him up.'

'And yet you did.'

'I did, didn't I? But I did want to ask you about something *concerning* him. Or rather, concerning a manuscript that we've received.' Hywel picked up his glass and took a sip, set it down in the exact centre of his beer mat and rotated it forty-five degrees. 'It's a sort of novel, written from the point of view of Molly—you know, from *Another Shore.*'

'Oh, really? Can you do that? Wouldn't it be infringement of copyright or whatever?'

'Yeah, you're right, it would be. Normally.'

'But?'

'Well, it's a bit of a funny one. The woman who wrote the manuscript says she was the person Molly was based on. She's saying that, in a way, she *is* Molly. So, you could argue that it was Gerald who infringed her. She could argue that she's just putting her side of the story. Moral rights cutting both ways and all that.'

Vickie paused with her glass half way to her mouth, put it down again. 'What's she called, this author of yours?'

'Emma Butler.'

Vickie's forehead corrugated and her thin, sweet face turned a whiter shade of pale.

'And she's sent it to you?'

'Yes. Haven't accepted it, though,' Hywel replied, with the unselfconscious grace of a man tiptoeing through a minefield. 'I need to figure out the implications first. The thing is, or one of the things is, that there's a character who is, or who resembles, the character of Caroline. And Caroline rather resembles … well, if I'm being honest, she rather resembles you.'

'Sorry, I'm not quite sure what you're saying. What are you asking me, exactly?'

'I'm just wanted to warn you. Before it comes out. There could be a lot of interest in the book, potentially.'

'Oh, I see.'

'No, don't get the wrong idea—that's not really the …'

'What else is it?'

'Well, the story as she tells it is a bit different from how it comes across in *Another Shore*. I mean, the events are basically the same, but she doesn't drown at the end, obviously, and in her version … there's a role for a character who resembles Gerald.'

'What kind of role?'

'Quite an important one. In a way, he's really what the book's about.'

'Oh my god. I'm starting to feel as though I need a lawyer present.'

'No, no, really. Sorry, Vickie. I didn't mean to freak you out.' He noticed they were both sitting in stress positions, and he sat back and forced a laugh. 'I'm just trying to understand what I'm dealing with. Obviously, if I don't take it, she'll just go to someone else. I can't bury it, or whatever.'

Vickie did not relax her hunch. 'Do you think that's a good

argument?'

'How do you mean?'

'If I don't shoot you, someone else will, so, why not? You still get the bullet, but this way, at least I get the money.'

'Who's talking about shooting anyone? If I could just back-track, I don't even know if *Another Shore* was based on anything that actually happened. We're just talking, as they say.'

Vickie poured herself another glass. Hywel thought: *She is Caroline. Definitely Caroline.* It was funny how he'd never quite seen it before.

'Why did this author send you the story?' she asked at last. 'I'd have thought you'd be the last agent in London who'd be willing to take on something like this.'

He shrugged. 'No idea.'

'Have you met her? Face to face?'

'Oh, yeah,' he said, carelessly. 'I have, as a matter of fact.'

'What does she look like?'

'You know, nothing special. Medium height, auburn hair, thin.'

'When did you meet her, Huey? Did she come to your office, or did you take her out for a three-bottle lunch?'

'What does it matter?'

'I don't know if it does. I'm just trying to work out what's going on here. I mean, there's *something* going on, isn't there?'

Hywel looked puzzled. 'I'm sorry, I don't quite …'

'I thought we were all friends, but you and Gerald have a massive falling out and nobody seems to know quite why, then you drop off the radar for six months, Gerald sets fire to himself on live television and turns into the bastard love child of Jim Morrison and Alexander Solzhenitsyn, Jocasta takes herself off to France without so much as a text, everyone grows a beard and suddenly there's this thin, medium-sized, auburn-haired author in the picture. You can't blame me for wondering if there might be some connections, can you?'

'Right, yes, I see … Look, Vickie … I was hoping we might have, you know, a bit of a truth and reconciliation session.'

Vickie waited for him to go on.

'It's just that things might get quite sticky.'

'Why? Because of this book? This book that *you're* handling?'

'I haven't done anything, have I?'

She hooked her hair. 'Haven't you?'

'I'm sorry; I'm sorry. I realise I'm rather dumping all this on you. It's just, well, who knows what might happen? … If the press gets hold of it …'

'Get hold of what?'

'Well,' he said, 'you know—in the present climate. Could be a bit sticky.'

Vickie shook her head, at a loss, evidently, for words.

'These ones free, yeah?'

Hywel looked up to find an encumbered couple hovering by the table. The man had two pints in his hands, the woman was pushing a stroller and holding a baby, rugby-style, in the crook of her arm. 'Sure, help yourself,' he muttered, and turned back to find Vickie still staring at him.

'Look, it's probably easiest if you just read what she wrote. I've got it in my briefcase.'

'You've brought the manuscript?'

'I thought you might want to look at it, so you know what I'm talking about. Should we go back to your place, perhaps?'

9

The streetlights came on as they walked back, side-by-side, in step and in silence, Vickie staring at the pavement but walking through the puddles, Hywel gazing into the empty park and shivering in the raw March wind. It was a cold house, too. Underwear on the hall radiator, dust and crumbs on the living room rug, books and bowls crowding the coffee table, a paisley duvet crumpled across the Stantons' red velvet sofa. He took up a fire shovel, crouched at the grate, poked it clear of ash and clinker, filled it with crumpled newspaper, added wood and coal, lit it and, for a moment, lost himself in the flicker and crackle.

Vickie came in with a tray of tea things. Hywel stacked the bowls, all of which seemed to have been used for cornflakes. They lingered at the kindling fire.

'You don't have a fag, do you, Huey?'

He reached into his coat pocket, tore the cellophane off a fresh pack, lit one for her.

She took a drag, pulled a face, coughed, threw it into the fire, flopped on the sofa and pulled the duvet around her. He poured the tea, added milk, sugared his own. She took hers, blew on it, stared at it. 'I'll give you the truth,' she said, 'but I wouldn't get your hopes up about the reconciliation bit.'

'Like I said, I just need a basic account. I'm really in the dark here.'

She sighed. 'Well, so, yes … it's true that the book was based on one of my cases. It was my first case, actually. Look Huey, it's a long story, but I was asked to write an account of what happened, for legal reasons. Gerald read that account and used it as the basis for *Another Shore*.

Hywel grinned, incredulously. 'Are you saying you wrote

it? *You* wrote *Another Shore*?'

'No.' She sighed, hooked her hair. 'Not really. Not the Norfolk bits, anyway.'

Hywel's turn to stare.

'It was a horrible case. Not just the abuse—I mean, that was bad enough; there were other things going on—in the department, the council, the diocese … I got too involved.'

'Like Caroline does.'

'Yes. In the end, when she'd become a problem for everyone, they finally found her a residential place. I think it was called Burnham Ovary College—'

'That's Waxham Pava, in the book?'

She nodded. 'After that, the file was handed over to Norfolk social services. I don't know what happened next. I didn't want to know, by that point.'

'So, Gerald wrote the Norfolk part?'

'Yes. Huey, you have to understand—that case was painful for me. The last thing I wanted was to get involved in writing a book about it. I didn't think it was a good idea at the time, and I always felt guilty about it after—but he was getting nowhere with what he doing. Two years working on that *Carceral* novel and he just wakes up one morning and deletes the whole file. You remember what it was like, don't you? You remember how we were living?'

Hywel nodded.

'What was she like when you knew her?'

'Emma? She was a strange girl. Nobody could really get close to her. That's why Molly's the way she is in the book—but it was just a guess, you know? I never really knew her. I mean, I never knew what she was thinking. She was … well, she was pretty cold blooded, if I'm being honest. Maybe that's how she

242

survived. Look, this is off the record, isn't it?'

'Of course.'

'What happens in Muswell Hill stays in Muswell Hill?'

'Absolutely.'

'Alright. So, can I ask you a question?'

'Yes, go ahead.'

'Are you sleeping with her?'

Hywel turned away from the fire, his face a mask of incredulity. 'What? No, of course not.'

She hooked her hair behind her ears. 'That's not what your wife thinks.'

'She thinks I'm sleeping with my client?'

'Not her particularly. But somebody. She thinks you're being unfaithful to her with somebody.'

He shook his head.

'Huey … truth and reconciliation, remember? Cuts both ways, my love.'

He peered at her face, blending, now, into the gloom. 'My relationship with Emma isn't really relevant. None of this is about me, is it?'

Vickie gave an unexpected chuckle. 'Huey, it's okay. I've spent the past ten years discovering all the the ways people find to go off the rails. Why should you be any different?'

'I'm not.'

'Yeah. Me neither.'

Hywel turned back to the fire, Vickie held the cupped mug to her face.

'Do you think I did the right thing?' she asked at last.

'The right thing about what?'

'Kicking him out.'

'I don't know. You can always let him back in, I suppose.'

'As if that would solve anything. But what about you? Why did you fall out with him? Jo said it was something to do with that *Sunday Telegraph* interview, but I don't think she believed it. Gerald told me you were the one that dumped him.'

'I fired *him?*'

'Yes. But he wouldn't tell me why.'

Hywel's turn to sigh. 'I don't know. It was … it's difficult to say, sometimes, why we do what we do, and afterwards everything's different and you can't quite understand yourself, what you were thinking. All the things that seemed so compelling and obvious … but afterwards you know you can't ever go back. It's all a bit … Humpty Dumpty … and you just have to deal with where you are …' He stuttered to a halt. 'I'm sorry, Vic, I'm not making much sense, am I?'

Vickie patted the sofa. 'Come and sit here.'

Hywel did as he was bid. She put her mug on the floor, shared her duvet, leaned her head on his shoulder.

'I'm glad you're here, Huey,' she said, and put her arms around him.

'Me too.' He looked at the line of white scalp that marked the parting of her hair.

'I wasn't looking forward to coming back today.'

'Yeah.'

The wind threw a handful of rain against the big bay window, and a billow of orange smoke blew from the grate.

'You know, there's a guy in the office …'

'There's a guy in every office.'

'Yes, well mine keeps offering to take me out for dinner so we can talk about our problems. He's married, of course.'

'They always are.'

Hywel put an arm around her shoulder, pulled her closer.

Little by little, his body relaxed in the warmth of hers.

'I met his wife once, at a charity do. She seemed nice. Very keen on snowboarding. And sometimes I think there's no way I'd ever, and sometimes I think, oh, what the hell—why do I always have to be the one who tries to kiss it all better. Why can't I break some bones for a change?'

Not knowing what to say to this, he said nothing.

'Did you fall out over this author of yours, Huey?'

'How do you mean?'

'You don't have to say if you don't want, but I have to tell you how it looks. I mean, you must know how it looks.' She raised her head. 'Don't you?'

Her eyeballs gleamed but he couldn't read the expression on her face. 'I suppose so,' he said, and with a sudden sense of stumble and lurch, of falling sideways into the void, he added, 'I'm in love with her.'

A heartbeat, and then: 'Oh, Huey … you're not …'

At once he felt obliterated by sorrow, and beneath, a rat bite of pain at the base of his throat. 'Yes, I am, I'm afraid. I wish I weren't …' He tried to force a laugh, but it came out as a sob. 'It's a bit inconvenient.'

'You *idiot.*'

'Yeah, I know. I know. Jocasta's asked for a divorce.' He exhaled. 'There: I said it.'

Vickie stared. 'She found out? How did she find out?'

'I told her. I had to tell her. I couldn't just … I just couldn't bear it any more.'

'You've abandoned your pregnant wife?' She pulled away from him, taking the duvet with her. 'Oh, well done, Huey— that's very classy.'

Hywel shivered, gripped his knees, bowed his head. Why,

245

he wondered, couldn't he play this scene better? Why couldn't he rise to tragic sorrow? A great soul overborn by passion? Stanton would shake the windows with his roars of anguish and rage; all he could manage was this self-pitying whine. 'I feel like I was in a car accident,' he went on. 'I didn't want it. I didn't want any of it. It just happened to me. I couldn't help myself.'

'Come on, Huey. That's a cop out and you know it. But I can't believe you would *do* something like that … You're the last person in the world who'd do something like that.'

He nodded. His chest heaved, convulsively. 'I know. I'm too boring, aren't I?'

'And Gerald—did he—?'

He took a gasp of air. 'No, not at all. Not at all. He was happy to see her go.'

A beat, and then: 'Oh, right. I was going to ask you if he gave you any support. But he was fucking her too, was he?'

'Vickie … I'm sorry, I'm sorry. It wasn't like that. We weren't … you know …'

'You weren't what?' Her voice rose to a shout. 'You weren't getting her drunk and roasting her in hotel rooms? Oh, good for you. Well done, Huey. What a splendid chap you are. No, I mean it, really.'

Hywel cringed. 'The worst thing is, she doesn't even like me. She doesn't bother to hide it anymore.'

'She's just using you. Can't you *see* that? Fucking Nora. I could kick you, you stupid man. I mean, I married a dog with two dicks, so it's not like I'm a honking great authority on relationships, but at least we had some good times on the way. I don't know what to say to you now, I really don't.'

She rose, threw aside the duvet, pulled the half-closed

246

curtains to, turned up the dimmer on a standing lamp.

'Vickie … you have to—'

'Please, Hywel. If you say one more word, I'm going to throw something at you. And it'll be your fault because I just won't be able to help myself.'

She took up the stacked bowls, and for a moment he wondered if she were about to make good on her threat. Instead, she marched to the door, opened it, and turned back. 'But I still don't get it. If he was happy to be rid of her, what *did* you two fall out over?'

'She hates him. She really, really hates him … I couldn't have stayed as his agent, not if I were going to handle the book.'

She stared, breathing heavily. 'And what does she say about him? In her book? Does he fuck her in that, too?'

Hywel addressed himself to the carpet. 'They have a relationship, but she's the one who initiates it, really. It's actually quite … quite moving …'

'Jesus. And this is really going to be published? You know it'll destroy him, don't you?'

Hywel nodded, but at once his fists clenched, his face reddened, and he turned to look at her with a defiant light in his eye. 'Yes, it's going to be published. I want to help her to tell her story. *Her* story. Doesn't she deserve it? I think she deserves more than your guesses about what she went through. Don't we owe her that much at least? You of all people should understand that. I wanted to help her. It's what everyone thinks about Molly when they read that book—if only *I'd* been there, I would have saved her. I would have been kind to her, made her happy. You couldn't. Your council couldn't. Gerald couldn't. I thought I could.'

Just for a second, Hywel thought his speech had somehow

got through to her—moved her to reconsider the situation and reassess her reactions to it. But it was just for a second.

'Spare me,' she said, and stalked out of the room. A moment later, he heard the sound of crockery being maltreated in the kitchen.

Hywel pulled the duvet round himself and laid his head on the back of the sofa, closed his eyes. A period of introspection then ensued. *Disaster, once it has befallen us, can bring a strange tranquillity in its wake*, he thought. He was like a man who's fallen from a third-floor window and, not having quite grasped the implications, lies on the ground wondering what kind of take-away to order that evening.

One thing was certain: Vickie would never see him the same way again. Their long, close friendship would not survive this day. The persona he'd crafted over two decades—of unassuming, trustworthy, level-headed integrity—would not survive either. He would appear, in her eyes, from here to eternity, as a weak and contemptible man.

And this was terribly unfair.

It was unfair because in his heart of hearts all he'd ever wanted was to lead a quiet, decent, productive life. To play the game in a spirit of patient acquisition. What was wrong with that? Although not particularly creative, he had a gift for marketing the creativity of others, and in this way he'd enriched his culture, his clients and himself. Not that he was what you'd call a martyr. His days had brimmed with small yet satisfying pleasures—squash ladders and dinner parties, wine clubs and organic farm deliveries, canals to chug down, beaches to lie on … And that had always been enough. More than enough. He'd done his pondering in car showrooms, contemplated his self in the mirrors of menswear departments, dreamed reasonable dreams, realisable through commercial channels. And by living his life in this way, he'd always assumed that he would, in the ordinary drift of days, accrue those things that gave that life its deeper meanings. He would fall in love and get married; children would be born and raised with affection and understanding; houses would be bought and would turn into homes. The world of teem and struggle, the poverty and confusion of those around him, the tawdry, debased history he was living through—these were things to read of in newspapers then ironise over in restaurants. Was that not, when all was said and done, what being his kind of Englishman was all about?

10

Jimmy Cliff was playing on the PA. Hywel Robertson sat alone on the worn pub Chesterfield, like a bird without a song. He'd arranged a fat pinch of Golden Virginia in a paper, now he distributed it evenly and rolled, taking care not to over-compact the tobacco. He dried his tongue a little on his lips and ran it along the slick strip of gum before stroking down the seal with a forefinger. He patting his pockets for an old business card; finding none, he settled for the lug of his Rizla packet. This was, of course, bad practice, since there was now a very real danger that the papers would come loose, andwould end up being stuck into a continuous sheet, and so be ruined beyond repair. Couldn't be helped. Nothing stays the same. He paused to take a sip of Guinness, then rolled the fragment of glazed cardboard into a cylinder and poked it carefully into the end of his cigarette; the other he twisted to hinder the escape of shreds. His work complete, he tucked the finished article behind an ear, noting as he did, that his hair had grown rather long. Should really get a trim at some point.

'Evening, cock. This chair taken?'

Hywel looked up to find Gerald Stanton standing over him. For a moment he froze, blinking and staring, as though trying to place the face.

'What are you doing here?' he asked at last.

'Straight in with the existential conundrums, I see. Normally, I like a bit of philosophical foreplay, get the juices flowing, but we can do it your way if you want.' Stanton unshouldered his rucksack, removed his overcoat and took what Hywel still thought of as *her* chair. 'So, anyway, I was ejaculated into the world in a bedroom in Shropshire in the summer of eighty-one, my father being particularly fired up by England's success in that summer's Headingley test match. It was the fact that he took a lengthy run up prior to initiating operations that I attribute my natural vigour—'

'Please, Gerald. Can you just … for once?'

The former writer and broadcaster looked at him curiously. 'You alright? You look like a schizophrenic at a Halloween party.'

'I'm fine. How are you?' Hywel replied, and wondered if he were about to be assaulted.

Stanton smiled, revealing gaps in his upper teeth. 'Look, there's been a bit of a hiatus, I know, but I'm pretty sure it's your round. I'll have a pint of the black. Get one for yourself, if you like.'

Hywel nodded and rose, keeping his eyes on Stanton as he did so. He walked to the bar and ordered. While the drinks were pouring and settling, he pulled anxiously on his beard and cast wary glances over his shoulder. Stanton had taken a newspaper out of his rucksack and was reading it. He carried the drinks over.

'Look, Gerald—about the book …'

Stanton looked up. 'Book? What book?' he asked, innocently. 'Oh, you mean *that* book. The one that made your oldest friend out to be a nonce.'

'Yes. I'm sorry. I should never have handled it.'

'No, you shouldn't. Let the side down there, didn't you? Well, young man, you've learned a bit of a life lesson. As have I.'

Hywel nodded.

'You know, I'm not the kind of obnoxious arsehole who goes around telling people he told them so.' He took a sip before continuing, 'Which is just as well for you, isn't it? Because I did, loudly and frequently.'

'I know. I know. But somebody else would have taken it on. She'd've got it published somewhere.'

'I very much doubt that. In any case, it probably helped that she had the best agent in London to smooth everything over, don't you think? Help her with her turn of phrase, package it for the publishers, negotiate the tricky legal aspects of the deal. Well, you did a good job, anyway. I read somewhere it was in *The New York Times* bestseller list for eight weeks.'

Hywel bowed his head. 'I wouldn't blame you, you know, if you …' He trailed off, and was suddenly afraid that he might start blubbing. He felt a heavy hand on his shoulder. It squeezed, withdrew.

'Come on. Let's not have any sentimental scenes. I don't blame you, not really. I never did …' Stanton paused and looked at him with a strange, inbetween, camera-caught expression on his face. Eventually, he went on: 'Well, that's not completely

251

true, but you lost the use of reason. It happens.'

'You're taking it very well.'

'Yes, well, good for the biography, don't you think? Bit of the old Lord George Byron? Bit of the old Oscar? Not sure *The Ballad of Haverigg Category D Open Prison* has quite the right ring to it, though.'

Hywel coughed, ran a hand across his face.

'Actually, now you're in a vulnerable state of mind, this might be a good time to ask you for a favour … I was wondering if you could put me up for a night or two, at your house. I'm going to Norfolk for a while, do a bit of—'

Hywel looked up. 'I don't have a house. Didn't you hear?'

'No. As you probably should've noticed, I've been out of circulation the past couple of years. What happened? You lose it in the split?'

'I lost it in the Canal Plus case.'

'What? What are you talking about?'

'Canal Plus—they sued, after they pulled the series. The house I lost in the divorce. And my parental rights. But I'd've had to have relocated to France, and—'

'I knew they'd dropped the series. Got a letter from that Armand person when I was in chokey. I didn't know there were afters. Were there?'

Hywel gave a bitter laugh. 'Jesus, Gerald: you make Harold Skimpole look like Jeff Bezos. Yes, there was a legal case. Actually, there were a few of them, because the French insurer sued my insurer, and then they sued me. My lawyer wanted to sue you for contributory damages.'

'Much good that would have done you.'

'That's what I told her. And it would have put Vickie on the street.'

'Well, then.' Stanton picked up his pint and offered to clink glasses. 'You made a noble gesture.'

'Not really. I was going to end up here whatever I did. It was settled out of court for €2.4 million in the end, including costs.'

Stanton laughed. 'Oh my god. You blew your own head off.'

'Only good part was that the insurer had to fund my lawyer.'

'You made a noble gesture,' Stanton insisted. 'Don't worry, I still love you. Here's to our renewed friendship … Well, go on then, pick it up.' Hywel did as he was bid. They clinked and drank. 'So, where are you now?' he went on at last.

'Stroud Green. She's letting me stay in her old flat. There's only one bedroom, but you can have the sofa if you like.'

'Are you still repping her?'

Hywel laughed a bitter laugh. 'Hardly. She's with Go Fish now. I'm not really in a position to … you know. Undischarged bankrupts can't really do that much.'

'You ever see her?'

'I went to the launch party. That was last June.'

'Where did they have it?'

'Kensington Roof Gardens. Just went to say hello, but she'd already left. With Will Self.'

Stanton nodded, scratched at his greying stubble. 'Thus the whirligig of time brings in his revenges,' he murmured, and they both looked at what remained of their drinks.

Hywel sighed, and without thinking took the cigarette from behind his ear and put it in his mouth.

'You know, it was a shame you didn't let me know what you were up to while you were up to it.'

'Yeah. I was a bit of a coward.'

'Don't say that. I'm not interested in that. Ask me why.'

'Okay—why.'

Stanton threw in a dramatic pause before continuing: 'Because she isn't who she says she is. Whom she says she is.'

Hywel shook his head. 'No, you're wrong there. I checked it all out with Victoria. And she should know—' He came to a sudden stop.

'Yes, well, all the same—she isn't. Do you remember the first time you met her? Do remember what she said in that taxi?'

'No, of course I don't—what do you mean?' Hywel saw that his cigarette had fallen onto the floor. He picked it up and put it back in his mouth.

Stanton drank the rest of his pint and wiped his mouth on his sleeve. 'Look, it's almost closing time,' he said. 'I've got half a bottle of Bells in my bag. Let's go back to hers and I'll tell you what I think happened in Norfolk. If I'm right, there might be a book in it … Well, come on, then—Best Kebabs will still be open.'

Robert sat forlornly under his pointy puce cupola, staring disconsolately through magical retinas at an unemployed purple hampton

Brigadier Robert D'Alby | Evan Hay
—A sweaty tale of soul-stirring desire in remote
and salty environs

Brigadier Robert D'Alby of the Glorious Roscommons was a fine hench figure of a man. As an impeccable Sandhurst officer cadet, it was crystal clear D'Alby was hewn from the right ornamental stuff; possessing athleticism, but devoid of narcissism, employing RP plus a military style of life, minus that all-too-familiar 'boot-polish-up-the-kilt' mentality. An unerringly Apollonian devotion to duty, ethics, & a Spartan indifference to discomfort made D'Alby splendid soldiering material; his ability to remain aloof (distanced from clamorous subordinates) enabled access to private thoughts beyond the woefully limited appreciation of rough-&-ready non-commissioned comrades. Additionally, uninventive fellow officers bored D'Alby: drunken mess parties, latent homosexuality, imbecilic gambling, & their monomaniacal brutalism, interdicted him from honourably pursuing a deep camaraderie. Above all, he abhorred their collective flat disregard for synthetic cubism et seq. Still, such wilful textural blindness didn't detract D'Alby, or prevent him from admiring Britannia's strength of character; nor could a variety of crude, spiteful behavioural patterns, intemperately disseminated amongst Blighty's privately educated landowning classes, annul the intuitive esteem in which he held this ruthless creed- neither did that nationalistic exceptionalism, existentially flaunted over generations of those deemed lower in rank, status, or quality, by English gents.

Remaining fighting-fit at thirty-seven, & well-cushioned by his index-linked Armed Forces Pension Scheme, D'Alby's subsequent induction into the Guild of Ancient Mariners & Venerable Fishmongers facilitated his pursuit of another lucrative opportunity to serve his country with insignia- via a stint of reclusive commitment as a generously endowed private-sector lighthouse keeper. Embellished with frilled epaulettes, as a proud wickie he kept Bishop Rock Lighthouse shining bright & spotlessly clean- during abundant spare time he manufactured basic collectibles such as hand-woven cotton rugs, novelty candles, or crafted model warships (embattled within bottles) & sundry other objets d'art to be sold as bric-à-brac at mariners' fêtes. Despite these crackerjack diversions, D'Alby's daily life grew into lonely, challenging, & surreal routines (although his dutiful service was made as comfortable as possible by paraffin heaters, frozen crabsticks, BBC World Service, *It Sticks Out Half A Mile*, & Scilly regional radio). In the fullness of time, Robert quietly observed how natural power emitted from those loose & fecund bowels of Mother Earth reigned supreme- that is, put simply- the everyman, that sentient nonentity, merely floated upon her ethereal waves. Yet one who could curry Poseidon's favour was blesséd indeed. So, weather permitting, Robbie irregularly attended an austere mariner's guildhall, where a gracious & most proper art of ingratiation was taught in confidence to select scholars. There, in Twisted Bobbins Sentinel Chambers, one could confidentially manipulate mystical gifts according to one's breeding, wisdom & talent; ancillary occult factors being two tools of divine provocation, each empowered with prodigious energies, enabling a righteous seeker to beseech & become adorned with those charmed privileges afforded to orthodox craftsmen. These were twofold: one pukka velvet wishing cap (immaculately derived from the legendary Fortunatus), & a pair of elegant ivory lorgnettes, proffering all-sightedness.

Now, amusing as this esoteric bourgeois scenario might appear, it was not entirely satisfying. Hence, influenced by the compelling literature of Aleister Crowley (on loan from Bobbins' hypnotic Worshipful Master), Robert sat forlornly under his pointy puce cupola, staring disconsolately through magical retinas at an unemployed purple hampton. Hallucinatory masturbation wasn't working- hard-core, no-nonsense skulduggery was called for. So one day, this abstemious xenophobe- inasmuch as his wasp's waist seldom played host to dodgy foreign foodstuffs- clipped his magnificent monkey wrench moustache, smeared petroleum jelly around his unloved ring- hole before purposefully penning a charmingly succinct advertisement, to be tastefully displayed in the lonely hearts section of *City Limits* magazine, ref: pubescent wantonness; which he dispatched post-haste by the utmost economic means of a tax-deductible supplies boat which fortnightly ferried rations of baked beans marinated in orange tomato sauce. 'Attention! Any cute proletarian teenagers hankering after admission to free pagan erotica in a lighthouse should call D'Alby now!'

'Oh, yes. London. Now there's a filthy big city chock-full of perverted deviants.' He thought fiendishly- inconspicuously revelling in anal imagery. On the surface both Robbie's deportment & attitude conveyed a cultivated character, a noble esquire who coveted beauty & classical repose above all else. But beneath this calm exterior, D'Alby naturally required a hard-knuckled fist fuck. Assimilating contradictory hyper-religiosity & hormonal pressures resulted in self-adjudged guilt; his pallid superego took waxen umbrage, wanly scolding a Dionysian id for its clammy, impure thoughts: 'just lay back & think of Merry England!'

D'Alby tentatively undressed in front of a full-length cheval mirror; perturbed, critically reviewing his ageing reflection- an inner resentment grew uncontrollably darker. Most shocking were his nauseating surly features which emerged outlandishly ugly, bizarrely misshapen- obnoxious in every detail. Each flaccid aspect called for slashing & expert mutilation. A self-defacing element imbued Robbie's mind: 'Oh, for a Black-&-Decker Workmate!' Bobby hated it. This damned chimera was alas no longer he; rather a mocking minacious curse. Giant hailstones crashed around toughened glass whilst D'Alby laughed uproariously, artistically smearing arterial blood across his gammon-pink nakedness. Having sliced off inverted nipples & super glued them to his knees, he took a rusty cheese grater to the ship's fringe benefit tomcat whilst ejaculating over vivid adolescent memories (of his gang goosing by House Apostles, all ceremonially attired in uniform coats & cocked hats with ostrich plumes) during his tour as a Charterhouse fag. Relaxed, he reflected upon the infamous full moon initiation rituals he'd witnessed; rough sleeping orphan Stan Crabbs- that plausible cephalopod became unstuck. A persona non grata, his rootless, ovoidal working-class disposition collected, drugged- bewitched by sinister decree. Manhandled by St Agnes' sturdy yeomanry downstairs into Old Lanes' spellbinding crayoned pentagram & forcefully shoved; Crabbs fell prostrate between scary cloven hooves- where he was instantaneously plagued by ankylosis & force-fed slough from millions of damned excrescences whilst his chafed homeless sphincter was invaded by vile swarms of chattering animalcules (besieging his cerebrum & infesting his congenitally stunted imagination with obscure forms of regimental Catholicism). Cruelly enough, metemsomatosis irretrievably undermined Crabbs' innate processes of perception, rendering his alchemical substitute frenetic, barren, snarling & regardant (why such random, forsaken educationally subnormal vagabonds were solemnly condemned to suffer so, fuck only knows).

'And then all of us nonpareils, chartered fishermen, aristocratic seafarers & the like, steamed the fat cunt & gouged out his oculi. He can't see nothing now.'

Following a bizarre, two-month long collage of auto-erotic overload (resulting in the first instance of little more than a sore willy- & secondly, through the latter period, only sensations of dizziness, nausea, acute futility & self-mutilation), having received no expressions of interest, nor any letters of reply, Bob nonchalantly applied enchanted Fastskin Elites before decisively jumping overboard, resplendent in top-of-the-range Speedos. Determined to swim ashore & hard ride Shanks's pony to central London immediately, in full picaresque personage, to get balls-deep into heavy-duty cottaging. He wondered what the precious all-seeing mincer would make of that. Beat off an all-penetrating stethoscope perhaps, or tickle an ever-swollen vulva? Because whatever it is, wherever it's coming from, unequivocally, it need a jolly good going over now & again. Seen?

Praise for *Elastic Waxes in Unbounded Media* ...

The messianic autoeroticism borrows a little too much from the Nietzschean playbook for my liking. Although I enjoyed some of its pieces individually, taken as a whole, it's not for me. I do sometimes invest in highly partisan material—articles attacking socialism for example—but my reading tends to be couched in a less fatidic register.
—Nadine Dorries

Ever since I was a wee bairn—about six or seven—I've wanted to be a deep-sea trawler. Many's the night I'd spend, lying in bed, imagining myself ploughing black furrows over the Iceland cod grounds, feeling the mighty engine vibrating in my belly, the thrust of the screw driving me onward against the thickening pull of the nets, the all-but-imperceptible tickle of the dungaree riders on my mighty back, my ice chest open in expectation of the glorious moment of up-haul and out-spill, when a thousands shining silver bodies would slide in slime across my plates and planks. That was when I'd usually have to reach for a tissue or two ...
    Sorry, what was the question again?
—'Demersal Dave' McIntyre

Barren, snarling and regardant—and that's not the half of it.
—Brigadier Robert D'Alby (retired)

Harringay or Haringey? Which is it? Who edited this? Have they not maps?
—Bill Bailey

Wow. Racially aggravated masturbation that makes no effort to pull its darned stockings up before setting out to alienate casual and committed readers alike. That's just about what we need right now.
—Count Indigo

All life is a flux of bioelectrochemical data, and all stories the trace it leaves across the white page of eternity.
—Issey Miyake

Having crap like this for sale on my site makes me yearn all the harder for the clean, black, emptiness of the void
—Jeff Bezos

All structures—and this anthology is no exception—appeal to a grounding metaphor that lies outside their purlieu; once one makes the deconstructionist move, however, structure dissolves into ludic play that is entirely subjective—signifieds being liberated, once and for ever, from their signifiers and children allowed to stay up late.
—Perry Anderson

Buttered my muffin. And you?
—Nancy Pelosi

We citizens from time immemorial have observed the actions of nobles, or studied books written about them, and in a sense taken their lessons; if we think we can discern in these infinitely detailed chronicles certain principles that appear to suggest the existence of a moral law here or there, we should try to govern our behaviour in accordance with such carefully sieved and ordered conclusions—all of which seems doubtful, perhaps nothing more than a game of logical inference. Because, quite possibly, those moral laws we try to guess at don't exist at all.
—Esther Liebmann (née Schulhoff)

Where are the forty scantily-clad Jewish women who speak neither English nor French? Where the cool shades of the Białowieża woodlands? The blind cellists? The soft trill of the sanderling? We woz cheated.
—André Gregory

Discursive, like my own sweet self. And certain passages attain a sveltely luminous transcendence, or else an enveloping darkness, complete with reassuringly soft, pink centre.
—Milla Jovovich

I for one don't subscribe to the maudlin tonality of such 'Shlimazels R Us' sob stories. If they don't want to work on my farm then leave. Head east, meet the lesser szlachta. They'll welcome you with open arms, like lambs to the slaughter.
—Richard Scott, 10th Duke of Buccleuch

Printed in Great Britain
by Amazon

86205160R00153